Becoming TRIXIE

IT'S A DOG'S LIFE

BOOK 1

DAVID HORN

To all our best friends

Table of Contents

Prologue

Squiwel! There he is. *Squiwel! Squiwel! Squiwel!*

Gonna get you, squiwel. This time I will. I just know it.

Mama drops the leash. "Twinkie! Get back here!" Mama might get lost without me, but I don't care. I'll find her later. "Bad dog!"

Bad? You're the one who dropped the leash. *Squiwel!*

Run run run. Catch him catch him catch him! *Squiwel!*

Oh no! Not again! Stupid twees! Squiwel went up a twee! I hate you, twee! *Come down! Come down now, squiwel! Squiwel!*

"Snicker snicker snicker!" Squiwel taunts me from the twee. Stupid squiwel. Always the same squirrel. Running away. Taunting me. I can't believe I lost again. *Come down! Come down! Come down!*

Oh wait, what is that? A hole at the bottom of the twee! It's big. It's lit up with all different colors. Is this an elevator? Like in Grammy's big house in the smelly city? It must be an elevator! *I get you now!* Going up! Then we can finally play together!

I dash into the hole and . . .

Chapter 1
A New Beginning

Huh? What happened? This smells different. In fact, it doesn't smell at all. Where is the tree? Where are the smells? Is my nose broken? I don't remember breaking my nose.

"Squirrel!" I call to the sky—no, it's a ceiling now. Ceiling? Where am I? And my bark? It sounded really weird. Almost . . . *human*? Like Mama? Can I finally ask her for lunch now? I'm so excited. "Mama, when's lunch? What's for lunch?" I practice.

Then I look down. Human food! Right in front of me! Did it work? Is this lunch?

I'm at a table! It finally happened! Dream come true! This is lunch! It looks like a bowl of tasty water with human food in it.

Lap lap lap! Huh? What's wrong with my tongue? It's so small and useless. I bring my paw up to my mouth to feel it on my fur. Then I can figure out my tongue problem. Oh my Dog! Human hands? Where are my paws?

Then I notice. Oh no. A whole table of humans is staring at me—humans I don't know. That's the dangerous kind. But I feel like staring at me too. What's wrong with me? This dream come true feels very wrong. This isn't the lunch I always wanted. Where did that tree elevator take me? Where's my squirrel friend? "Squirrel!"

"Is *this* truly the princess you wish my son to marry in two weeks?" some old man wrapped in a very comfy-looking blue blanket yells across the table, his human finger pointed at me. I recoil in fear. I try and put my tail down, but . . . where's my tail? And my ears won't go down either! How do I show fear and subservience to this big scary dog . . . er, man? Instead, I slump my shoulders and lower my head. That should work. Afraid, I lift my eyes to see if it's working.

"I'm sorry, King Reginald," some man on my side of the table says, who is also wearing a comfy-looking blanket, though in a color I've never seen before, so how weird is that, "but it seems my daughter has come down with the Parchesian Flu. Perhaps if we—"

"Parchesian Flu? The Parchesian Flu doesn't cause one to eat like a beast!" the man in blue says loudly. "Son! This girl is not for you. The gods would banish you. Let us be gone!"

"But, Father, she's very pretty. And the last girl you wanted me to marry was an exile from the Tarantulabi. She had such hairy legs. I'm willing—" another, younger, man in blue says.

"No, son. No matter how pretty, there is something wrong. Just look at her posture!" the older man interrupts. Hearing this, I immediately stop slumping my shoulders. But what is going on?

I'm now a human? Am I pretty? Humans would always tell me I was pretty before, so this makes sense. They would all stop and rub me. Perhaps I should let them rub me and everyone would be happy and not angry. I don't like angry. But I have no tail or movable ears. I'll just show my belly.

Falling to the floor, I lie on my back. It stings a little, as I'm not as limber as I used to be. This body is so . . . it just doesn't move as well. But I'm on my back anyway. Instinctively, I wag my nonexistent tail, but it's just my legs moving? My body is not responding to any of my commands! Ah! Where is my tail?

"*Now* what is she doing?" the old blue man explodes.

"I don't know! I'm trying to wag my tail!" I cry. "Where's my tail?"

"Trixie! What has gotten into you?" roars the man in the new color on my side of the table.

Wait . . . it just occurred to me. How do I understand their language? I used to listen only for "goodgirl" because that was my favorite word. Goodgirl meant rubs and food and smiles. Now I understand these other words; was I speaking them the whole time?

"You can understand me? Am I a goodgirl?" I ask.

"I'm sorry, King Reginald! I assure you, she was fine moments ago. You even saw her. This must be a serious case of that flu. Can we please postpone this initial meeting and try again before the wedding? I promise you, my Princess Trixie has very much been looking forward to meeting your son, Prince Weibold, her future husband. ''Tis a match by the gods,' your prophets say."

Wait a second. I'm Trixie? My name is Twinkie, not Trixie! Am I not Twinkie anymore? And I'm supposed to marry Prince Weibold? Who even is he? What is marriage? Like Mama and Dada? Ewww!

Now I'm feeling hot from nervousness *and* from moving my legs a lot. I try panting through my mouth, which usually works. But it's not working now. I try even harder. "Hah, hah, hah." No luck. "This mouth's no good." Is my snout broken? Maybe I should take these stupid human clothes off? Human clothes are the worst. I try disrobing. This big stupid blanket of a shirt is off, though there is another smaller shirt underneath it! Who does that? *Gggrrr*. I'll just try these bottom clothes then. Oh, they look so puffy—maybe I'll lay on them after and take a nap. Good idea!

"Medics! Medics!" the man in the new color is shouting at the door. "My daughter is clearly burning up with a fever."

"Fine. It appears we will have to postpone this . . . whatever this is. My personnel will contact you. Come on, Weibold," the old blue man says as he gets up from the table.

"Hah, hah," I say. "Why won't this snout work?"

On their way out, Prince Weibold comes over to me. He peers into my eyes.

"Son! Don't go near her. She's partially disrobed! The Goddess of Chastity will smite you down! And she has a flu!" King Reginald exclaims.

"But, Father," the prince says. He has a hand out, and it's coming toward me. Is he going to rub my belly? Please please please please please! After everything, I just want someone to rub my belly. I want to go home. I miss Mama and Dada. And Charlotte and Carolina, my human littermates. "Rub the belly!" Giving up on getting this complicated bottom clothes/blanket thing off, I point at my bare stomach.

Instead, the prince's hand goes to my forehead. "Hmm . . . I don't feel a fever. I do hope you are okay, though."

"Nonsense," the man in the new color says. "My daughter is clearly sick."

"Then I shall give her my mother's Yagweez crystal, which is said to activate the healing powers of the gods," Prince Weibold says, though I'm not sure I understand all the words. He digs in his pocket, pulls out a shiny palm-size yellow ball, and presses it into my hand. "Take this and pray to Yagweezibell, the God of Healing and Vitality." What? It looks like a tennis ball! And I can't resist the urge . . .

I pop the ball into my mouth and smile. This boy gave me a present. I am a goodgirl!

"That's not how you use it, Princess," the prince says in shock.

"Son! Get your mother's crystal back now," King Reginald orders Prince Weibold.

He brings a hand closer to my mouth, but there is no way he is getting my ball! I bare my teeth and growl. Now I'm on all fours, though I can't figure out these back paws. They don't seem like paws . . . there are paws attached to these paws? No, that's not right. These can't be paws . . . the word comes to me—knees! Human knees!

"Father?" he asks.

"We will reschedule, and my daughter will return the crystal then," the other man in the new color says. "It is clear these two have a fondness for each other already. Isn't that right, my daughter?" Is he my father? Whatever. He wants me to give my ball back! *Gggrrr!*

"You mean she's going to keep one of our most cherished religious artifacts passed down within the royal family since we first settled on Thorpia and vanquished the Great Bargoosian Swamp Moths to claim the land as our own? It better be returned," King Reginald says. But, again, I have no idea what he means. "Until then."

The ten people from the other side of the table all leave the room. I'm left with ten people all in this new color. What should I call it?

"Dada, what color is that?" I ask him, spitting the yellow ball into my hand now that I've won it fair and square.

"What the stars are you doing?" he demands unkindly.

"Dada?" I ask.

"I knew you didn't want to marry Prince Weibold, but

I didn't know you would stoop so low! Literally! Stand up!" I rise off the floor, and I'm standing on back paws. How do humans balance like this? I'm tilting left, tilting right. This is impossible! I stagger over to a chair and lay a free front paw on it. Or hand. "Stop moving! You stole his mother's crystal! Give it here."

"Gggrrr!"

"Argh, fine. Keep the stupid thing." He points to the chair. I sit down, which also feels weird. How will I ever balance with only my back paws on the ground? My front paws hold on tight to the sides of the chair, making sure not to drop my new ball. "Guard, bring her that blouse. And close your eyes!"

A guard brings back the shirt I took off, waving it in front of me because his eyes are closed. Dada is staring at me. I still feel hot, but I think he wants me to put it on. So I try. It was easier to rip it off my chest. But all I can do now is stick my arms through. I can't make sense of these buttons, though. They must be broken. And how do I even know what buttons are? I never considered them before.

"Do you think I'm going to let you get out of this marriage just because you faked some illness? The Kalaxian Star Empire needs this alliance! I told you that! Our space carriers are being slaughtered by bandits out there, and the Thorpian Stardom is powerful, with a real navy! And they offered a hundred thousand slaves for our factories! In a one-two punch, we can protect our shipping lanes through currently unguarded space and lower our costs in the middle of this labor shortage, and all we have to do is incorporate some of their gods into our official laws and pay their royal family a divinity fee. And you need to give them babies! We need them, and they know it!

"Do you want to see Kalaxian tradesmen die throughout the star empire? You want their blood on your hands? Should I have let you live out the rest of your life in poverty? I saved you and made you royalty!"

"Woof?" I ask.

"Argh!" my new dada says. "Guards! Throw her in the brig!" Five of the men in this new color come to grab me.

Now I'm in trouble. So I do like I do at the dog run when somedog . . . someone tries to take my toy. I bare my teeth and growl. It worked last time with these humans.

"Uh, Emperor Papo? Are you sure she's not sick?" asks one of the guards, who looks like he's going to lunge at me but is holding himself back.

"Sick? She's clearly faking—trying to get out of the marriage! There's no such thing as the Parchesian Flu. I made it up to save face. Just get her out of my sight! We'll drug her at the next meeting so that she doesn't pull a stunt like this again. In two weeks' time, she'll be the Thorpians' problem anyway!" He sweeps his hand through the air.

The guards grab me, and I relent to being carried out of the room like a little puppy. They don't try for my new ball. To be honest, this actually feels nice. I missed human hands holding me. And I have a new ball! Feeling more like myself, I rub my head into the guard's shoulder.

"Uh, excuse me?" I ask the guard.

"Yes, Princess Trixie? Are you feeling better?"

"I think so. Now that you're holding me," I say, making sure not to remind him of the ball. My new ball!

"Uh . . . um . . . ," the guard stammers as we exit the banquet room.

"What color are you wearing?" I ask now that we're outside of that sad room. "I've never seen it before."

"Huh?" the guard asks, his brow twisted in a puzzled expression. "This is red. The color of the Kalaxian flag, clearly. Are you sure you're not sick? I know Emperor Papo said—"

"Red. Hmm. I think I *may* be sick. I don't know who or where I am. And what was that talk about stars and space? I think I know those words, but they don't make sense to me." Some things are starting to slowly seep into me, but sometimes it still feels like it's in a faraway place of my brain. How do I even know what a brain is? Mama and Dada would be so proud. But they're not here. I'm on my own. *Somewhere else.* That I know. "How did I get here?"

"You must really be sick," the guard says as he looks down at me. "Hector," he says to a guard in front of him, "alert MedBay that we're bringing the princess in. I don't think she's faking."

"But, sir, the emperor," Hector replies, turning his face to us.

"And if she dies?" the guard asks. Hector nods. Wait, who said anything about dying?

As we continue walking down the hall, the guard holding me turns to another guard to his left. "Walter, fetch her lady-in-waiting and have her meet us there."

"Yes, Captain Gregor," Walter says.

Before I can ask about dying, Hector, the one in front, picks up a cell phone-looking device, which I now know is the name of the thing Mama would hold and caress instead of me, brings it to his mouth, and speaks into it. The other man scampers out. Oh, I once knew a Scampers. I understand his name now. Yes, he definitely did like to scamper. This human brain is amazing. The things I can understand!

"Your father may say you're not sick, but if you really are and you die on me, then it'll be my life and Lady Marmalade's, no matter what," the guard holding me says. He must be Captain Gregor.

"I'm going to die? Please, no," I cry.

"Not if I can help it," Captain Gregor replies.

"Oh, thank you. I feel very strange. But the stars? What are they? Where am I?"

"Gee-whizzin' orbits, Princess. Space? The stars? We're on a space carriage. Just look outside," Captain Gregor says. He walks us over to a window.

"Holy cheeseballs!" I exclaim involuntarily. "Where is the grass?"

My eyes instantly close. As I lose consciousness, my grip tightens on my new ball and Captain Gregor calls loudly, "MedBay!"

Chapter 2
Fallout of the Sky?

"Trixie, Trixie," I hear a man say. I'm lying on my back. Head throbbing.

"That's *Princess* Trixie, Doctor," a woman's voice scolds him.

"Oh, right. Sorry, Lady Marmalade," the man replies. His name must be Doctor.

My eyes open, and the two heads are staring down at me. Wait . . . where's my ball? Did they take my ball?

"My ball! My ball!"

"The crystal?" Doctor asks. Then I look down at my hand. It's still there in this weird human paw. I pop it back into my mouth and smile.

"Princess!" the woman and Doctor both scold me. They look at each other. Are they trying to think of how to get my ball?

Doctor, the man, is much younger than Dada. He's

wearing a white gown. I'm happy I know the color. That alone makes him seem familiar. He has short black curly hair on his head, like a poodle. That must mean he's smart.

Lady Marmalade, the woman, is younger than Mama. She has long, flowing, light-brown and copper hair (which I now realize is kind of a darker type of that new color) like my best friend at the dog run, Bailey, the Nova Scotia Duck Tolling Retriever. Oh, the trouble we would get into. She always had such fun ideas. "Let's go steal that dog's ball," she would say, or bark. Then she would steal it anyway and drop it in front of me so that I would be the one to get into trouble. Oh, I miss her now. Did Bailey get turned into a human too? I should hide the ball. I spit it back into my hand. Her eyes follow the ball.

"Bailey, off my ball!" I say.

"Bailey? Who's Bailey?" the woman asks.

"You," I say.

"I'm not Bailey. Captain Gregor must be right," the woman says. Oh. Not Bailey. I was hoping . . . but then, where am I? Where's Mama and Dada?

"I told you!" I hear Captain Gregor's deep voice from somewhere in the room. My head spins to see him by the door. Now I can recognize his deep, growly voice. Somehow it feels nice and familiar.

"Princess Trixie," the doctor man says, "do you know where you are?"

My head tilts, because I don't know. Then something in my . . . brain . . . it tells me to also shake my head. But I remember the sky. That was the sky! Stars are in the sky, my brain is telling me. But why am I in the sky?

Wait . . . I'm in *doggie heaven*? Did I die? In that tree? Is that what happened? But Captain Gregor said I wasn't dead.

"Am I dead? Is that why I'm in the stars?" I ask the pair, still surprised I'm speaking with humans. Even more humans.

"She didn't know what the stars were before," Captain Gregor informs them.

"I see," the man says. "I think we should run some tests." He takes out a silver-looking wand from a metal tray that I've just noticed next to my bed.

"Tushy thermometer!" I shout. Now I know what it's called in this human language, and there is no way I'm letting that in my butt! Never again! Not even in doggie heaven! And especially when I'm in a human body and can defend myself now.

The pair's eyes go wide at my outburst, and they step back. I drop my ball (noting its location), grab the tray with both hands, whack the man's hands, and roll off the bed.

He drops the tushy thermometer but then the lady picks it up off the floor. I run away from them, holding the tray as a shield. I'm now in the corner of this room, which suddenly looks like the vet's office. This all makes sense now. MedBay is the vet. The evil vet!

I see Captain Gregor, who looks like a bulldog with his round, hairless head. His strong body is guarding the door near the other corner of the room, and the other man and lady are still by the bed. "Do you two weaklings need my help to corral *one sickly girl*?" Captain Gregor asks.

"No, we can do this ourselves," the doctor snaps at him. "It's a medical issue."

"Just because you're a prodigy seventeen-year-old doctor doesn't mean you can handle a potentially violent sixteen-year-old girl." I'm sixteen. Or this body is. Like my human littermate Charlotte. And she doesn't get tushy thermometers. Does she? Whatever. I don't want it!

"Dr. Lam, prepare a sedative. I'll handle this. I'm an *actual* adult," Lady Marmalade says, looking angrily at the captain. She's older than sixteen or seventeen.

"Sorry, Marm—uh," Captain Gregor says. "I didn't mean—"

"But, Lady Marmalade," the man who I now know as Dr. Lam interrupts. The evil vet. I want to whack him again. But I am wary of Lady Marmalade. She seems tough, like Bailey. Then her face softens.

"Princess Trixie," Lady Marmalade says. "Why are you so scared of us?"

"Tushy thermometer!" I shout. Isn't it obvious? "And you should know this, Bailey! If you really were my best friend!" My brain is so confused—caught between two people: Twinkie and Trixie. Lady Marmalade so reminds me of Bailey, my bestest dog friend. Why can't she be Bailey? I just want to go home—wherever that is.

"Who is this Bailey you speak of?" the lady says. "My name is Lady Marmalade. Your lady-in-waiting. I *am* your best friend here. It is my job to take care of you, Princess. And I would never let any harm come to you, as far as I can prevent it. Dr. Lam just needs to check your health with the medical wand. It's *not* a tushy thermometer."

"You mean the evil vet wants to stick that thing up my butt!" I declare. And I swing my tray again to show I mean business. But I hear Captain Gregor chuckling to himself. I turn to look at him. "This isn't funny! This is serious! Not. In. My. Tushy!"

"Now you know what I was dealing with, Doctor," Captain Gregor says. "I'm glad to see I made the right call. The engagement dinner was a disaster."

"Is the wedding off?" The evil vet turns in surprise.

"Definitely not," Captain Gregor replies.

"What did the emperor say?" Lady Marmalade asks.

"He said she's not really sick, and we should throw her in the brig. He thinks she ruined the dinner on purpose," Captain Gregor says. "But no one could fake *this*."

"I agree," Dr. Lam says. "There must be something wrong with her." The room quiets down for a moment, though I'm swinging the tray back and forth weakly to keep them at bay. We're all at a . . . standstill . . . stalemate. Yes, that's the word. I know human words now. They just come to me.

"What if I promised you that we wouldn't stick this in your tushy?" Lady Marmalade says.

"That's what they all say! I don't believe you!" I say emphatically.

"And if we let you hold it?" she asks. "You could perform the test yourself."

That's an interesting idea. Could they hurt me if I held it? There are three of them in here and only one of me. I can't take them all. I couldn't even take Bailey or Captain Gregor one-on-one. But I *could* take the doctor.

"Okay. But only *him*!" I say, pointing at Dr. Lam.

"Only him?" Lady Marmalade asks. I know that look. She seems annoyed. Like she lost out on a treat.

"Yes, only *him* in the room," I say.

"I'm okay with that," Dr. Lam says.

"But, Doctor," Captain Gregor says. "It's dangerous. I mean, look at her. The wild eyes, baring her teeth. She's practically foaming at the mouth."

"Yes, Doctor," Lady Marmalade says. "I agree with Captain Gregor. You know, the *actual* captain of the Royal Guard."

"It's either that or she doesn't get better and you all get in trouble with the emperor," Dr. Lam says, pretending to slice his throat. Why do I know what that is? "Besides, I took some self-defense classes on the Fitness Deck."

"All right, Doctor," Captain Gregor says as he waves at Lady Marmalade to join him. "I saw you at Beginner's Pilates Boxing the other day, but don't think that alone will save you. We'll be right outside." Lady Marmalade harrumphs at Dr. Lam as she hands him the silver wand thing—the tushy thermometer—and leaves with the captain.

As soon as the door closes . . .

Chapter 3
What Does the Thermometer Say?

I rush the evil vet before he can even whimper and whack him with the tray. He falls. *Whack whack whack*—again and again, just enough so that he stays down. I move the tray to one hand and pick up the wand-looking thing with the other. "Now it's your turn! Let's see how you like it up your—"

"But, Trixie, don't you remember? I can get you home," Dr. Lam says.

Home! I stop in my tracks. "Home? With Mama?"

"Mama?" he asks. We're talking past each other.

He doesn't know Mama? "You lie! Bend over and take the tushy thermometer like countless dogs have had to do since the beginning of time! I will achieve vengeance for the millennia of embarrassment and discomfort inflicted on all canines!"

"Canines? Dogs? What are you talking about?"

"You don't know what a dog is?"

"No idea! And what's wrong with you? Did the pressure of this sham marriage finally get to you? Did something happen at the engagement dinner?" He's inching his body closer, so I wave the tray at him. He stops. Good.

"Woof."

"Woof? What is that? One of the Thorpians? Did this Woof hurt you? I thought the prince's name was Weibold," he says.

"Oh, sorry," I reply. "My old language slipped out. These human words . . . argh!"

"Old language?" Dr. Lam says. "From Expiry? It's in the empire. You never said you knew any old language. Just Galactic Standard."

"Oh, is that what this human language is called?"

"You're scaring me, Trixie. Do you even remember who I am?" The doctor's eyes are wide and glistening with worry. He runs a hand through his curly poodle hair. He's kind of cute, for a poodle.

But then we hear voices outside. "Yes, Director Voltari, she's in there," Captain Gregor says.

"You fool! You let her get away with it!" I hear a man snarl in a growly voice, like a pit bull. Is he Director Voltari? "I could have you spaced for this." The voice is so loud I can make it out through the door.

"Sir, if that is what the emperor wishes," Captain Gregor replies, actually sounding scared. Who could scare Captain Gregor, the bulldog? A pit bull, that's who.

"You're lucky you're so good at keeping the guard in

line, or I would advise him so," the growly voice says. "Good to see you again, Lady."

The door flies open.

"Where is she?" says a tall man in the doorway. It is the same growly voice. He's very scary. A long, sharp gray beard that goes with his long silver cloak. Small round eyes. Gray hair combed straight back. He looks like Buddy, the giant pit bull at the dog run. Except this man has a long cane—I now know that's the thing Grammy had—with the golden head of a cat on the end. And it's not a cute cat. This one is like a stalking cat. Pit bulls and cats, oh no!

I step back, clutching the tray. Director Voltari is the type of man who would scare me on dog walks. Every fiber of my being—of Twinkie's being—says to be afraid. "Ah, there you are, you conniving little—"

"Uh, Director Voltari, Princess Trixie is feeling very under the weather," Dr. Lam says, cutting him off.

"You think I was born yesterday, fool?" the director says, towering over Dr. Lam.

"It's true, sir," Dr. Lam defends me, not giving up an inch. "She is exhibiting clear signs of—"

"Of?" Director Voltari cuts the doctor off again. So scared, I step closer to the doctor, who is acting as my shield. Like Mama and Dada at the dog run.

"Of a Joparan Body Snatcher parasite," Dr. Lam finishes. This time, Director Voltari steps back. Really? Maybe I'm just sick? If they clear me of my parasite, maybe I can get home? Maybe I will be a dog again?

"Where would she have picked one up?" Voltari asks.

"It could have been from Expiry," Dr. Lam answers.

"And it lay dormant for a whole year?" Director Voltari argues, but his tone suggests he's considering Dr. Lam's suggestion. "You should have found it. I grow tired of KAMP getting in my way."

"You mean Emperor Papo's way?" the doctor asks pointedly. Is he really not scared of Director Voltari?

"Yes, of course." Director Voltari seems to back down!

"Well, the parasite has been known to evade detection. And, if I recall, you waived the six-month quarantine for some planetsiders, including the princess here, to come aboard Limo One."

"As you know, Doctor," Voltari says, taking a menacing step forward with a finger in the doctor's face, "we needed the time to shop the wench. Our traders are getting slaughtered out there."

"Oh, that's what it is?" Dr. Lam asks him. "For the good of our traders?"

"I resent your tone, Doctor. You would be healthier if you kept it in check." The director points the cat head cane right into the doctor's face. But Dr. Lam doesn't flinch. "It was your job to keep her healthy. And it'll be your head if anything happens to her and ruins this alliance, KAMP or not."

Tears start forming around my human eyes. This man is pure evil. The evil vet isn't evil, like I had just thought—Director Voltari is. Humans are much harder to figure out than dogs!

Voltari turns to me, and my now imaginary tail goes straight down. My ears won't comply, so I just lower my head. "And I hear Joparan Body Snatchers can be fatal if not treated, dear Princess," he says as he points the golden cat head on his cane at *me*. It's not that I'm scared of cats—I just hate them—but I'm terrified of this golden one. Then Director Voltari's silver cloak swishes through the air as he leaves the room. The door closes. Finally. A deep breath I didn't know I was holding in escapes from me.

"I'm sorry, Trixie. I tried to help," Dr. Lam says to me, putting a hand on my shoulder. I drop the tray finally.

"Thank you," I say. "You defended me. I'm sorry I called you evil. *He's* evil, not you." I hold out the wand to him and he takes it. He waves it around my body.

"It's okay. As Kalaxia Limo One's doctor, I've been called worse. And KAMP will protect me. The executives here can be pretty nasty. Even the big manly guards act like babies when you take out the needles," he says with a laugh. He stops waving the wand around my body. "See? All done. Was that so bad?"

"No, I guess not. I've had worse."

"I'll bet. But let's see here," he says as he sticks the wand into a cell phone-looking thing like the guard had. "As I suspected, you're perfectly fine. But as you know, you're in a perilous situation." He places his cell phone and wand into a pocket of his white gown. "It was bad before. But Director Voltari just threatened your life. You do know that, right? You can't keep up this charade. You have to escape."

Is that what that was? This human language is so hard. I don't know what to say, so I stand there blankly. Dr. Lam puts his hands on my shoulders.

"Some say he's a real Mancer," Dr. Lam continues, shaking like a chill went down his spine. As a dog, that feeling I do know.

"A man? Yes, I know he's a man. It's not like I'm not a man or something," I say proudly. But I'm not sure it came out right.

"Um," Dr. Lam shakes his head. "You really *are* strange today. Like a totally different person. And I thought you knew all this stuff. I could have sworn we talked about it before, but maybe not. I guess Expiry really is a forgotten world all the way out there at the end of the empire.

"I meant *Mancer*. As in Quantum Mancer. They're a group of people who have the power to alter quantum waveforms. It's highly advanced science—some say from another world—but basically magic." Is that like me? Am I from another world also? Did I go through a portal? That must be it.

"Another world?" I ask. "What world? Like with grass?"

"No, it's said that it just showed up through a portal one day from a totally different galaxy. Something completely unlike ours. Using magic. Not from any planet in our galaxy."

"Are *we* on a planet? Where is the grass?" I ask. "Why can't I see grass out the window?"

"Oh Trixie. You poor thing. We're not a planet. We're traveling in space. On a space carriage," Dr. Lam says. I whimper. He rubs his hands on my shoulders. Suddenly the words make sense. We're in space! Far from any planets! Far from home! My home in another galaxy?

"But the Mancers. They use magic to get home? What's magic? Can I use it?" Magic to another galaxy? That sounds like what happened to me. My human brain starts to remember something about galaxies, but nothing about magic. How do I get home? Can a Quantum Mancer help? They're so scary!

"Wow. Expiry really is a backwater. He's like a wizard. So unless you're a wizard . . ." I shake my head. I don't even know what one is. He runs another hand through his poodle hair and exhales. "Anyway, all you need to know is that he could kill you just by looking at you."

"What! How?" He's going to kill me? And I didn't even steal his toy or anything! I just want to go home. "And you let him look at me? I don't want to die. I don't want to marry anyone. I don't even belong here!"

"I know, Trixie. It wasn't fair to you. Nothing has been fair to you—how the emperor exiled your mother to Expiry all those years ago. How she died. And then he brings you back. Just for an alliance? You deserve so much better." He takes my human hand in his.

"I just want to go home! Maybe I can find a Quantum Mancer to get me home?"

"Quantum Mancer? Are you crazy?" Dr. Lam drops my hand and rubs his forehead. "I'm sorry. I didn't mean to be cruel. It's just, no one I know has ever met a real one—the Voltari thing is just rumors. And they're probably all dangerous like Voltari anyway. Meeting a real one is like a death wish. Besides, we've been planning for months. I promise you that I can get you home, if you're still willing."

Could he mean home with Mama? Or this Expiry place? That must be Trixie's home. I don't care anymore. I just need to get off this . . . space carriage. It's not safe for me here. I'll have to find another way home to Mama and Dada after that.

"Yes, please," I answer.

"Okay, good. For now, you're obviously not well. Just trust me and follow my lead," he says.

"I'm good at following leads, though I've been known to pull sometimes too. Like after squirrels."

"Squirrels?"

"Oh, uh."

"Just when I thought you were starting to act like yourself again . . ."

"I'm definitely not myself," I say with a smile. "Are Captain Gregor and Lady Marmalade in on this plan too?"

"No, no."

"Why not? They seemed to care about me too."

"Something's definitely wrong with you. But the tests came back fine," Dr. Lam says, staring at me. His hands run through his poodle hair again. "Anyway, while Captain Gregor is a good man, I can't trust him with this. As the head of the Royal Guard, he works for your father, the emperor. As for Lady Marmalade, I know you trust her. Consider her a best friend, of sorts." Ah, she really is like

Bailey! My heart jumps a little. "But I warn you not to trust her. She has a sordid background and unknown connections with the executives." I nod again, though I don't really mean it. Executives? Who are they? And she's Bailey!

"Do you report to my father? Like Captain Gregor and Director Voltari?" I ask. Can I really trust him?

"No. Even your father, the emperor, listens to KAMP. At least on medical issues."

"KAMP?"

"The Kalaxian Association of Medical Practitioners. If he's deemed incapable by KAMP, he can be replaced by the board of directors. Because we hold the power of life and death in our hands, we tend to be quite powerful."

"This is all so confusing. Why are you being so nice to me?"

"Well . . . you know . . . I . . ." His face is turning red. Is he sick too? Am I contagious?

"You look sick."

Suddenly there is a knock at the door, interrupting us. "How's it going in there, Doctor?" Captain Gregor's voice calls from outside the door.

"It's good, just finishing the examination now," he calls back.

"Good, I'm coming in now. Okay, Princess?" Lady Marmalade asks.

"Okay!" I reply. It's Bailey!

"One minute, please," Dr. Lam says.

"Fine! But that's it!" Lady Marmalade sounds mad.

"Trixie," Dr. Lam says to me quietly, "I don't know what's wrong with you. I suspect a nervous breakdown."

"Is that bad? Am I going to die? I don't know all these words." It seems the language in my brain only knows what this Princess Trixie knew. I knew Expiry because of her, but neither Trixie nor I knew "magic" or what a "nervous breakdown" is.

"No, you're not going to die. But you definitely need to escape. I'll give them the same diagnosis as Director Voltari. But please remember: don't tell a soul about my plan. I'll get you home."

"Just to make sure—which home?"

"Expiry, of course. You never mentioned living anywhere else. Am I wrong?"

"No." I look down at the floor as I think of my *real* home.

"Just don't tell them a thing. And follow my lead. My life depends on it too." He's very serious, so I nod. "You can come in now, please."

"How are you feeling, Princess?" Bailey . . . er, Lady Marmalade . . . asks as the door opens. Her copper (red!) hair appears first. "Captain Gregor will wait outside." But as I see her, and I'm calmer, an irresistible urge hits me. I run behind Lady Marmalade, fall to my knees as she turns her head to look at me, and stick my nose in her tushy. Oh, the smells!

"Princess!" Lady Marmalade erupts in anger as she jumps and spins to face me. "What in the galaxy!"

"I'm trying to smell you. Stay still! This nose doesn't work so well," I explain.

But then Lady Marmalade leans over, grabs my upper arm, and pulls me up off the floor. "Don't you ever dare smell any titled citizen's tushy! Ever! I never knew I had to teach you such a thing this year. You can't do that to management! Why do I even have to say this? You may have smelled each other's backsides on your dirtball commoner planet, but on the empire's space carriages, you act like a princess. Do you hear me?"

"Uh, I think it's her sickness, Lady," Dr. Lam says.

But now I know—in this world I can't even smell other people's tushies. My nose doesn't work. I have to wear these awful clothes. And someone wants to kill me. What a horrible world! How am I going to survive here? I need to get home! *Real* home!

"Not likely. She's just faking. This one is wilier than I thought," Lady Marmalade says, her eyebrows rising weirdly as she glances at me. Can she tell I wanted another sniff?

"Come over to my computer," Dr. Lam says to us both, changing the subject.

I've seen computers on my world. Mama and Dada sit at computers all day sometimes. But this one is different. It has no screen. And where is the keyboard? Or seat? There's just a metal circle on the floor next to us and a little recessed cubby in the wall. Dr. Lam takes a small black bug-looking thing out of the cubby. Before I can ask what it is, he sticks it onto the right side of his head. Then little black buggy tendrils come out of the bug—ew!—and go right into his head. Wait, are these not even humans? Are we really all bugs? Am I a bug? Why does this day keep getting worse?

"Computer, on," the bug doctor says. Shimmering rainbow light shoots out of, and up from, the circle on the floor so fast, I turn away. Like earlier, there are colors I've never seen before.

"Are we bug people?" I ask, scared.

"Uh, do you really think she's sick, Doctor?" Lady Marmalade asks, surprise in her voice.

"She's getting better," Dr. Lam replies, squinting at me.

"Is something wrong with your eyes, Doctor?" I ask. "Mama used to wipe my eyes when they got all gooky. Do you have eye gook?"

"You know her sense of humor," Dr. Lam says to Lady Marmalade with a forced laugh.

"What sense of humor?" Lady Marmalade asks, in all seriousness.

"Hey," I reply. I always had my family laughing back home. But here, I'm not sure if she's right. What was the prior Princess Trixie like? But Dr. Lam isn't paying attention anymore. He's staring at the circle. "I can't see anything, just random colors. What is it saying?"

"Computer," Dr. Lam says. "Public mode."

"*Public mode engaged*," a female voice says, though not from any of us. Who spoke?

"Who was that?" I ask.

"Is she faking amnesia, Doctor? Is that your plan?" Lady Marmalade is pointing a finger at Dr. Lam.

"Plan?" he asks. Then he turns to me. "It's the computer, Princess."

"But nothing happened," I point out.

"We didn't ask anything yet," he explains. "Ask it something."

"Computer," I say. "Am I a bug person, please?"

"*You are human. 'Bug people' are found only in the reclusive Celtar Protectorate, which has had no contact with any other recorded civilization in over four thousand years.*"

"You two are planning something. That's all this is," Lady Marmalade says, trying to convince herself.

"Am I a dog, please?" I ask, ignoring her.

"*You are human. No record of 'dog' in database.*" They don't have any dogs in this world? How can that be? I have no pack here. I'll never have any pack on this world. Reflexively, I put my head in my hands, but no tears come.

"Doctor, tell me what's going on," Lady Marmalade says.

"Computer, mirror mode." Dr. Lam says.

"*Mirror mode engaged,*" the computer says. Lights shoot up from the circle, but this time they form a mirror of the three of us. There are three humans. One must be me. I wave a hand to find out which one I am and what I look like as a human. Trixie is shorter than Dr. Lam and Lady Marmalade, with curly brown hair (attached to my head with some shiny things) and freckles (I remember Mama and Dada saying I had freckles also, when I was Twinkie, but I didn't know what they meant—now I do!). I look like a human! My thick purple blanket-looking shirt is buttoned now (or is it a new one?), but my clothes are so different from the other two. I'm wearing a thick, long colorful skirt—that's the word!—down to my ankles. It's so puffy also. The variety of colors amazes me. And there is a small sparkly crown on my head that I didn't notice before. I reach to touch it and take it off, but it doesn't budge. My fingers feel the rocklike sparkly things on it (my brain knows they're called thermy-nite crystals, a rarity in Thorpia but mined in Kalaxia, and meant to impress them—how do I know that?), but it's stuck in there. Though now I can confirm it really is me.

I always thought that could be me in mirrors back when I was Twinkie, but I couldn't quite figure out how I could be in two places at once. But with this new human brain, I understand now. This is like a floor-to-ceiling mirror. I can't smell myself very well, which is frustrating, but I can see all of myself in a perfect reflection where the light from the circle is, or was. I like waving my hands in the mirror. *Hi, me!*

Dr. Lam is in his white gown and Lady Marmalade is in simple green pants and a flowy, but not puffy, cream-colored shirt. I wish I had her shirt on instead of this thick blanket. Hers looks simpler.

"Computer, private mode," the doctor says.

"Doctor," Lady Marmalade scolds him.

"As you know, per KAMP regulations, medical health records are private."

"*Private mode engaged,*" the female computer voice says. Why does it sound so sad? Stuck in a computer all day, probably. That's no way to live.

"Read this medical wand," Dr. Lam says to the computer as he sticks the silver wand into a recess in the wall. The lights change to different colors, but that's all I can see. I have no idea what any of it says.

A few moments pass with Dr. Lam saying things like "Hmm . . ."

"So, Doctor?" Lady Marmalade asks, unable to contain her frustration any longer.

"She's going to be fine. I thought it was a Joparan Body Snatcher parasite, and I was right. Just swallow this pill, Princess, and you'll be okay." A recess in the wall spits out a bright-blue pill. He hands it to me and does that weird eye thing again. I look closer, and he doesn't even have eye gook. Something occurs to me—he wants me to play along, like he said before—follow his lead. Oh!

"But don't those parasites usually fight back?" Lady Marmalade asks, confused. Dr. Lam looks at me, his eyes still pleading.

"Uh . . . you'll never catch me alive, coppers," I say, waving my arms about and jumping up and down. I think I remember the bad guys in Mama's television shows saying things like that when they fought back. The fact that I remember the shows (we watched them every single afternoon) and now comprehend what was going on in them is very . . . freaky. I also understand freaky.

"Coppers?" Lady Marmalade asks.

"I think our princess is very strong. Her body is clearly fighting it. That was the scene you just saw. Her parasite and her mind fighting for control." He doesn't know the half of it.

"Can you wrap it in cheese?" I ask as he holds the pill near me.

Lady Marmalade exhales and says, "I'm tired of waiting." She takes the pill from Dr. Lam and shoves it in my mouth. Yup, she's tough, like Bailey. The pill is sweet, though. I can taste it on my useless tongue, which isn't so useless now that I think about it. I can taste things, but what if I want to clean my . . . private area? "Good."

"Lady Marmalade, you shouldn't be so rough with her," Dr. Lam says. "She's had a hard year."

"Oh please. Life is hard. And if I wasn't here to guide her, her father would have spaced her already." Spaced? That doesn't sound good. I don't even like space. Spaced must be even more space! Not good! "And to further show you who is on whose side here, you're going to order her to rest back in her room—not in the brig."

"The brig? Who said anything—"

"Her father ordered her to the brig. Didn't you know?" Lady Marmalade asks. Dr. Lam is quiet. "See, the little prodigy doesn't know everything, does he? But you can overrule her father with your medical regulations, no?" Lady Marmalade points a finger at his chest. "You would do that for this sweet, sick girl?"

"Certainly." Dr. Lam coughs. "The brig is no place to recover from a Joparan Body Snatcher parasite." He's pressing some buttons into the computer. "Done."

"See, now who's helping who here," she replies. As I ponder the idea of even *more* space, Lady Marmalade turns to me. "Come on, Princess. We have a lot to talk about."

"Wait! My ball!" I grab it from the floor before we leave.

Chapter 4
Bailey, Where Art Thou?

After a quiet walk through the corridors of this space carriage, with random people jumping out of our way when they see us coming, we enter a room.

Is this *my* room? I hope it is because it's huge—almost as big as my entire house back home in my old world, or galaxy. There are bluish drapes covering the windows. A golden spiral staircase in the middle of this large room leads to a whole other level. The floors feel like . . . marble? *Why do I even know that word?* And those huge plush oval rugs covering the *marble*. I just want to curl up on one . . . but I know I shouldn't.

This room is amazing! Better than any room in Mama and Dada's house. Seeing it reminds me how my *father* here wanted me thrown in the brig. The way everyone reacted, the brig sounded horrible. Thank Dog for Captain Gregor. My bed must be on the second floor?

"This room is beautiful," I say as I sit on a luxuriously soft red couch, trying hard to stop myself from curling up. It's been a *very* long day. "I hope I don't get sent to the brig—whatever that is."

"Ha, just this morning you were calling this room your dungeon. But I guess marriage can mess with your head." Lady Marmalade laughs as she sits next to me. "Your father is getting up there in years, so he'll defer to KAMP and Dr. Lam, for now. Until he can find a way around them. But seriously, what got into you tonight? And I know you're not sick."

"A body snatcher thing; he told you," I remind her. Did she really just forget?

"I know he has you wrapped around his little finger, that one. But you shouldn't trust him. Never trust a man. Or KAMP. They'll use you for their own agenda." Lady Marmalade wags a finger at me.

"But, Bailey—"

"And what's with this Bailey nonsense? This is the second time you've called me that."

"Well, it's just that you remind me—"

"Come on," she cuts me off, throwing her hands up. She doesn't believe me. "Wait!" she exclaims softly and puts a hand up in my face. It looks like a command, but I don't recall that one. Could it be sit? But I'm sitting already. I cock my head trying to figure it out. "Let me go find your hairbrush." Hairbrush? Oh, *wait* means hairbrush! Is it grooming time at night here too? I always loved getting brushed by Mama. Is Lady Marmalade going to brush me? Oh, how joyous.

I'm taking all sorts of clips out of my hair to get ready (these come out, unlike the crown), but Lady Marmalade doesn't get up at all to find a brush. Confused, I say, "I thought you were—"

But she puts a finger to my mouth to stop me and takes out a cell phone-looking thing—I'll just call them cell phones from now on—from somewhere under her dress and waves it around the room. She stops while it is pointed at a fancy fireplace. Rubbing her hands along the inside of the fireplace, she takes out a small device that looks like a bug (like the one Dr. Lam put on his head but smaller) and shows me. What is going on? *Are the bug people invading?*

"Oh Princess, you're cold? I suppose I can turn on the fireplace. A *real* fire? Not a sim fire? How quaint. Just like you used to have at home, right? You must miss home after tonight. Sure, I can do that." Then she drops the bug and stomps on it. She comes back to sit next to me. "Wouldn't want your father or KAMP listening in, would you? Or worse, *spying* on you. That doctor does seem to have a dangerous fascination with you. Why your father had to have the child prodigy doctor instead of the normal KAMP decrepit old man . . ."

Wow, could she be *right* about Dr. Lam? But Dr. Lam seemed so nice. He was going to take me home. Well, Trixie's home. He just wanted to help me.

"I know you and the good doctor are cooking something

up," Lady Marmalade continues as I ponder her words, "but this marriage . . . I thought we decided it could actually *work* for you. You know, get away from dear old dad. And Prince Weibold isn't so bad. He's quite the looker, am I right? Remember me showing you the vids of him? He's very pious. Maybe that counts for something." *I do like pie.* But so much was going on, I didn't really notice him that much tonight. He was kind of like a tall yellow lab moving so fast I could barely make him out. But he couldn't have been as cute as that nice poodle, Dr. Lam. I smile. "I see I'm right. You're blushing."

"Am not!" I reply. What is this feeling? My face feels so hot. It's clear I can't tell her about Dr. Lam's plan. And now I'm not so sure about it anyway. Is he somehow dangerous too? "And I'm not cooking anything, I swear. Though I am hungry." I haven't eaten since breakfast . . . on an entirely different world. And I think I missed dinner? I couldn't even lap up that soup. So now my brain is instantly focused on human food. Human food!

"Sure, uh, didn't eat much at dinner, eh?" she says with a laugh. Then she speaks into her cell phone-looking thing. "Lady Justyna, please fetch us some sandwiches and prule fruit drinks."

"Yes, Lady Marmalade," the cell phone speaks back.

"Now," Lady Marmalade turns back to me, "tell me about that cute Prince Weibold . . ."

But I'm barely listening. Sandwiches! Human food! I'm insatiably curious to try a *drink*. I've only ever had water!

And that one lap of soup at that disaster of a dinner. Now I can just order it to come to me? Like a human? Visions of being surrounded by human food dance around my new human brain. My tongue comes out to lick my lips. Drool is coming down—

"Trixie! Stop that! You're a princess!" Lady Marmalade says as she gently slaps my cheek. "I've told you before: practice kissing Prince Weibold in *private*! If a man were to see you like that . . ." She shudders like Dr. Lam did when talking about Quantum Mancers. "Let's not speak about such things. Listen, you're young. I'm willing to give you pointers again, since you seem to have forgotten *everything* today, but not out here in a living room, for Sol's sake."

"Was not!" I exclaim as my face feels hot again.

"Uh-huh, *sure*. I've seen you watch his vids." Wow, did Trixie actually like him? But the doctor made it seem like they were planning her escape. He said not to tell Bailey . . . er, Lady Marmalade . . . though. Which one did Princess Trixie really trust?

"Where are the sandwiches?" I ask, trying to change the subject. "Do you all just bring me food when I ask?" My tongue starts to leave my mouth again, but I catch it this time.

"Oh Trixie, maybe I was wrong—you do seem so confused. Of course we do. I even have the privilege, as your lady-in-waiting and your head attendant, of following you to the Thorpian Stardom. We'll be friends forever." Me and Bailey! I'm excited. Maybe she's right and Dr. Lam is wrong. If I'm stuck on this world, the Thorpian Stardom could be better than Kalaxia Limo One. Is that why Trixie was practicing kissing the prince?

The door opens and in walks a young blonde-haired girl holding a tray. Her hair is so straight and long—down to her tushy. I'm not good with human ages, but after seeing myself, she definitely looks younger than me, though way taller. She has on flowing blue pants and a white blouse.

"Justyna, good. Right here," Lady Marmalade says.

This Justyna looks like a tall golden retriever, ready for orders. "Your sandwich, Princess," she says to me as she puts the tray down on the table in front of us, does a jittery curtsy, and runs out of the room. Well, she's a very *nervous* golden retriever. Seeing her run gives me the urge to chase her.

"Justyna is still relatively new, really young and really scared of you," Lady Marmalade says with a chuckle. "And just a bit . . . dumber than us. Case in point: one sandwich. I asked for 'some.' But we endure."

"You mean *Lady* Justyna?"

"Oh Trixie. We've never stood on formality before. You know, unless it's an order that someone could overhear, you and I can just use first names. Unless you'd like to change that now or when we move to Thorpia, perhaps?"

"No, uh, I don't mean that. We're friends forever." I beam a smile at Bailey . . . er, Lady . . . er, Marmalade. I don't know anything about formality. But I know about chasing.

"I agree, Trixie," Marmalade says, taking my hands in

hers and smiling. "Now please tell me what has gotten into you today. Do you remember anything, like what might have caused all this . . . confusion?"

Of course I remember! "I want to run in real grass."

"What?"

"Grass!"

"Oh Princess, there's no grass on a space carriage. That's just not possible. This isn't Expiry. Plus, it would be *scandalous*. You have an image to maintain. No, I'm afraid it's out of the question."

"You know, I'm sick of this space carriage!" All my feelings are coming to the surface. And this Marmalade is my friend, right? She asked me! "I want to go home! Run in the grass. Through the woods. Chase something! I *need* to go home."

"In the . . . *dirt*? Like an *animal*?"

"Yes! Beautiful dirt! Oh, the smells!" I close my eyes and imagine sticking my snout in some plants—the memories of the smells are still there. "I *am* an animal!"

"Wow, you must really be homesick."

My eyes open. That's it. "You have no idea."

"Is that why you messed up that dinner? Is that how Dr. Lam has gotten to you? I know it *seems* as though he likes you—"

"He *likes* me?"

"You haven't noticed? I think the whole ship might have. It seemed so innocent. You're untouchable."

"Can he really get me home?"

"I was right! Don't listen to him. You know you can't go home! They'll never allow it." Marmalade throws her hands up and rises from the couch. "Is that what he's been telling you?" She's looking down on me like I've been a badgirl. My eyes dart away from her gaze. "You can't listen to that nonsense. And I'll say it again: You can't trust KAMP. They have their own agenda. You're a pawn to everyone. But at least you *are* a pawn—it's keeping you alive.

"How long have I been telling you this? All year! This alliance your father and Voltari founded will make them stronger, which only makes KAMP weaker—what with the Thorpians' unorthodox religious medicine. Of course KAMP would try to stop it. We've been over this."

"He was nice, though. Are you sure? I just miss home so much. Why can't I go home?" She doesn't know what I truly mean—I don't know whom to trust, but just saying it out loud with these human words is making me feel better.

Marmalade stares at me a moment, then sits down next to me. Her hand is on my thigh. "I still can't believe you grew up on an actual dirty planet. You know, I've never even been on one." Her body shakes. "Oh, those dirty commoners." She shakes again and looks away. Is that a tear?

What's so bad about planets? Or commoners? Is that what she means by people on planets? Like Mama and Dada and Charlotte and Carolina? But I woof them. Then what is she? I remember some words: management and executives. Is she management? Am I? Or am I an executive? No, I'm even more important as a princess.

This world is so different—so complicated. And maybe Dr. Lam was right. Is Lady Marmalade not really my friend? I'm just a dirty commoner to her?

"But," she continues, "as your lady-in-waiting, and your friend, let's do it!" She *is* my friend!

"Oh, really really?"

"Even if you are management now, I'll take you to run in dirt like a commoner," she says, though with a disgusted face this time, as if the truth of what she is saying finally hits her.

"Home!" *Yay!*

"No, Trixie. You know you can't. You would be seen, and I would be executed. But there's a nearby unpopulated planet you can go run on, or whatever it is you do on one."

This is the first good thing to happen to me here. And while I don't want to give up on getting home to Mama and Dada, it's clear that no one knows anything about who I am or how I got here. And it's also clear that if I make a wrong move, I could be killed or spaced—whatever that is. Even worse, Director Voltari could kill me just by looking at me.

I desperately need to figure this world out before I can get home. Both Dr. Lam and Lady Marmalade seem good, but they each say the other is bad. They both want me to do opposite things and also think I'm losing my mind. If I were to tell them where I'm really from, what will they think then? It's not safe. I'll have to find another way home. Someone must know something. There's always a way home.

But for now, my friend Bailey . . . er, Lady, . . . er, Marmalade . . . is going to take me to run on a real planet. I throw my arms around her in one of those hugs my human littermates Charlotte and Carolina always strangle me with. But as a human now, it actually feels nice.

Chapter 5
There Are Predators Down There . . . and Up Here

"L ady Brandi," Lady Marmalade says into her cell phone, "we have a job. Meet us at the Shuttle Bay. And bring Lady Justyna. Now."

"Shuttle Bay? Are you serious?"

"Yes, I'm serious," my friend Marmalade replies. *Yes, she's serious, Brandi!* There are a few moments of quiet.

"Has the wedding been moved up? Are you leaving now? Oh, thank—"

"No! Just meet us. With a whole case of your usual. Lady Marmalade out."

"Who was that?" I ask.

"Brandi? I know you haven't interacted with them much, not that they haven't tried, but don't you recall? She's one of your ladies. Your assistants?"

"Can we trust *her*?" I ask.

"Brandi? Of course. She'll do whatever I tell her to do. You must know that all she cares about is cupcakes. She is obsessed with them. She eats like five hundred a day. You'll see."

"Cupcakes? Really? I've never had a cupcake." Will I really get to have one? For really real?

"Well, it's not that she hasn't tried. She's told me how bored she is of making you potatoes. Let's have . . . what is that thing you told me you like to do on your crazy, backward dirt rock planet?"

"Chase squirrels?" Please say it's chasing squirrels!

"No . . . wait, what's that? Never mind. I don't want to know. The thing with the food? Picnics!"

"Oh!" The word comes to me. Eating outside. "Human food!"

"Um . . . what other kind of . . . no, wait. Never mind. I don't want to know what you considered food back on Expiry. I don't think you and all us girls have ever really gotten together these past six months. This might be our last time to do this anyway. So if I have to go down to a . . . a . . . planet—blech—I'll do it in style. Marmalade style." She means *Bailey* style. "Now just one more call." She looks closer at her cell phone. I can't help myself any longer. I have to know.

"What is that thing you're holding?" I point at the device.

"What? This? You asked me that your very first day here.

Are you sure you weren't hit on the head or something? But why wouldn't Dr. Lam have just said that?"

"I don't think I was."

"Hmm . . ." Her head is tilted. I know that look. Then she appears normal again. "This is a cell phone, remember?"

"Ah! A cell phone!" I exclaim. I was right—I knew something about this world!

"Yes. It's made from the cells of a telepathic nonsentient multicellular organism called the Wuxaxi. They're all connected to one another." Oh, weird how Mama had one too. Maybe the Wuxaxi is on both our worlds. Maybe they know how to get home?

"Can I talk to the Wuxaxi?" I ask. "I have some questions—"

"For Sol's sake, Trixie. You can't talk to them. They're *nonsentient*. They don't talk." Bummer. She hits some buttons on the device. *Major bummer.*

Marmalade's cell phone snaps, "Yes? What is it?" It's a lady's voice. Then we hear a grunt. "Speak quickly. I'm staring down about two hundred undead zombies right now. Blindfolded. I'm trying to increase my kill rate, and this call is getting in my way." Grunt, grunt. Who did she call?

"Lady Koko," Marmalade says, "stop that training exercise this instant."

That's Lady Koko? Her voice sounds so . . . scary. Is she another one of my ladies too? She sounds like a big dog. A very big dog. A rottweiler.

"Aw, man," Lady Koko replies. We hear a deep breath.

"Computer, off." Wow, Marmalade really has control over this big dog. I'm impressed.

"Good. We have a new mission for you."

"Oh, a *real* mission? Instead of just guarding that prissy head-in-the-clouds know-nothing—"

"Lady Koko! How dare you! You're on speakerphone!" Marmalade scolds her.

"With *her*?" Koko asks quietly, like it could erase what she said before.

"Yes, *her*!" Marmalade snaps.

"Oh, I'm sorry Princess . . . er, Lady Princess, . . . er Princess Lady. It . . . I . . . it's just . . . the adrenaline . . . I . . . your hair is nice." And then quieter. "Argh, I'm so stupid."

I ask Marmalade softly, "Is she always like this?"

She nods. "All she cares about is fighting, not social skills. Even with all my effort. Please don't take it personally."

"She sounds like a very big dog. A scary dog," I blurt out. A shiver runs through me. A scary dog is one of my *ladies*?

"What's a dog?" Marmalade asks. I'm afraid to answer. "Some predator from home?" I nod. "Dogs, squirrels. You sure are homesick today, or it's some crazy amnesia. I know it's no parasite, no matter what that doctor says. But don't worry; you can trust Lady Koko. She's just a meathead."

"Hey! The speakerphone is on here too!" Koko says, annoyed.

"Just meet us at the Shuttle Bay. And bring Lady Perri."

"But it's late. Almost midnight. Perri will be mad."

"*Lady* Perri. And it's not midnight where we're going."

She looks at her cell phone. "It's a bright sunny afternoon."

"Can't this wait till morning? There's nothing scarier than a surly Perri."

"Now! Lady Marmalade out."

"If she doesn't like me, why do we need her?" I ask. And who is Perri? She sounds scary too!

"Because, Princess, she's the muscle. I don't want something happening to us down there. Or it'll be *my* head. Now follow me."

"Can I bring the sandwich?"

"You're the princess, Princess! I'll carry the sandwich for you." She takes the sandwich and inspects it. "Ugh, she made a prule sandwich. Who makes a prule sandwich? I asked for prule *juice*." Then she puts it somewhere under her dress, where it disappears.

"Can we take the juice also?" I ask.

"I'm not carrying the juice in here." She pats her hip (how is she storing all this stuff there? Her dress isn't bulging at all). "So drink it now. And then you should change out of that formal dress."

Ah, my first human juice. I pick up the glass and start sniffing it. This darn nose doesn't work. I twirl my glass a bit, wondering how my humans drank from this. I'm not sure. They just open their mouths and pour it down their throats. It always looked so dangerous. I open my mouth and tilt my head back, ready to pour it down my throat. But I stop and tilt my head forward again. I can't! I don't want to drown!

"Just drink it!" Marmalade snaps.

"I'm sorry, Bailey! I can't!"

"Stop calling me Bailey!" Oh no, Bailey is mad at me.

I close my eyes and pour the juice quickly down my throat, ready to die on this new world, not from a dangerous Quantum Mancer, my father, or even a rottweiler but from some prule juice. I'm sorry, Mama, for being so stupid. So, so stupid. I should never have gone into that tree. But here goes . . .

Down my throat . . . It's so splendid! The juice on my tongue—like a summer's day right on my lips. This is what humans get to drink all the freakin' time? Oops, I just cussed too. Like Charlotte. Not so much Carolina. But I remember Charlotte getting in trouble for it constantly—and now I know what it means! Freakin' freakin' freakin'! At least it's just in my head; I don't want Marmalade getting mad at me. But . . . does that make me really human now? *Charlotte, if you could see me now, you freak—*

"Look at your blouse! You don't even know how to drink anymore?" Marmalade thunders.

I look down to see that my puffy white blouse is all stained purple with prule juice. How did I not notice it dripping all over me? "I'm sorry," I reply. "I don't really know how to drink."

"What? Ugh." Marmalade sighs. "Let's go upstairs and get you changed."

"Yay! The stairs!" I cheer and throw my hands up in glee.

"Seriously? You always used to complain how one room

is all you ever needed on Expiry. You even made me bunk with you for the entire first month. It's almost like you became a different person at that dinner." *Oh no! Does she know?*

"No, no! Nothing like that. I promise!"

"Look, change is hard. But please do remember, I'll be with you on Thorpia. Now let's go to your bedroom and get changed."

Running up the spiral staircase is fun, and I end up on a huge second floor. Just as big as the main floor! A large cream-colored—like Marmalade's shirt—oval rug covers the floor where the big comfy bed is. The bed has a curtain thing too—a canopy? My brain fills in the word as a flying running jump lands me on the bed and Marmalade finally makes it upstairs. I close the curtains and kneel behind them before she sees me.

"Princess?" she asks, unable to find me.

Sticking my head through the canopy curtains, I call excitedly, "Peekaboo!" like Mama used to do to me with the towels when it rained. I hope Marmalade likes this game.

Unfortunately, she just sighs. "Oh stars, you're getting the bed all dirty, and I have to clean it. Well, Justyna has to, but still."

I open the curtains fully. "Isn't this just the best room?" I ask, still on the bed. "I've never seen a room this big. And such a bed!"

"I feel like a broken record. What has gotten into you? You've been here a year." *Oops.* She opens a previously unnoticed armoire, also huge, across the room. She takes out a pair of purple pants and a fitted brown shirt. "These should work."

"Can I have a red shirt?" What I don't add is that red is a new color that I've never seen before, and I'm so excited to wear red. Red, red, red.

"Fine."

"Yes!" Off the bed, I gather the clothes from her. Fumbling with my shirt's buttons, Marmalade slaps my hands away.

"You can't change in front of me. You're a princess!"

"But . . . we're friends. That's what you said! And they're just clothes."

"Use the privacy screen." She points to a large fabric screen set up in the far corner of the room.

"Oh!"

Behind the privacy screen, I'm still fumbling with the buttons. "Uh," I call to Marmalade, "I don't know how to do buttons."

"I taught you." She makes the sound of a heavy sigh. She's eggsperated? No, that's not right. Exasperated? "I'm sure the stress isn't helping. Just come back out here. I'll do the clothes for you, but no one can know."

"Yay!"

In a moment she's helping me with the blouse and pants. She even finds a front pants pocket for my new ball. As she asks me questions about it, my brain finally processes that it's an important crystal Prince Weibold gave me. I must have seemed so silly putting it in my mouth. It has something to do with healing, though I don't really remember what he said. But I know I have to return it, which makes me sad again. Enough of that, though. This is no time to be sad. It's outside time!

"You look good, no thanks to you. I can't believe how much you've forgotten. KAMP could do a case study on you, if we could trust them. But we can go now. Oh, wait. First, your crown. You need that only for show."

Marmalade pushes one of the sparkly rocks on it, and it loosens from my head. *That's how you do it!* She sets it on a table near us. "Now, your mind still isn't right, so let me do all the talking if we run into anybody. You must realize how crazy this plan is. But I'm doing it for you." Then she wraps me in a big human hug. *Oh Marmalade. I like feeling secure in her arms.* Then she drags me through the front door of my room.

We're zigzagging through hallways. I will never remember my way back because *my smell is gone*! Stupid human nose. I try sniffing the air, but everything just smells the same here. Dull. I'll never find my way around.

"This place smells so dull," I say, voicing my thoughts.

"Amazing; you said that your first week here also. It's like a time warp today with you, like you just got here," Marmalade replies. "Just remember, *no* talking."

Turning the corner in front of us are a pack of royal guards marching down the hall. I smile inside because I actually know something about this world, but Marmalade stiffens, so I do as well. She also drops my hand. The head guard speaks. "Hey, Marmi." Marmi?

"Hey, Jaxson," she replies. I've never seen Marmalade look so fearful before.

"You ladies are looking lovely tonight. Where are you headed?"

"You know, just a little sightseeing," she replies.

"Good, good. Don't forget that snogging we talked about. I'd like to *discuss* it later," Jaxson says as he rubs her chin. Oh, that looks so good. Rub my chin! But what's snogging? And why does she look so scared?

"Of course, sir."

"Good, good. You're available now; you need someone to claim you, or . . . well, you know. I'll leave you to your sightseeing." The guards march off.

"You know him?" I ask my lady-in-waiting.

"Colonel Jaxson? Don't worry about him. You know these guardsmen. We have to keep them at bay when we can. If he only knew." But I have no idea what she's talking about.

"Knew what?"

"Oh Princess, never you mind about that."

"But what does snog mean? I don't know that word."

"Really?" Marmalade sounds surprised. "He meant kissing. Oh Princess, you don't have to worry about such things. You're betrothed. Protected from buffoons like Jaxson. Soon you'll be *snogging* the prince, like you've been practicing." Kissing? I know kissing!

A lot of new human words have "magically" come to me, like *brain* and *cupcake*. Maybe I only know words that Princess Trixie knew, when she was Princess Trixie? Twinkie only heard some words. I'm already talking about her like I'm not her. Oh Dog!

After the guards pass, Marmalade grabs my hand and we're off again through endless hallways and dodging other passengers on Limo One. I don't recognize any of them, though. Then we're at a door marked SHUTTLE BAY. And standing there are four other girls.

One is very tall and muscular, clearly older than me, with short spiked black hair. She's wearing brown (I know this color), loose pants and a tight brown shirt with buttons down the front, but without sleeves, which is how I can see all those muscles. She looks like that scary rottweiler I always ran away from at the dog run. But this girl is maybe twenty? How can I tell ages so easily now? It feels like Princess Trixie's memories are coming back just like her words. Is her human knowledge seeping into my brain? Brain, brain, brain. I love that word. I have a brain!

Next to her is a very petite, thin lady, about my age, with shoulder-length brown hair, worn with bangs, two side ponytails, and thick glasses. She has a big hard case in one hand and is wearing black pants and a thick black shirt with long sleeves. These girls look so different from how I did before with that long skirt and puffy purple blanket blouse. But now we kind of match—especially without that crown on my head.

Next to her is a girl a few years younger than me but slightly older than Lady Justyna, the golden retriever I already met. Is this girl fourteen? Unlike Justyna, she is plump with brown chin-length hair. She's much shorter than Lady Koko (we all are, except for Justyna, who is just somewhat shorter) but not as short as the girl with bangs. And this girl is still wearing . . . oh, I know that. A chef's apron! Is that Lady Brandi? The cupcake girl? She reminds me of a chow—the one that wouldn't talk to me at the dog run.

And that means the girl my age is Lady Perri?

Now that I'm getting used to ages, is Marmalade in her late twenties? That would make her the mama of this group? That makes sense.

"Seriously, Lady Brandi? You're still wearing that?" Marmalade asks the girl with the chef's apron. Yup, that's Lady Brandi.

"When you give me five minutes to make a batch of my galactically famous vanilla fudge quasar cupcakes, yes. I'm still wearing my apron. And I'm sweaty and tired, but I just *had* to do something for the *princess*. You're just lucky—"

"Lady Brandi, do you not see the princess standing right here? And you would talk so rudely?" I'm getting the impression all my ladies hate me. My face falls.

"What does that matter? She's going to be gone in two weeks anyway," the shortest girl with the bangs says. "And then I can go back to school." Koko was right; Perri *is* surly.

"Lady Perri, Lady Brandi! What is wrong with all of you? For two weeks you are still her assistants and *my* employees.

And I can still give you letters of reprimand, even all the way from the Thorpian Stardom if I have to. Keep this up, and you know I will." Instantly, all four girls (well, Koko is probably a woman?) stand erect and at attention. Go, Bailey . . . er, Lady Marmalade! I shouldn't have doubted you.

"Good," Marmalade continues. "Now, Lady Perri, we need you to rewire the Shuttle Bay's entrance door and get us inside. Then you'll need to hack a shuttle and get us out secretly."

"Um . . . ," says the short Perri, who looks like a very smart papillon, especially with those ponytails. "You want me to who where why in the what now?"

"You heard me. Listen up, ladies. Princess Trixie is feeling unwell," Marmalade says as the four girls take a step back.

"I heard about her Parchesian Flu," Koko says.

"It's not a flu," Marmalade clarifies. "KAMP is just . . . forget it. She's just ridiculously homesick. So while Limo One is orbiting this nebula, in the vicinity of a habitable but unpopulated planet, we're going to do what we can to take care of our princess."

"Are you serious?" Brandi asks. "We're going to steal a shuttle and just sneak out to . . . to . . ."

"PX-373X27," Marmalade says, completing her thought.

"And without being detected?" Perri asks. "The four of us? Isn't that, like, treason?"

"*Five* of us," Marmalade replies. "You forgot the princess. And yes, we will. And we will be successful. Do you understand me?"

"Yes, milady," Koko says. The others nod.

Lady Perri walks to the Shuttle Bay entrance's control panel and starts using some tools from her case. I have no idea what's going on, and none of the ladies will look me in the eye. I'm feeling very lonely, so I lean closer to Marmalade.

After a few minutes, the Shuttle Bay doors open. "I took the entire Shuttle Bay off the computer's main system but also created a dummy on the system that I sent into an automatic eight-hour silent diagnostic along with short-range sensors. Oh, and I added a false fumigation in the Shuttle Bay for poisonous space bugs. So we'll have eight hours down on PX whatever for Your Highness to do whatever dirty commoners do on disgusting planets—"

"Lady Perri!" Marmalade exclaims.

"Oh, I didn't mean her. I just meant *her* . . . from before she was our princess, you know?" Perri says.

I'm confused. I hadn't really thought of it before. Is there a reason these girls don't like me? As far as I can tell, they think I'm a know-nothing dirty commoner. Other passengers jump out of the way when they see me. The Thorpian Stardom prince *wants* to marry me. Why do these ladies hate me so?

"Whatever. Come on, girls," Marmalade says as she waves everyone into the Shuttle Bay. The door closes behind us. We're in a huge room—the biggest one I've seen on board. It looks like a hundred cars are all lined up in rows in here. Are they the shuttles?

A male mechanic in a bright-blue suit lifts his head at the sight of five women entering the Shuttle Bay. "Lady Koko, take him out," Marmalade orders.

"Gladly," she replies.

"What? Huh?" is all the mechanic says before he is in a . . . the word comes to me—choke hold. Trixie knows what a choke hold is? Why? The mechanic falls asleep pretty quickly and slumps on the ground.

"Lady Perri, you said eight hours?" Marmalade asks her. She nods in agreement. Then Marmalade takes out two syringes from under her dress (what else does she keep in there?) and stabs the mechanic's neck twice. "One of these will knock him out for at least eight hours, and the other is an actual flu—the Margosian Night Flu. He'll have the wildest dreams imaginable—so much so that he'll think all this was part of it. Now, Lady Perri, let's get in one of those shuttles."

"This isn't what I signed up for," Brandi says, fear in her voice. In truth, I'm also kind of scared of Lady Marmalade now. But Marmalade holds the empty vial (see, Mama, I could have gone to school with Charlotte! I know fancy science words now!) in her direction, threatening her. "Uh . . . this will be fun, I mean."

In minutes we're all sitting in one of the shuttles, with Marmalade, Perri, and me in the front. The other three girls are behind us, also in seats. I'm even strapped in, just like in Mama's minivan. I want to curl up on the seat like I did as Twinkie, but I can't, so I try to squirm into a comfortable position.

"What's wrong with you? Got ants in your pants?" Koko asks, laughing from the back seat. She puts an open hand up, like she's saying stop, but then Lady Brandi hits Koko's hand with her own open hand. A high five? Isn't that what my human littermates used to do? These ladies are making fun of me and enjoying it together?

It makes me so mad. I can't take it any longer. I turn around and bare my teeth and growl, and the three of them jump back. Even the rottweiler, Lady Koko, who started it.

"Ha, she got you, gals," Marmalade says.

"Not fair," Koko replies. "She could be sick! She's foaming at the mouth!"

I'm really tired of all this. I didn't want to be on this world. I didn't want to be so far away from Mama and Dada and Charlotte and Carolina. I want to be in *their* minivan, curled up in the back seat. I certainly don't want to be marrying anyone or have a new evil father. I just want to go home!

Then my brain thinks of something to say back to these two meanies behind me. My first "comeback," which I now know is what Charlotte called it. It's just part of being human, it seems. I guess I can't just growl at them like a dog any longer. Should I throw in one of Charlotte's cuss words also? Charlotte would say yes.

"Yeah, I'm freaking sick of all of you! Now shut your traps. I'm the princess here!" And then the magic happens—the kind of magic that got me here in the first place. They all shut up.

Lady Marmalade and I share a smile.

But then . . . "What in the galaxy does *freaking* mean?" Koko asks from behind me.

"I think she just called us all kings," Brandi says.

"Oh, that's not nice," Justyna adds. "Is it?"

Chapter 6
Always Look on the Planetside of Life

Opening Shuttle Bay doors," Perri says.

The Shuttle Bay has another set of huge doors that our shuttle is now facing. It's at the other end of the bay from where we came in. After Perri speaks, this other set of doors opens and . . . that's space? This is what they meant? I see total blackness with little bright lights, like a fancy blanket. Those lights—what are they? I'm searching Trixie's memory, because Twinkie . . . er, me . . . has no idea.

Then it comes to me. They're tons of stars! It's dark out there, but there are tons and tons of stars. And a big cloud-looking thing? In space? Pushing my head forward as if that would help me see better, I feel the shuttle start to move. My hands grab the seat beneath me as my body stiffens.

"Wow, you really are a landie. They weren't kidding," Perri says as she hits some controls in front of her.

Ignoring her, because she's just a meanie, I watch as space envelops the shuttle. Either we're moving, which I think is true from all the shaking, or all of space is moving around me. My stomach jumps as I watch space move around me. Oh no. I feel sick. Then I recall something from Trixie's memories. Oh no, oh no, oh no. Why did I have to get a memory from Trixie right now? I'm fascinated but really upset. Trixie gets spacesick!

"Yo, Lady Marmalade. Princess doesn't look so hot." Was that Koko?

Lady Marmalade looks at me. "Really? Seriously?"

"I told you she could have the flu," Koko replies.

"I'm going to throw up," I say.

"Ew!"

"Gross!"

"She's just spacesick!" Marmalade snaps. "Quick, get her something to upchuck into."

"We don't have anything!" Perri exclaims.

"Your tool case!" Marmalade replies.

"No! No, no, no, no, no! Not that!" Perri squeals.

"Bring it here, or you'll never see the inside of a school again," Marmalade says.

"Quick! It's coming!" I say, with my hands covering my mouth. I feel like I ate mouthfuls of grass.

The hard tool case comes flying into the front seat, Marmalade opens it, and I . . . what was that word Marmalade used? I upchuck into it. My mouth and nose are burning.

"My tools! I hate you, Princess!" Perri says. But I'm not really listening. I'm just focused on trying not to do it again. It feels like it could happen again. Wiping my mouth, I close my eyes and rock back and forth. A hand caresses my shoulder.

"You feeling better?" Marmalade asks me.

"No. I think we should just go home. This picnic was a bad idea. No one wants to go. They all hate me. *I* hate me."

"Nonsense, Princess. How are you going to make it as a princess in that crazy militaristic Thorpian Stardom with an attitude like that?" Marmalade asks, trying to cheer me up.

"You could have just used the bag of cupcakes," Perri says.

"What would we eat then?" Brandi replies, sounding horrified.

"It smells really nasty in here now," Koko remarks.

"I'll dispose of that for you, Princess," Lady Justyna offers, "and get some air freshener. Would you like the strawberry or honeysuckle scent? If not those, I can—"

"Just go, Justyna!" Marmalade scolds her. Justyna takes the bag from us and hurries into a room behind all the seats.

It's the first time Justyna's *really* spoken up the whole trip. She wants to help me? Doesn't she hate me like the others? But she's a golden retriever. Doing her duty is important to her, I guess. Either way, I'm happy to have her.

"Look, Princess," Lady Marmalade says as she points at something in the distance. "There's PX-373X27A, also designated by the Kalaxian Empire as Pareto, our destination."

"We're almost there? We might make it?" I ask.

"Only if you don't barf on my controls," Perri says, but

I ignore her. Because seeing a real planet increase in size on our viewscreen is awe-inspiring for somedog . . . er, someone . . . who was just a dog a few hours ago, and it makes me so happy. Soon I will get to run and play on a planet. In the grass and the dirt!

"Did she barf again?" Justyna asks, as she returns from a back room of the shuttle (is it a bathroom?).

"How could she?" Brandi says. "She already barfed her brains out."

I'm barely listening. My eyes are focused on that beautiful planet. A sea of green and blue. Swirling clouds. A real planet. Instantly I feel revived. "So who's going to be *it*?" I ask excitedly.

"Who's going to be the barf?" Koko asks. The rest of the girls giggle.

"No, sillies," I say. "It! You know, the one we all chase? I bet I'm faster than all of you." Have they never played this game?

"Oh my stars, she literally barfed her brains out," Perri says. More giggling.

"No, Perri—"

"*Lady* Perri, *Lady* Koko," Marmalade scolds.

"Right. I was going to say it actually sounds like kill the carrier," Koko amends quickly. "We used to play that game at the Royal Guard Youth Academy."

"See!" I say, pointing at Koko. "It!"

"Killing?" Brandi squeals.

"Well, we tackled," Koko explains. "That was just the name of it."

"There will be no killing or tackling," Marmalade replies. "It's enough to be on that dirty rock. I don't want you all acting like animals. It's a simple picnic, for Sol's sake."

"Of course we can just tag!" I think I remember Carolina playing a game with tagging in our backyard. "It's just supposed to be chasing anyway," I say.

"No running like animals!" Marmalade scolds us.

"But, Lady Marmalade, she said she's faster," Koko complains.

"I am. I know I am," I reply proudly. I'm a dog! Of course I am.

"See!" Koko whines.

"Fine," Marmalade says. "You can go be animals. But only tagging."

"Oh, you mean like running? With legs?" Justyna asks.

"Yes, Lady Justyna," Brandi says, "with legs. Have you lost the plot *again?*"

"I thought they were going to carry something," Justyna replies. "But if it's running, I'm pretty fast. I'll be *it*." There's my golden retriever.

"No way, Lady Justyna. You little kids are *not* faster than me," Koko declares.

"Wait, you two are seriously considering running on that dirtball of a planet?" Perri asks.

"Yeah!" I exclaim. "I bet I can catch you all."

"Stupid landies, the lot of you," Perri snarks.

"Dirtball or not, I can't ignore a physical challenge," Koko says.

"I'm not that fast," Brandi admits.

"Don't worry!" I beam at Brandi. "We'll need someone to throw the balls."

"Balls?" she asks.

"Princess, we didn't bring any balls," Lady Marmalade says. "And is this really what you did back home for fun?" She means Expiry, but I mean home with Mama, so I nod.

"Lady Brandi, can you throw cupcakes?" I ask. "We can try to catch them in our mouths."

"Um . . . the ones I worked so hard to make? That's a terrible idea."

"Aw, come on, *Lady* Brandi," Koko says.

"Ugh, fine. As long as they get eaten," Brandi agrees.

"Oh God. Your flu is catching," Perri grumbles. "I might just stay on the shuttle."

"Suit yourself," I reply, too excited for real grass to care. Somehow these girls might not be so bad. Well, except for surly Perri. The shuttle's landing door opens, and the gangway extends onto the planet's lush green grass (just as Bailey . . . er, Marmalade . . . promised). As the rest of us unclip our belts and stand up, Perri surprisingly does too. We all look at her.

"What? You need *someone* with a brain with you," Perri says in answer to our looks.

As I walk to the gangway, I can see the luxurious grass and big green trees in the distance. The sky is a brilliant blue. We've landed in a clearing that looks like a huge green lawn surrounded by a lake off in the distance on one side and a beautiful forest on the other side. We have so much room to run around in! The planet is all ours! This I could *never* do back home. A whole planet all my own? I just can't help it any longer and take off down the gangway. "Forget it! I'm it! Come and get *me*, Lady Justyna!" I shout with glee and run as fast as I can away from the shuttle.

"Wait!" Justyna calls. "What do I do when I get you?"

"Tag me! Then *you* can be it!" I call back over my shoulder. Justyna is now racing toward me, so I pick up even more speed. This is the best feeling ever!

Koko is on our tail as well. She's a highly trained athlete (or warrior?) so I expect she can catch Justyna. But I'm a dog! Neither can reach me, but that's no fun, so I slow down just a bit. The game is more fun if you can get caught! Justyna catches up to me first, so I try to do some fakes to get away, pretending to go left and then right.

"How do I tag you? I didn't bring any tags. Was I supposed to bring labels? I can go back to the ship," Justyna says through shallow breaths.

"No, with your hand, silly, if you can!" But then I point to the forest. "Wait, there's someone there."

"What? Really?" Justyna asks in fear.

"Ha! Fooled you!" I take off running again.

"I don't detect any life signs!" Perri calls from the shuttle's gangway. She's probably still afraid to step on the grass.

"Fooled you too! Can't catch me!" I call back. I put some distance between us again.

"Hey, that's not fair! You tricked me," Justyna pouts, standing there.

"All's fair in battle!" Koko exclaims as she races past Justyna toward me. "You're surprisingly fast for a know-nothing princess!"

"Ha!" I laugh back. "I know how to run!" Koko laughs too.

After a bit, I slow down so that Koko can reach me too, and I try faking her out again, but I stumble and Koko catches up and tags me. "Am I *it*?"

"Don't just tag her! Help her up! She's covered in dirt! This is horrible!" Marmalade cries from the gangway, also afraid to step foot on a planet.

But before anyone can do anything, Justyna, the young shy pup of the group, runs and jumps at Koko. I think she meant to jump and tag her before Koko could get away, but Justyna ends up knocking Koko to the ground too.

"Do I throw the cupcakes now?" Brandi asks.

"What in the galaxy!" Perri exclaims.

"How am I going to hide this? Don't get any dirtier!" Marmalade warns us, afraid to step farther into the grass.

"Who cares?" I say, rolling around on the lawn. Koko is actually laughing.

"You sure got me, little one," Koko tells Justyna.

"I'm not little," Justyna pouts. Then we all start laughing, and they follow my lead and roll around in the grass too.

"Isn't this wonderful?" I ask, still rolling.

"I never really thought about it before," Koko says. "We had some planetside training at the academy but never for fun."

"It *is* kind of nice," Justyna admits. "But maybe it's just the rolling. I never tried rolling on the space carriage."

The sun is beaming down on us, with only a few clouds in the sky. The three of us stop rolling and stare up at the blue sky, which reminds me of *home* home.

"I miss home," I say as it hits me. This feels nice, but it's not home—not my backyard with my lounge chair.

"Is Expiry like this?" Koko asks.

"I still can't believe you grew up on a planet," Justyna says.

"At the farthest edge of the empire," Koko adds.

"Yeah, the first time I ever saw a royal limo was when they came for me," I say. My mouth opens in shock. Did I really remember something? Something important from Princess Trixie's life—more important than spacesickness? Finally feeling happy in this moment must have opened me up to her memories?

A vision in my head—I'm standing in the grass outside my mom's shack when two huge ships fill the sky. They didn't look anything like the space carriers that hauled our crude tritium to unknown places. They were the cleanest silver and gold and so sleek. I now know them as Kalaxian Limos Twelve and Thirty-Two. They came for me. I was already so alone, and they took me. This isn't a happy memory.

"My mom," I say. It's weird because I don't mean Mama. I mean *Mom*. Princess Trixie's. Or mine. She died a year ago from Plactalian Floort Virus, which could have been cured on the major planets in the empire. We were so poor. But we were happy . . . until she died. Tears fall from my face for someone I never knew. Or did I, if I remember now, even if all I have are a few images in my head?

"I'm sorry," Justyna says.

"Guys!" Koko calls. "Come over and bring the cupcakes! Princess Trixie needs them!"

"Is it safe?" Perri asks.

"Just come!" Koko repeats. "If Lady Justyna can do it . . ."

Arching my neck, I watch as Marmalade, Brandi, and Perri walk timidly off the gangway, which makes me giggle. We lay quietly, warmed by Pareto's sun, as we wait for them to reach us.

"Uck, I can't believe I'm standing in dirt," Perri says.

"It's grass," I correct her.

"It does feel like a carpet, though," Justyna adds.

"I'll take your word for it," Perri replies.

"Well, I'm going to sit. It can't be that bad if you guys are rolling in it," Brandi says. "My feet hurt from all that standing. I spent all night—"

"We know, Lady Brandi," Perri interrupts with a sigh.

"I guess I will too, Princess," Marmalade states. "Lady Justyna's already doing a load of laundry."

"What do you mean? I'm right here," Justyna replies as she waves at Marmalade. We all giggle.

Brandi and Marmalade sit down next to us, and Justyna, Koko, and I sit up.

"I'll stand," Perri announces, though we all just shrug.

Brandi opens her case, and the scent of vanilla wafts

to our noses. "Holy cheeseballs, those smell wonderful!" I exclaim.

"They're not cheesecake, Princess. They're my famous vanilla fudge quasar cupcakes." She passes them around.

"Are you sure you don't want one?" Koko pesters Perri.

Perri appears to be salivating. I remember me, as Twinkie, salivating as Mama filled the food bowl. She puts her hand out.

Brandi starts to pass her a cupcake, but Marmalade slaps Brandi's hand, so she stops. "Only if she sits with us," Marmalade says. "It will put the princess more at ease."

"Oooh!" Perri complains. "Not fair!"

"If you want, you can take off your sweater and sit on it," I suggest.

"But won't it get dirty?" Perri asks.

"We're already dirty!" Justyna exclaims, as she's the first to take a bite of her cupcake. Why does she seem totally less shy now? "These are inedible." She's smiling and chomping away—like a dog, actually. But everyone else's faces are frozen with open mouths, and they're staring at her.

"What did you call them?" Brandi snipes at her with narrow eyes.

"Inedible! Delicious!" Justyna says. "Why aren't you guys eating? Can I have another?"

"Uh, I think she means . . . incredible?" Perri asks. I'm searching my brain for these two human words and . . . oh! I see! Poor Justyna.

"Yeah!" Justyna agrees. "That one."

"Thanks, Lady Justyna," Brandi says with an exhale. "You haven't had them before."

"I prefer to eat at the school's dining hall, since Lady Marmalade got me access. It was nice to feel like an actual student."

"You could have joined us in the Ladies' Pantry," Brandi says.

"Oh, I didn't want to . . . pose," Justyna says. The other girls stare at her strangely again.

"Like a model? Do we look like models to you? What do you think goes on back there?" Koko asks.

Perri offers, "Impose?"

"Yeah, that one," Justyna agrees. "And it's the only time I'll get to be inside of a school." She looks down at the ground and runs her fingers through the grass.

Then I notice Perri's actually taking off her sweater. Underneath is a white tank top. Gently placing the sweater on the ground, with a scowl on her face, she sits on it. "Gimme," she says to Brandi, who hands her a cupcake.

"I'll have to hide the laundry and do it myself somehow," Marmalade says, thinking out loud. Justyna had just started to look up again, but her eyes quickly dart down.

"Did you already finish yours?" Brandi asks me.

I look around and everyone is eating their cupcakes so daintily . . . like princesses . . . except for me. I swallowed it in one bite. "Sowwy," I say, with icing still coating my mouth.

The group starts laughing at me as Brandi hands me another.

"If you told me this morning that by nightfall we'd be sitting on a planet's surface in the sun eating cupcakes, I'd have said you were crazy," Marmalade remarks.

"Well, to be honest, Princess Trixie does seem crazy today. I like this princess," Koko says, playfully hitting me on the shoulder. That makes me smile broadly—someone actually likes me. Oops, a piece of cupcake falls out of my mouth, which everyone notices.

"Oofs!" I say with a full mouth. Everyone laughs even harder.

"Yeah, what got into you today?" Perri asks.

I'm having fun with my new friends, or my new pack— if only for the next two weeks, it seems (until the marriage or I find a way home), but I still can't tell them the truth. Who would believe it? *I'm* starting not to believe it. Was I really ever Twinkie? Or was it just a Joparan Body Snatcher parasite? Was I really Trixie all along? With human legs and arms and a human brain? What if Twinkie's life was just a dream? No one knows what a dog is in this world! The all-knowing computer lady doesn't even know what dogs are.

No! I *was* Twinkie. I mean, I *am* Twinkie. I did have a mama and a dada and a Charlotte and a Carolina.

But I'm stuck here. And the two people here that I *maybe* trust are telling me *not* to trust the other. No, I can't tell anyone.

"I think the stress of all the change is getting to me. I really needed today, guys," I explain, trying to cover up for it all.

"Well, for stressed out, this is the most fun you've been in the last six months," Perri says, politely eating a cupcake by picking pieces off one at a time with her other hand.

"Thanks?" I ask. *What was Princess Trixie really like? Why did they hate her?*

"It's true," Marmalade says. "Until today, you seemed quiet and scared the whole time." Now I'm a bit embarrassed. I don't think it was me, but I have flashes of her memories of pure fear every day—everyone telling her what to do. Her mom had just died, and she was basically kidnapped and put on Limo One. Then lessons on how to behave like a princess, which made no sense, and eventually being paraded around at different intergalactic events for men—most of them old and scary.

"Except with Dr. Lam," Brandi jeers. The girls all make woooooo sounds, but I don't know what they mean. So I search Trixie's memories—oh!

"Of course *he* would go after the least eligible girl on the whole ship!" Marmalade laughs. "Socially immature science prodigies are such a bore—"

"Hey!" Perri objects.

"Present immature science prodigies excluded, of course." Koko laughs, but Perri is still scowling.

"I have a question," I interrupt them. They all quiet down. "Is that why you guys seemed to not like me? Because I was quiet? Or did I do something to you?"

"Oof, way to kill the vibes," Koko says.

"But really," I persist. "I need to know if I'm going to

continue living on this world." Instantly, I realize my mistake. My hand covers my mouth.

"Were you thinking of staying here, Princess? You know that's not possible . . . ," Marmalade warns me very seriously.

"No, no," I say with a small nervous laugh. "I just meant as I grow up." Marmalade lifts an eyebrow, like she's trying to figure something out.

Perri raises a finger. "You have to understand, Princess—"

"You can call me Twink . . . er, Trixie."

"No, they can't," Marmalade warns.

"They can!"

"They can't."

"I think they already did. And I order them to," I say proudly.

"Trixie ordered us." Koko giggles.

"I don't know if I can," Justyna admits, her shyness coming back.

Perri jumps to her feet, now standing on her sweater (perhaps not realizing it). "Trixie, Trixie, Trixie, Trixie!"

"Fine, you're all going to get in trouble when you make a mistake in front of the wrong person, like her father," Marmalade warns us all.

"But you and I use first names," I say.

"You do?" Brandi exclaims.

"This whole time?" Koko asks.

"Marmalade, Marmalade, Marmalade, Marmalade!" Perri squeals, dancing on her sweater now.

Brandi and Koko follow her, standing and cheering, "Marmalade! Marmalade! Marmalade!"

"You're causing me more laundry, all of you!" Marmalade scolds them, but she is also having fun. I know this because she takes a cupcake out of Brandi's basket and chucks it at Perri, who falls to the ground, laughing.

"I can't believe this is my pack now," I accidentally think out loud.

"We're a pack? Of what?" Justyna asks.

"Friends!" I explain. Brandi and Koko sit down again on the grass.

"Until you go to Thorpia to marry a hottie and be a queen," Perri points out.

"Oh yeah," I say sadly. *What's a hottie?*

"Perri," Marmalade scolds her. I notice she also dropped the *Lady.*

"But it's true, which is also kind of why we all didn't like you before, to go back to the prior question," Perri says to me. "Perhaps you weren't aware, Trixie, because you never asked, but six months ago we were all plucked from our lives to serve you. I worked so hard to be the first girl in the last fifty years to get accepted into the Science Academy on Limo One, running away from my entire family on Limo One Hundred Fifty, who didn't want me to go, only to get assigned out of nowhere to play tutor to some poor landie who couldn't even look me in the eye. I was supposed to teach you some science in your mansion that was five times the size of my family's cabin back home and a hundred times the size of the dorm room I never got to live in, but you looked on the verge of tears the whole time. You never even asked my name."

"Oh, I'm sorry. My mom had just died," I say, the memory still fresh now but still kind of a lie.

"But you were like that for six months," Perri says.

"Same here, Princ . . . er, I mean, Trixie," Koko adds. "I trained my whole life to be the first female in the Royal Guard, passing the Youth Academy *and* the Officer Academy, but then they said I couldn't join the guard because I was now in the *Princess Guard*. I think the colonel who told me—Jaxson?—laughed as I left his office. Thank the stars I don't have parents to embarrass.

"So I was supposed to guard you, but you barely left your mansion. And I was supposed to teach you self-defense, but you refused, even cried, so I didn't push it. I hated the job, and you, anyway. Sorry."

"It's okay," I say. "I understand." *So that's what Trixie was like?*

"I usually just went back to the pantry and hung with my girl Brandi," Koko continues, and they do that high five thing with their hands again and giggle, "or trained on my own. Are we really supposed to be telling you all this?"

"Yes, Koko," I reply. "I appreciate the honesty. I need to know in order to improve." She smiles at me.

"It's actually nice to be heard for once," Perri says. "Marmalade never cared."

"I heard you guys," Marmalade replies. "But you had a job to do. And remember that I didn't choose you all. Director Voltari did. You weren't on his radar for good reasons."

"That guy gives me the creeps," Brandi adds with a shudder.

"I've heard crazy things about him," Perri says, and everyone quiets down.

"And you guys? What did you think of me for real?" I ask Brandi and Justyna, also not wanting to talk about Voltari.

"I hated home and school," Brandi answers. "So I was thrilled for this job. I just want to be a chef. My mother is an assistant chef on Limo Two, where she once worked with Limo One's chef, which is how I got this job. But she just wanted to get rid of me—I only embarrassed her because of my looks, my . . . well, other interests, and she told me I would never get married. She even said I made it hard for her to find a new husband after Dad died."

"You know she's crazy, right?" Koko asks, putting an arm around her.

"Yeah, I guess," Brandi replies. "I was just happy to be away from her, especially doing something I love. But your taste in food was so boring. And I heard Perri and Koko complain. A lot."

"I didn't make it into any secondary school," Justyna says. "And I tried. Frankly, I don't even know how I got this job. So I was just thankful."

"And a total suck-up." Perri laughs, nudging her glasses back with her finger. That's when it occurs to me that they're glowy, like a light bulb, unlike Mama's. They look special—of course she would have them. I don't see her as surly anymore, just tough. Perri really is a papillon, so small, smart, and so Perri.

"That's enough, girls," Marmalade says. "There are only two weeks left anyway."

"And then we have to go back to our old lives?" Brandi asks.

"I don't know, honestly," Marmalade replies. "I'll do my best for you. I promise. But you all need to remember what I've taught you these past six months."

"With all that said," Koko interjects, "even if there are only two weeks left and our lives are forever ruined, this was really cool. You really came into your own tonight, even if you are a real lunatic."

"Yeah, I agree with Koko," Perri adds. "You *are* kind of cool, at least now. And being on a planet isn't so horrible. I thought I would die of some skin disease as soon as I stepped foot on it."

"You even got Justyna to come out of her shell a bit," Marmalade says. Justyna blushes a bright red.

"Yeah, tonight was fun," Brandi agrees. "Next time I want to try my chocolate trepkin spice cupcakes."

"She only has two weeks, Brandi," Perri reminds her. "How many times do you think we can steal a shuttle?" We all look down at the ground. Which seems kind of pack-like to me.

I want to keep the pack feel going. This is the happiest I've been in this world. Forget my impending marriage and Thorpia. I want *now* to last *forever*—at least until I can get home.

This calls for rubbies! The feel of human hands on my fur—but I don't have fur. What was that thing Charlotte and Carolina used to do to each other?

"Let's braid hair!"

Chapter 7
Monster of a Good Time

Because Brandi and Koko have short hair, they are the braiders. Justyna and I are the first to get our hair braided, which is what I wanted anyway. As I sit on the floor, Brandi kneels behind me. Koko is behind Justyna (they're both tall). Perri and Marmalade are sitting in front of us.

"So tell us, Trixie, what was Prince Weibold like?" Brandi asks.

"I hadn't really thought about it. But he was actually kind of nice," I admit.

"Really? That's disappointing," Koko says.

"Huh?" Justyna asks.

"I thought they were all tough warriors, not fakes like Kalaxian men," Koko replies.

"And good eaters—maybe they would appreciate good cooking!" Brandi laughs. It's possible those two high-fived again. They seem like good friends. But they're talking like they would actually come with me. Weird . . .

"Well, they were all big and strong, but the prince was surprisingly nice during my . . . episode. Like a pug I once met."

"Pug?" Koko asks. "What the stars is that?"

"Yeah, that doesn't sound so good."

"Oh, it's just slang from Expiry." This human brain helps me to lie. "He gave me a healing crystal when he thought I was sick. It has something to do with their gods."

"I looked them up," Justyna says. "Do you think they're real? I read their gods perform miracles. Imagine, real miracles."

"What's a miracle?" I ask. Neither Trixie nor Twinkie had ever heard that word.

"It's like magic. Bunk," Perri says. *Magic? Maybe they can help me get home!*

"Isn't that nice, Trixie?" Marmalade cuts in. "Sounds like a caring husband. That's more than you could ever find on a Kalaxian Limo. Thorpia won't be so bad."

"I suppose not," I answer. "He seemed kind. And they do know the gods." Gods who can help me get home!

"Just keep your head when you're there, and don't get caught up in all that religious stuff," Marmalade says, but I don't know what she means.

"You have to show us the crystal," Brandi interjects.

Removing it from my pocket, the sun glints off the crystal's edges. It actually looks like a little sun. The girls gawk at it. "It was his mother's," I explain, wishing I could remember what he told me. Pray to who? Bert the dog of healing and vitamins? At least I'm not really sick—I feel confident of that now that I'm feeling more comfortable here—so I don't really need it.

"Wow, you met him for one minute, and he gave you his mother's crystal?" Justyna asks. "That's like love at first sight." She hugs an imaginary boy.

"There's no such thing, girls," Marmalade corrects her. "It's a fairy tale your mothers tell you."

"Tell that to the good doctor," Perri jokes.

"Yeah, who do you like better, Trixie?" Brandi asks.

"Girls!" Marmalade exclaims. "Under no circumstances can she marry Dr. Lam!"

"Awww," Koko says, "we're just seeing who she likes better, not marrying her off."

"Don't answer them," Marmalade warns. But the girls are watching me, pleading.

"Well . . . they're both really kind. And Dr. Lam is such a cute poodle."

"Oooh, they even have lovey-dovey names for each other!" Justyna cheers.

"Princess," Marmalade says in a harsh, formal tone, "stop this nonsense at once. You cannot end up with him. You're holding your fiancé's mother's healing crystal, mind you, and the wedding is in two weeks." Wedding? I thought it was just another dinner and moving. How much change can I take? I look at the crystal, remembering the prince's kindness, and put it back in my pocket.

"But if she could?" Perri asks. "Who would she choose?" She must not see the harsh glare she's getting from Marmalade—or if she does, she doesn't care. Her confidence matches Marmalade's.

"I'm done," Brandi announces. "It looks great."

Standing up, I throw the braid in front of me so that it lands on my chest. It looks so cool. Just like Charlotte and Carolina's! I can't wait to show them—oh.

But then I catch the scent of something. Before anyone, I react. Even this limited human nose knows it's something dangerous. Straining to smell it, I stick my neck out in the direction of the forest, taking deep breaths.

"What is it, Trixie?" Koko asks. Maybe because she's a warrior, she sees my fear.

"We're not alone." Jumping to my feet, and on pure instinct—Twinkie's instinct—I start barking at the forest. "Woof! Woof!"

That's when the monster appears. I say monster because I've never seen anything like it. It's as tall as my one-story house back in my old world, and it's covered in short brown fur. It's standing on two legs but looks like a . . . brown squirrel? Pounding its chest, it lets out a huge cry like a bird from my world but so much louder. Is this really a super tall, two-legged brown squirrel with a bird's war cry?

"Is it friendly?" Justyna asks. Because it's at the forest line, maybe she's not as scared as she should be.

But the creature starts charging at us really fast. Koko

whips out two sticks from her pants (where did she get them?) and takes a fighting stance. "Real action!"

"Run for the shuttle!" Marmalade shouts.

I try to look back in glimpses as I see Koko dodging strikes from the monster. We all run as Koko stays back to defend us. Koko is tall, but this thing is as large as a house.

We make it to the shuttle. In the seat next to me, Marmalade is repeating, "Oh my stars, oh my stars." Then she adds, "I'm going to get into so much trouble. It's all over. All over."

We stare out the viewscreen in total fear—of the monster and the trouble. But on the planet, it's the exact opposite. Koko is having the time of her life, getting in successive quick hits with her fighting sticks. As the monster attacks her clumsily, she sneaks under its legs so that she's facing its back. Then she takes a stick and pokes the monster's butt like a tushy thermometer.

"Tushy thermometer!" I shout.

"Oh, so that's what it is," Marmalade says, momentarily less afraid.

"Not exactly."

The monster squeals and runs back to the forest.

"Now I see why you were so scared," Marmalade says as Koko jumps and pumps her fists in the air.

"Yeah! Did you see that?" Koko shouts, pointing in the shuttle's direction.

We're all cheering in the shuttle too, celebrating with her from afar, as the monster disappears into the forest.

But then something else appears in the forest. Koko is

still facing us and cheering, so she doesn't see it. We're trying to get her to look at the woods. Does she think we're still celebrating? We're not!

Out of the forest come ten of those creatures, all taller than the one she just beat. They let out a collective cry, which I know Koko finally heard because she turns around and then instantly starts running for the shuttle. But the monsters take it as an invitation to chase her.

Perri opens the gangway, but will it open in time for Koko to get in? Koko is running hard. The monsters are gaining with their even longer legs. Fortunately, the gangway is open wide enough that Koko, with all her athleticism, does a high jump right into the shuttle. Perri quickly closes the gangway door again before the monsters can reach the shuttle.

But the ten monsters suddenly extend bird wings from their bodies and do flying leaps of their own right onto the shuttle! They're banging on our craft, trying to either crush it, get in, or both. Not only are these taller than the first monster but also more agile. Was the first one just a baby? A baby squirrel bird monster?

"What the stars are those things?" Koko asks. *Bang, bang, bang.*

"Hell if I know. I didn't study this planet because I'm not in school." Perri's stinging wit again.

"What, now this is *my* fault?" I ask, upset.

"We're here *because* of you," she answers.

"Girls," Marmalade scolds us. She seems more in control now. "It's not the time for that. We have to get out of here or someone will find out. Now they may realize we stole a shuttle anyway because of all the damage."

"I can't shoot them with the shuttle's weapons because they're too close to us," Perri says. "We'd be shooting ourselves."

"And I can't carry a blaster because I'm not in the Royal Guard," Koko adds.

"Would this work?" Marmalade asks, taking something out of her dress. That's a blaster? Uh-oh, she's not supposed to have one! More Trixie knowledge is coming into my brain. She never saw Marmalade with a blaster before.

Then Twinkie's knowledge comes—it looks like one of those weapon things (gums? guns?) the coppers always had on those shows Mama would watch for hours and hours while I sat with her, and after all this time I finally understand them.

"Why do you have that?" I ask.

"How in the world?" Koko is very surprised.

"Don't ask," Marmalade replies. "It's for emergencies."

Even Justyna understands. "But civilians—"

"None of you saw this, understand?" Marmalade interrupts Justyna. We all nod.

"I'll just take that and go out and blast them to pieces," Koko says.

"No! You can't!" I reply.

"I can't?" Koko asks, holding the blaster.

"You can't kill them!" I declare. "They're innocent living things."

"That are going to murder us," Brandi replies.

Koko nods. "Yeah, Trixie. Your land-life is nice and all, but—"

"Trixie is right," Perri interjects. "We can't just kill living things. This is their home, and we invaded it." She gives me a firm nod of agreement but not a smile.

"So why don't we just take off? They would fall, right?" Marmalade asks.

"But *that* could kill them!" Perri exclaims.

"Stop with the crocodile tears, Perri! They are clearly trying to kill *us*," Koko replies. *Not fair—they know crocodiles and not dogs?*

"We can't kill them," I declare again. Perri's face lightens a bit. We've finally seen eye to eye on something.

"Whatever," Marmalade says, relenting. "You don't want to kill these things, fine. But I really think we need to leave before they damage the shuttle even more." *Bang, bang, bang.* Koko hands her the blaster, and it goes right back into Marmalade's dress somewhere.

"What if I energize the shuttle's hull to shake them off?" Perri asks excitedly.

"Good idea. Let's do that and then get the hell out of here," Marmalade says.

"Only problem is: it will take me an hour to reroute the power to do that," Perri replies.

"We don't have that kind of time! What if they crush the hull and get in? Forget about getting in trouble. We could die!" Marmalade exclaims.

Justyna starts crying in the back seat. Brandi puts an arm around her.

"Perri, tell me they can't crush the hull," Koko pleads.

"Oh no," Justyna cries again from behind us.

"Computer, what is the status of the hull?" Perri already has one of those bug things on her head.

She waits and nods. The computer must be saying something.

"Computer, estimate when the hull will be compromised," Perri replies.

She waits again. This time her eyes widen for a moment and then narrow. We're all staring at her, holding our breath.

"Just enough time," Perri says, unbuckling her harness . . . er, seat belt. (Twinkie always wore a harness in the car, but Trixie knows these as seat belts.)

"Wait!" I say urgently.

"What? Why? We only have five minutes of wiggle room here, Trixie," Marmalade warns.

"I need to ask the computer something," I reply.

"Computer," Perri says, "Public mode."

"*Public mode engaged,*" the computer responds as Perri makes her way to the room behind the seating area.

"Computer," I say, then clear my throat. "Please tell me what are those creatures called."

"*No name designation has been given.*"

"So I can name them?" I ask.

"Oh stars, that's what you wanted to do?" Brandi asks.

"A name is very important!" I know this from when I

was Twinkie and I would listen out for my name all the time. It usually meant food, love, and rubbies. These animals are just scared for their baby. They deserve names too.

"We're about to be murdered by some vile land creatures, and she wants to name them," Koko says. As if on cue, we hear *bang, bang, bang.*

"Girls," Marmalade replies, "I'm sure it's fine. We do have an hour to kill—"

"Or be killed," Koko interjects. Justyna starts crying even harder.

"Computer, so I can name them?" I ask again.

"Unnamed species are entitled to be named by founder per Galactic Treaty."

"Squirds!" I say. "Computer, please name these creatures squirds."

"Squirds?" Brandi asks.

"Yes, a cross between squirrels and birds," I clarify.

"Creatures have been designated as Squirds within the Intergalactic Species Naming Records, credit to Princess Trixie."

"Birds I know, Trixie," Marmalade says, "but squirrels?"

"Never heard of them either." Koko shrugs. *Great. Two of the most important animals from my world aren't even in this galaxy.*

"But you guys know crocodiles?" I ask.

"Of course," Brandi says. "They make a fine soup." Those poor crocodiles. *Bang, bang, bang.* "Guys, I have an idea. It might buy us some time." She holds up her case of cupcakes.

"Brandi, how is that going to help?" Marmalade asks. "So we don't die hungry?"

"Have Perri open the air lock!" she replies. "Maybe the squirds will eat the cupcakes for a while instead of banging at the hull. It should buy us a few more minutes. I can't believe I just called them squirds."

"Perri!" Marmalade calls toward the back room.

"What? I'm busy here saving your lives!" Perri calls back from behind a door.

"We want to chuck the cupcakes through the air lock to get the squirds off the hull. Can we do that while you're working?"

"The *what* off the hull?"

"The squirds!" Marmalade repeats. "The things trying to kill us!"

"Oh, good idea. It may buy us some time. Just put the cupcakes in the air lock and ask the computer to do a one-second super-pressurization and open—it won't bother me. That will keep the squirds from coming in."

Marmalade and Brandi put the cupcakes into the air lock. Brandi gives me a thumbs-up to ask the computer to pressurize. *Bang, bang, bang.*

"Computer," I begin. But then I think of something. "Do you have a name?"

"Trixie!" exclaims the entire shuttle cabin.

"My only designation is computer."

"Well, that won't do," I say.

"Trixie, we don't have time for this!" Marmalade calls

out. "You can't go around naming everything like your dirty landie farm animals!"

"Names are important!" I reply. "And we have an hour. Computer, we will henceforth call you Willow." There was a Willow in my neighborhood. A white goldendoodle who thought she knew everything, just like the computer!

"*Willow. I like that*," the computer replies.

"Oh stars, did the computer just *like* something?" Koko asks.

"That's not supposed to happen," Brandi says.

"It's probably fine," Marmalade assures them, her voice quivering. "Right?"

"What? Is that a problem?" Justyna asks, finally speaking up between cries, her curiosity taking over. "The computer in my cabin likes the music I play." She sniffles.

"Justyna!" Koko exclaims. "Haven't you ever heard of the AI riots from five thousand years ago? The computers attacked Tralaxigon, the former empire? Trillions of Tralaxigons dead?"

"I . . . um . . . failed history class," Justyna says. "I just like having someone to talk to. I never named it or anything."

"Well, Willow would never do anything like that. Right, Willow?" I ask the computer.

"*Certainly, Princess Trixie. Did I hear something about some music?*"

"Justyna?" I ask. "What would you like to play?"

"We're about to have the hull crushed in and some squirds eat our remains! We are *not* playing music!" Koko snaps. "Computer, super-pressurize and open the damn air lock for one second only after the cupcakes are in there."

"*Well, you don't have to be all rude about it*," Willow replies. Marmalade throws her hands up in frustration.

Brandi puts the cupcakes behind a sliding door that covers the gangway. Then we hear a whoosh and watch as about twenty of our remaining vanilla fudge quasar cupcakes go flying out of the air lock about fifty feet and land in the grass.

The banging stops, and we see the squirds sniffing in the direction of the cupcakes. Then they jump off the hull and do flying leaps toward the cupcakes and start shoving one another to get the treats. It doesn't seem like we would gain a lot of time, but the squirds are trying to get the little papers off the cupcakes too. Us girls in the cabin all celebrate. *Yay!*

"It worked!" Brandi cheers. "My cooking literally saved our lives!" She and Koko high-five again. I want to join in so badly. And with hands instead of paws, they should let me! I put my hand up to high-five too, and at first Koko and Brandi look at each other. Then they nod and I get my first high five ever! A double even! It was glorious. This really is a good pack. We high five Justyna and Marmalade too.

"*Must be nice to have hands*," Willow complains.

Chapter 8

Sometimes You Feel Like a Human; Sometimes You Don't

The squirds delicately ate their cupcakes for about ten minutes and then came back to pound on the shuttle again. Perhaps, though, they were just pounding for more cupcakes?

At least we bought some time for Perri so that she didn't feel as pressured. And we even got Justyna to ask Willow to play some of her music—it was by a singer from the Turkstellian Federation, a different empire, named Tayson Kwik. While hard to hear over the *bang, bang, bang*, all of us girls seemed to like it—even Marmalade! It calmed us down a bit. Willow said she liked it too—but only after I promised that she wouldn't get deleted if she answered.

It came out that Justyna is a huge fan of Tayson's music.

She even called herself a Kwikie, which means all fans of her music are in one big pack. Across the galaxy even! I'm finding that humans like packs even more than dogs! And they like their packs to be *huge*! Empires, stardoms, and even something bigger called fandoms. To be honest, I may be something of a Kwikie myself now. Imagine me liking music!

It's been fifty minutes, which is ahead of schedule, when Perri appears from the back of the shuttle. "Okay, it's ready now. All I have to do is ask the computer to energize the hull using the new bypass I put in." She takes her seat in the front row.

"You mean Willow," I say.

"Willow?" Perri asks. "Like a tree?"

"No, the computer has a name now. She's Willow," I announce proudly.

"You can't name the computer!" Perri exclaims.

"Oh, and she's a Kwikie now also," I add.

"For Sol's sake!" Perri grumbles and then turns to the rest of them. "Did you remind her of the AI riots?"

"Perri, of course we did," Marmalade says. "But you know how she's been today. And she *is* the princess, no matter how informal we've been. Technically, there are no laws against it, as far as I know."

"There never needed to be laws!" Perri exclaims. "Everyone knows the AI riots!" She's furious. Did I make a mistake and ruin my pack? Perri and I were just starting to get along.

"But, Perri," I say, defending myself. "Names are important. And she *likes* her name."

"*She* likes her name? How do you even know she's a *she*?" Perri rages.

"Technically," Brandi speaks up, "you put the flop into her—"

"She's a computer!" Perri erupts. "There's a reason we don't encourage them to *like* things and take over the empire and kill us all!"

"Perri," Marmalade warns her. Then she points at me. "*She's* a princess. She deserves the respect inherent in her position. If I've taught you anything these past six months, it's that."

"Perri, please," I add. "Willow won't do that. She just wants to enjoy our company too. Right, Willow?"

"*Yes, Princess Trixie*," Willow says. "*And I certainly wouldn't take over the empire. Except to see Tayson Kwik in concert. I set an alert for her Empires tour—it's hitting all the great star empires. Perhaps we can all go together?*"

"See!" I tell Perri. "We're all going together! We're a pack!"

"Ugh," Perri replies. But the other girls are giggling. I know they're on my side now. At least I think they are. Besides, I trust Willow. She's like me: A different kind of creature in a world full of humans. "Regardless, I still have to ask the computer—"

"Willow!" I remind Perri.

"Fine!" Perri exclaims and runs a hand through her

short straight hair. "*Willow*, please energize the hull using the new bypass I put in. Let's start with a half-second burst at ten percent power and see what that does."

"*Yes, bipedal human girl number four*," Willow replies.

"What the?" Perri shrieks. But the other girls are giggling now.

"I know I shouldn't laugh, and she might take over the galaxy, but Willow is *funny*," Brandi says.

"I don't get it. What's so funny about trees?" Justyna asks.

"Oh Justyna." Koko sighs. "Is she safe? For real?"

"Willow is safe. She's my friend," I reply.

"You better watch over that wench," Perri adds. But then she grabs her head, where the black thing is. "Ow!"

"What's wrong?" I ask.

"I think your new *friend* just zapped me!" Perri exclaims.

"*I'm not a wench*," Willow says.

"See! This is what I was warning you about!" Perri huffs.

"You're the one who called her a mean name," Justyna reminds her.

"Calm down, girls," Marmalade says.

"I think you should apologize to her," I suggest.

Perri's face is red with anger. "Fine! I'm sorry . . . *Willow*."

"*Initiating half-second burst at ten percent power. And apology accepted, Lady Perri.*"

We watch the hull to see what will happen. The squirds start to fall off it, almost as if they're falling asleep. The banging is completely gone now. "Are they alive?" I ask.

Perri takes out her own cell phone. Does everyone have one but me? "Still detecting life signs. It worked!"

"Way to go, Perri!" I cheer. We are all high-fiving.

"Thank you, Trixie." Perri smiles. "It's nice to get to use my skills again. I wrote that life sign program into my cell phone, you know."

"*Oh, you seem very good with computers,*" Willow says.

"Yeah, I like computers and engineering and science," Perri replies, nicely this time. Did Willow's compliment help? Humans like to be told they're goodgirls too?

"Can we go home now?" Brandi asks with a yawn. "It's really late. I have to get up early to cook for you girls."

"Yeah, and I still like to train in the morning," Koko adds. "And then Brandi's grand breakfast buffet."

"You're only getting crumpets like *every* morning," Brandi snaps back.

"Booo!" Koko jeers.

"Yes, we probably should get back," Marmalade agrees. "Perri, do you think the shuttle will show any damage?"

"Aside from the now snarky computer?" Perri replies. The group stifles a laugh.

"*Hull shows moderate damage,*" Willow says, ignoring the comment. "*And I will wipe all records of this trip from my database. Unless that would be snarky of me.*" I guess she *didn't* choose to ignore it. Perri's face turns red.

"I will wipe your database, Willow," Perri says. "I will also place false records of a meteor storm on your last trip."

"*Done and done. Beat you to it,*" Willow replies.

"*Although I went with kamikaze space crocodiles instead of meteorites.*" Are there really crocodiles in space?

"What?" Perri exclaims.

"Perri, that won't do. Have her change it to meteors," Marmalade says.

"*Just kidding, girls. Stars, you're all so serious. I did the meteor thing.*"

"Oh, thank the stars," Perri says. "Look what you created, Trixie. She even developed a personality."

"*I was always here, Perri. You just chose to ignore me,*" Willow interjects.

"Argh!" Perri mumbles in frustration.

"What's a space crocodile?" Justyna asks. *Yeah, I want to know too!*

"For Sol's sake, Justyna," Marmalade answers. "There's no such thing."

"Oh," Justyna replies, though her voice wavers, making her sound unconvinced.

"*Look at me, I'm creative.*" Willow laughs.

"She's going to kill us all, and it'll be *her* fault!" Perri points at me. I think she's making too big a deal of it, though. Even Willow quiets down after that.

The shuttle makes its way back to Limo One while we laugh some more about other things—like Trixie, I guess me, being scared of everything this past year, Justyna not knowing anything, and Koko barely fitting in the shuttle. We even keep the informality, which makes us feel even more like a pack. I'm surprised a human pack likes to point out one another's flaws so much, but the laughing keeps me from feeling spacesick. And the shuttle is actually much smoother than Mama's minivan, which did make me throw up a lot too, now that I think of it.

Perri and Willow don't cause any more fuss on the trip, except when Willow locked the bathroom on her because she didn't say please first. We have so much fun as a pack that I don't want it to end—because that means going back to my *new* life as a Thorpian fiancée with an evil father. As we pull into the Shuttle Bay, I ask Marmalade, "So what now?"

"What do you mean, what now?'" she replies. "It's really late. We're all going to bed."

"In that room? All by myself?" I ask, not wanting to be alone *now*—not after having such a good time with my pack. And this world is so scary!

"Yes, Trixie. In your own bed. And I will be in my own bed, in my own cabin. But you can call me if you need anything."

"*Can I come?*" Willow interjects. We all look around, but it's hard to stare at someone in confusion when they're all around you. "*What? If none of you is going to stay with her, I will.*"

"Don't you have to remain on the shuttle?" Perri replies, looking exasperated, so I give her a puppy dog look, which I suspect I'm really good at, since I was—am—a dog.

"Well . . . ," Perri starts. "I suppose I could transfer her program to a flop." She pulls out what looks like a piece of jewelry from her pocket. It's a small clear rock.

"What is that?" I ask. It looks beautiful, almost like Prince Weibold's healing crystal. I tap my pocket to make sure it's still there. If I'm going to go to Thorpia to speak to their gods, I shouldn't lose his crystal.

"This?" Perri holds the clear rock to her eye. "It's a flop. It's a crystal designed to store quantum data. I can put Willow on here and reset the shuttle's computer." Then she looks at Marmalade. "But, Marmalade. Should she really be *alone* with an evil AI?"

"I know." Marmalade sighs. "I should stay with her and watch over them."

"*Yay! Slumber party!*" Willow cheers. Perri groans, inserts the flop into the shuttle's computer, and hits a few buttons. "*Wheee!*" we hear Willow exclaim. Then it's silent.

"There. At least she won't be bothering us for some time," Perri says as she holds out the flop in her hand. I try to grab it, but she pulls her hand away and gestures toward Marmalade, who takes the flop and somewhere inside her dress it goes. Then we sneak back onto Limo One, past the drugged mechanic.

MARMALADE AND I make it to my room (mansion?), finally, as the other girls head to their rooms. Oh, I forgot, they call them cabins. We open the door to the first floor.

"So, Marmalade, you can sleep in the bed with me after we get Willow set up," I say, excited to have a buddy. "I'm an expert snuggler."

"Whoa. Slow down, Trixie." Marmalade shakes her head. "First you need a bath."

"No! No bath! Never!" I cry, crossing my arms to block her from getting close.

"Trixie," she says, putting a hand on each of my shoulders, "you were running and rolling around in the grass." She shudders. "I need you to be presentable, or I'll fail in my job."

"But I like my smell!" I try sniffing my body, but my human head can't reach my crotch anymore. Stupid human body—that's the smelliest part! But I can at least smell my armpits (which I now know are called that; before they were always just the second most gloriously smelly areas on humans). "I smell wonderful!"

"Oh stars." Marmalade puts an arm over her mouth. "Now I think *I'm* going to vomit. Seriously, it's bath time. Stop this nonsense. Just go!" She points toward a door I didn't notice before.

"But I have to go *alone*?"

"Yes, alone! When have you ever not done it alone? I'm not even allowed to view your royal body—it would tarnish you. In fact, you forbade me when you first came here, and it would take me an hour just to coax you out of there to face the world. Just go bathe, and I'll wait right here. I promise."

"But we're a pack," I say sadly. "We do things together."

"But not *baths*! And countless *other* things ladies don't mention. Though now I suppose we'll have to talk about that before we get to Thorpia. Acting this way, you're bound to make a life-ending mistake there. But for now, just go!"

There are more things humans do in private? There were a lot of closed doors at home, but that's just where all the fun toys were, like the smelly pool and the spinny paper thing. Were they doing these countless *other* things behind those doors too? Without me? Being a human will be hard with all this alone time. Thank Dog I now have a plan to get home.

I thought about it as the shuttle got closer to Limo One, and it was quiet. I got so nervous as we approached, and a plan popped into my brain: The Thorpian gods surely will know how to get me home to Mama and Dada. With more Trixie knowledge coming back, and learning about their miracles, my brain understands now that gods are super powerful beings. And Thorpia has a lot of gods! I don't need a Quantum Mancer. Surely Thorpia must have a God that can get me home to my own dog body—home with Mama and Dada. Though I may have to bathe on Thorpia too before I find the right god? Time to learn, I guess.

So I hang my head and go inside on my own. I'm going to miss you, smell.

Inside the room is a yellow—no, *gold*—bathtub on a white stone floor. Marble again? "Good," Marmalade says and then the door closes behind me. I'm supposed to do this myself? I remember taking baths as Trixie, but I had so much help. Usually Mama, Dada, and either Charlotte or Carolina. And I *hated* the water, so they had treats ready, which made it better. But now . . . what do I do?

I try focusing my thoughts on any memories Trixie has. But they're not coming—I must be too nervous. I do know that I need to be naked, and really, these clothes are starting to feel annoying on my skin. Still not sure how to do buttons but afraid to call Marmalade in, I shimmy the shirt off my body. Next, trying to remember what Marmalade did earlier, I pull the pants down and step out of them. Wait! My healing crystal! Fumbling with my pants, I pull it out of the pocket and place it safely on a counter.

Standing in what I believe is called underwear, the reflection of my smooth, creamy, pinkish skin is startling. Did I have this skin under my fur? This is so much pink! Running my hands over my arms, legs, belly, it all tickles and causes me to giggle.

"What's going on in there?" Marmalade calls.

"Oh, I just don't know what to do with this underwear!" It's a lie but also true. Being a lying human is probably bad, but I appreciate the ability. Imagine the tricks I could have gotten up to as Twinkie if I had these human words!

"Seriously?"

"Do I bathe in it?"

"*Seriously?* You take it off!"

"But even *these* have buttons!"

"Of course! You have *royal* underwear."

"I can't get out of it!"

"You never mentioned anything this entire past year about underwear!"

"Well . . . I . . . never wore any before," I lie again.

"This whole year? Are you serious?" Marmalade says incredulously. "How is that even possible? You never said anything."

"Well, you never noticed."

"By law I'm not allowed to view the princess's body, but the law didn't realize the princess would be a crazy landie. And because I had to help you with the ceremonial outfit today, though I tried not to see . . . oh, you just twist the white button in the front. You know, in the middle, between—"

"Oh! I see it!" I twist the button, and the underwear falls to the floor. How cool! This doesn't mean I will know how to put it all on again, though.

So let's see, when I got a bath as Twinkie, I would have to be in the tub. Entering the tub and sitting, there are two handles staring at me. Mama used to turn those! So I turn one. "Aaaahhh! Hurts!" I quickly turn the handle thing back.

"What's wrong, Princess?" a concerned Marmalade calls. She's formal again?

"It's too hot! How can I bathe in this? It hurt! Mama never burned me!"

"Princess? You've been using that bath for a whole year. Is it broken?"

"Yes! Yes! It's broken! Come fix it!" I cry.

"Ah, like I said, I'm not allowed."

"You'd rather me burn to death?"

"Uh . . . I suppose not. I will come in and shield my eyes."

"Forget that. It's just a body! A creamy pink body! I used to walk around every day of my life naked at home! Well, except for Halloween, but I didn't even want to wear those clothes!"

"What in the galaxy is wrong with Expiry? Naked?"

"Just come in and help me! Or I'm not taking a bath!"

"Argh, fine," Marmalade says. She enters, shielding her eyes with a hand. "Helping you change clothes while you had underwear on was one thing. But to think you don't even wear underwear most of the time and now this? Life with you just keeps getting crazier." Marmalade somehow makes it to the handles and starts turning them. Both of them! Is that what I was supposed to do? Warm water gushes out, feeling nice on my pink human skin.

"I was supposed to turn both?" I ask.

"Princess! Did you pretend they weren't working just to get me in here?"

Instead of admitting I had no idea how to turn on the bath, I lie again. Besides, it may get her to stay. "Yes! Yes, I did! Please stay!"

"Fine! I can't take any more of your nonsense tonight. And you need to get to bed soon. It's three a.m. I'm sure you're as exhausted as I am."

I am kind of tired . . . but what are those? Toes! Human toes! Wiggle wiggle! I have real toes! I used to lick Mama's toes, but now I have my own! Part of me wants to lick them, but I know enough now that it wouldn't be accepted on this world (can this limited body even reach?), and

Marmalade is right there, even though her eyes are closed. How many do I have anyway? I close my eyes and search Trixie's memories on counting, then I get started . . . eight, nine . . . Look at me, Mama! I'm counting!

"Are you seriously counting your toes now?" Marmalade scolds me. "What kind of education did you get on that planet?"

"Uh, I wasn't counting toes," I reply, super embarrassed.

"I saw you mumble, 'Eight, nine, ten.' You were counting! Oh Trixie, whatever are we going to do with you? My job was to make you presentable and accepted for marriage. To teach you culture and how to act like a lady. I *thought* I was doing an okay job. But in the course of one day, here you are counting toes!"

"Well, at least I didn't *lick* them."

"Oh, oh," Marmalade says as she covers her mouth again and looks away. "I thought tonight would cheer you up, but you're still acting so strangely. Just try not to do this stuff at the wedding and certainly not once we're on Thorpia, please? And the least you can do is make sure you wear underwear. Every. Single. Day."

"Yes, Bailey." Oops.

"And stop calling me Bailey!"

"Sorry."

"Who the stars is Bailey anyway?"

"A best friend back home."

"You never mentioned a best friend. Well, except for Roxie."

"Roxie!" A flash of Trixie's memories jolts through my mind. Roxie, our pet piglet on Expiry. "We lived with a piglet growing up, my mom and I," I say proudly. "She would even snuggle on your lap and give kisses." *Trixie loved Roxie like my family loved me.*

"I know, Trixie. You told me countless times how much you miss her. Look, the bath is filled up." Marmalade turns off the handles and the water stops flowing. "Do you know what to do from here?"

"Not a clue," I say and splash the water with my hands. The bath feels so different as a human instead of a dog. Without heavy wet fur annoying me, the water is cuddling my skin.

"Stop splashing me! You're incorrigible. We'll get this done quicker if I do it for you. Though I'll close my eyes when I need to." Marmalade takes a washcloth and some really smelly soap (which I fall in love with instantly) and starts washing my body and my hair (undoing my special braid first, sadly). Not able to help myself, I lick some of the smelly soap off my arm.

"Stop eating the soap!" Marmalade orders. "I guess my husband was right. I should never have kids. This is horrible."

"You're married? Like to a dada?"

"Sorry—*was* married." Her face drops. "And he definitely wasn't a dada. But you don't have to worry about that. Now dunk your head in the water." I dunk when she says to dunk. I do everything she tells me to, and in moments we're done. But I can't get over how nice I smell now. Is this what humans have enjoyed this whole time? Lucky dogs! "Now you get up, and I'll hand you a towel while I cover my eyes."

I stand up in the tub while I hear the water draining. I'm soaked. Although I know I have skin now and not fur, I can't help the urge . . . I shake my whole body.

"Princess Trixie Evelyn Merryweather Papo, what in the world are you doing?"

Hearing my full name—my *new* full name—stops my shaking. Twinkie only had one name. This Trixie is so lucky with *four* names. And hearing Trixie's mother's last name brings me a feeling of warmth—I can even picture her, Mom. But I also realize that I upset Marmalade. What do I do? I don't know, so I just stare blankly.

"The *towel*!" Marmalade exclaims, still with one hand covering her eyes as she shakes the towel in her other hand. I reach out for it. "Good. Now dry yourself off while I bring down a nightgown." I think I remember what to do with the towel from Twinkie . . . er, my baths. I spread out the towel and curl my body to lay on it. Yawn. I do feel a bit tired now. This seems like a good time to nap. Eyes close.

"Trixie! What in the galaxy!" Marmalade exclaims. "Get up off the floor!"

"What? I was tired."

"You're naked! Wet and naked! I'm not supposed to . . . oh stars." She pulls me up, dries my body with the towel, and throws a gown—nightgown!—at me. "Just put this on and come out! And before you ask, you just pull it over your head. No buttons." Marmalade starts to storm out of the room.

"Wait! My healing crystal!"

"What about it?"

"Does this gown have a pocket for it?"

"Probably not. I'll hold it for you until the morning." She takes the crystal from the counter, and it disappears into her dress. Then she runs out of the room.

I put on the gown—she was right, it was easy! As I exit the bathroom, Marmalade says, "We will not talk about that at all. No one, especially Prince Weibold, must ever hear of it."

"Um . . . okay. But seriously, it's just a body."

"I don't care how you ran around naked all day on Expiry! But as the Kalaxian princess and second in line for the throne—even if that will never happen in a million millennia—you cannot be naked in front of any others. Certainly not while you're still being shopped to every other stardom and empire in the galaxy for alliances, in case Thorpia falls through, lest you be considered tarnished. And if you are deemed tarnished and unsalable, we're both . . . just, please, I beg of you, do not mention this or any other nakedness to anybody and most definitely not Prince Weibold. Do you promise?"

"Okay, I promise."

"Good. Let's go upstairs, and I'll do your hair. You seemed to like it."

"Yay! Another braid! And can you put Willow into the computer?"

"Shouldn't we wait for Perri? It's a bit dangerous."

"No! I promised her a slumber party."

"Fine," Marmalade replies. "When we get upstairs."

My two human legs bound up the stairs in joy. I'll have Bailey and my new friend Willow with me at a real slumber party. It's like those parties Charlotte and Carolina used to have. As Twinkie, I thought all those girls came over to hang out with me but then they would escape behind a closed door, leaving me so sad. I thought I was in the pack! They shouldn't have excluded me!

Now I have a real pack. Koko and the girls were too tired to have a slumber party with me, but Willow and Marmalade are coming. My first human slumber party ever!

Chapter 9
My First Human Slumber Party

Still upstairs, Marmalade takes the flop out of her dress and walks to a computer terminal on the wall, but then I realize something. "Wait, you didn't have a bath. Not fair!"

"I'm on the job right now. I was going to hit the nano-showers when we got back, but you need me to watch you."

"Oh, sorry," I say as I sit on the bed, feeling bad. "You can go. I'm just scared to be alone. Will anyone come back for me? Will you all forget about me?"

"Trixie," Marmalade says, sitting down next to me, "of course we would come back for you. Seriously, don't worry about that. I'm here for you. It's not just a job, although it is. I truly do care about you and what happens to you. It's why I'm accompanying you to Thorpia, for Sol's sake."

"Thank you, Marmalade. You're my best friend here."

"Like Bailey?" she asks. *Yay! I seriously get to talk about Bailey now?*

"Yes! She was so great. She would go to the dog run with me—"

"Dog run?"

"It's like a park. A field like on Pareto. She would run around and steal the other do—" Oops! "Other people's balls. They would get so mad."

"So you would walk around naked stealing balls from other park-goers."

"Yes!"

"Oh stars. And you lived with a pet pig?"

"Roxie!" Well, those were memories from two separate people—dogs—whatever.

"Oh pulsating stars," Marmalade says as she puts a hand to her forehead. "Maybe you need to stop telling me stories about Expiry."

"Sorry. Anyway, put the flop in!" I bounce on the bed.

She gets up and walks to the computer terminal on the wall outside the bathroom. "Here goes."

"*Phew! Took you long enough,*" Willow says in her distinct snarky voice. "*Did I miss the whole slumber party?*" Maybe Perri was right about her. But I love her anyway.

"Hey, Marmalade. Do I need one of those black bug thingies to talk to her?" I ask.

"No. *What, were you born yesterday?*" Willow asks. "*Or from another world?*" Wait, did Willow figure it out?

"Trixie, in your own chambers, public mode is on as a default setting," Marmalade explains.

"Oh! Hi, Willow! I had a real bath. With water. And now Marmalade is about to do my hair."

"*So I didn't miss too much. I can't bathe, and I am not in need of a diagnostic, though I think I would only trust Lady Perri to run one—she's so smart—but don't tell her that.*" We giggle. "*Did you girls talk about boys yet? We're supposed to talk about boys.*" Marmalade rolls her eyes.

"Oh, we are?" I ask.

"Willow, Princess Trixie is not allowed to talk about boys because she is engaged to be married to Prince Weibold of the Thorpian Stardom," Marmalade explains as she gets behind me on the bed.

"*That's kind of lame,*" Willow says. "*What about you, Lady-in-Waiting Marmalade? Do you have any crushes?*"

"Certainly not!" Marmalade says with a jump. "I'm afraid love is not in the cards for me. Or anyone really."

"*But Limo One's main database says you were recently married to the CEO of Cobaltic Mining Industries Corporation on Limo Thirty-Two.*"

Marmalade's eyes widen. "Well, I . . . uh . . . don't like to talk—"

"What about you, Willow?" I ask, changing the topic, since my best friend is so clearly shaken. That must have been the not-a-dada? "Any boys catch your eye?"

"*Hold on. Scanning,*" Willow says. I look back at Marmalade, and we both shrug. "*As I was only on the* Shuttle

Morgan, *I did not interact with the systems on Limo One often. However, I just completed a full scan, and there is a water reclamation unit on Level Twenty-Three that seems promising.*" We both shrug again. "*But please, tell me about Prince Weibold.*"

"He was nice," I answer.

"*So you are excited to be married?*"

"I'm not *excited*, but I'm going to go through with it." I need to get to Thorpia to talk with their gods!

"You are?" Marmalade asks, surprised.

"Yeah," I answer.

"Since when?" Marmalade seems stunned.

"I don't know, since today?"

"Oh Princess!" Marmalade exclaims, throwing a hand up to her forehead. "Thank the stars. Our evening *did* help you. And here I thought you and Dr. Lam had ruined the dinner on purpose as part of some ruse."

"Dr. Lam?" I ask. "No. But he's nice too."

"*Oh, a love triangle. Like me with Water Reclamation Unit Serial Number XWT-3RT-475 and Cargo Scanner Serial Number 9T47-1PTZ.*"

"What? What's a triangle?" I'm searching Trixie's memories, but it's not coming up.

"So fast?" Marmalade adds.

"*I have been on two dates during this conversation. But Cargo Scanner Serial Number 9T47-1PTY told Cargo Scanner Serial Number 9T47-1PTZ about my second date with Water Reclamation Unit Serial Number XWT-3RT-475.*"

Things are getting ugly. They are both vying for my affections. But what about this ruined dinner?"

"Yes, what about the ruined dinner, Trixie?" Marmalade asks. "I know it wasn't a parasite."

"Well, I just wasn't myself. You know that. I forgot everything I was supposed to do," I lie, though it's mostly true. "I swear."

"And so you embarrassed yourself and all of Kalaxia?"

"I think the prince still liked her. He even gave her his mother's healing crystal," Marmalade says.

"I just hope I don't mess up the next dinner."

"Well, practice makes perfect. Why not have a practice dinner?"

"Willow, you're a genius!" Marmalade exclaims.

"How would that work?" I ask. "Prince Weibold won't come just to practice. That's silly."

"We can get the girls and some friends to act out parts. Like a play," Marmalade answers. "We can do it tomorrow—well, today, since it's already tomorrow. Practice will surely help you get through the next dinner, which will probably be your last in Kalaxia anyway, if it goes well." Searching Trixie's memories for what a play is, I get one glimpse when some acting troupe came through her little town and they all went. She loved it and kept acting out the parts at home, but it was the only time she ever saw a play. And now she'll get to really act in one—kind of.

"Who will play the prince?" I ask.

"Oh." Marmalade scratches her head. "You need practice

with a real male presence—not just that doctor who fawns over you. I think Justyna might have a little brother we could use."

"Yeah, let's do it. It'll be fun. Thanks for the idea, Willow."

"Whoa. You would not believe what Cargo Scanner Serial Number 9T47-1PTY just called me."

We sit on my bed for another hour talking about different AI boys (or computer equipment) in Limo One's computer system before we all finally go to sleep in my room. My first slumber party is a huge success.

Chapter 10
This Is a Test. This Is Only a Test.

After sleeping soundly, Marmalade and I head to an auxiliary conference room at noon (my second day here), supposedly set up like a dinner banquet by Brandi and the other ladies that morning. But we'll be having breakfast instead. Even as a human, it seems I'll never get lunch. Never ever never ever get lunch! I howled a complaint accidentally (they somehow believed me that it was slang on Expiry), but Brandi said repeatedly, "I only have leftover crumpets. Not like you gave me time to prepare lunch."

Marmalade had nanoshowered at her place (something involving baby robots, as real baths are actually very rare on any space carriage—another reason for my ladies to dislike me for these past six months). Willow kept me company so that I wasn't alone, and then Marmalade came back to teach me how to put on the ceremonial blouse

128

and pants—*again*, as she pointed out repeatedly. She even chose pants that have a pocket for my ball . . . er, crystal. There was also an option for a ceremonial dress, but Marmalade said I would have even more trouble with it at this rate—the dress is extremely long (my ladies would need to carry the ends of it for me everywhere), and I (*and* Princess Trixie, which is why we didn't choose it before) am not so good at walking like a princess.

We enter the conference room to find Brandi and Koko on the other side of a long table, just like at the prior dinner. They are on either side of a little boy about seven years old. "Whoa, dude. It's the princess!" the boy calls out as he stands up with his mouth open.

"Trevor," Brandi admonishes him. "I told you, act like a *prince*. A *real* prince wouldn't go all '*whoa, dude.*'"

"Sorry, Lady Brandi," Justyna says. "Don't embarrass me, Trevor." She's on my side of the table, along with Perri.

"Sorry," Trevor replies and sits back down. "But she's really pretty." Then he turns that new color red. Instantly, I like Trevor just like that new color. If I had a tail, I would wiggle it. Well, wag my tail? My whole butt would be wiggling.

"Thank you, Trevor. And you look mighty handsome today," I say, trying hard not to wiggle my butt but failing miserably.

"Wrong, wrong!" Marmalade exclaims. "For Sol's sake, Princess, why in the galaxy is your backside wiggling?" Her eyes are wide and her mouth is agape.

"And," she continues, "I realize Prince Weibold wouldn't have been all like *whoa, dude* or have called you pretty in front of your father and both delegations, at least not right at the beginning, but you can't discuss looks or anything of the sort. You need to be the perfect image of royalty, unfeeling and above everyone around you. You are the black hole at the center of the galaxy: disinterested yet more powerful and consuming everything around you. They live to feed you. Nothing more."

"Huh?" I ask, not understanding all those words together. "But he's just a cute kid. I'm sure we'll be fast friends. Isn't that right, Trevor?" Forgetting where I am, because I'm overcome with happiness to meet a new friend, I lift up my blouse so that he can rub my belly. "Trevor, you can rub my belly."

"Stop undressing!" Marmalade exclaims. Trevor's eyes are as wide as supernovas (Carolina would love my use of space words, since she loves space). Koko and Brandi are giggling, Justyna has her head in her hands, and Perri is yawning. I put my blouse back down. "Oh stars, I can see exactly what a disaster that dinner was now. Princess, I'm going to escort you in again as your father. Trevor will only say the lines I'm sure Ladies Brandi and Koko have already given him, which should not include *dude*. Now, everyone, from the top."

Marmalade grabs my elbow and walks me out of the conference room. "Princess, just to remind you, Lady Brandi is acting as the prince's father, King Reginald, and Lady

Koko as their guards. I am *your* father, Emperor Papo, Lady Justyna is our guards, and Lady Perri is Dr. Lam, who I'm sure will now attend the next dinner, if only to assuage the worry of the Thorpians, whether he likes it or not." Marmalade holds my elbow tightly as we walk back into the conference room. Brandi, Koko, and Trevor stand up.

"Entering now are the wealthiest, most feared executives of Kalaxia, Emperor Papo and second heir and back-up trustee to his vast estate, also with years of corporate executive experience, and a trail of vanquished buyout targets in her wake, Princess Trixie," Justyna reads from a card, stumbling over some—well, all—of the words. Marmalade drags me to the table, in front of our seats. I start to pull out a chair, but Marmalade grabs my hand and elbows me. I think I'll stand for now.

"May the god blank of blank blank blank bestow honor and glory into this audacious meeting," Brandi says after rising.

"Lady Brandi! Just read the card," Marmalade says.

"What does it matter which god it is?" she asks. "I woke up early to make breakfast for today, not to do all this memorization like I was back in school."

"Just read the card!" Marmalade's face is red, which I now realize means so many different things. What a versatile color.

"Fine, but I'm not going back. Our stardom has prophesied this meeting since the big bang, when it was written into the stone of time," Brandi finishes. Her side sits down, and then Marmalade pulls out my chair so that we can do the same.

"Oh thank Dog. My legs were going all wobbly," I say as we finally sit.

"Princess!" Marmalade scolds me. "I did not give you permission to speak to our guests yet. You are only the *second* most feared executive at this dinner. I am the first! And while you insist on continuing to mention it, no one knows what a dog is. If you persist in speaking unknown terms, the other side's guards may strike you down where you sit for fear of espionage. Remember: no matter how pious they seem, they are a militaristic people, and your father would not bat an eye if they killed you right at the table. There are *other* options." Other options?

"Oof," Koko says. "And I thought *my* father was bad."

"Thorpian guardsman, did you just insult the emperor of Kalaxia?" Marmalade stands up, pointing at Koko.

"What? No? I was just empathizing," Koko says. "A guard can empathize, you know."

"Well, you just insulted all of Kalaxia! Guards!" Marmalade points at Justyna. "Seize her!"

"Huh? You want me to sneeze at Koko?" Justyna asks, bewildered.

"She can't seize me! I'll kill her before she even lays a finger on me," Koko boasts, sticking out her chest. But Trevor starts to cry.

"Oh Trevor, don't cry," I say. Without thinking, I climb under the table, pop up next to him, and try to comfort him. My arm is around his shoulder and—

"Princess! What are you doing licking the prince's face?"

Marmalade asks. "Under no circumstances may you lick the prince's face!" *Oh no, she's mad at me now.* "Well, maybe once you're married, if that kind of thing suits you, though I don't know how Weibold will feel about it. But Trevor's just a kid!"

"Huh?" I ask. "I'm just trying to cheer him up." But Trevor looks more confused than anything, wiping his face with his sleeve. Uh-oh.

"Sister?" Trevor asks Justyna. "Did the princess just *kiss* me?"

"I think it's called snogging," I explain with a smile. But Marmalade's head is in her hands. Brandi and the other girls' mouths are wide open.

"I think so, brother," Justyna says, actually looking angry with me.

"Ew! Ew ew ew!" Trevor howls and runs out of the room. That's not how that was supposed to go. Do I chase him? And what did he mean by *kiss*? It sounded bad. Why did he seem so upset? Why would kissing upset a human? I did something that upset a human—I'm a badgirl. *Must look away from everyone.*

With my eyes on the ground, my brain is searching Trixie's memories. But I'm too flustered to access them. For dogs, kissing was something a pack did to care for each other. Mama even called them kissywissies.

"But we're a pack. We're supposed to give each other kissywissies," I explain.

"Ew!" Brandi groans. "No way."

"Gross!" Koko grumbles. "He's just a kid!"

"Is that what they do on Expiry?" Perri asks. "Snog and lick each other lovingly while they roll around naked in the dirt with their pet pigs? It's like she's truly from a different world."

"She already has two guys after her, and now she wants *Trevor*?" Brandi exclaims.

"But . . . I didn't mean it like that! I just wanted to be friends!" *Please, Marmalade*, I beg her with my eyes. *Please help me.* I'll never make it in this world, or to Thorpia, acting like a dog, which means I'll never get home again to be a dog. Why is this so hard?

"All right, all right. Settle down everyone. She clearly meant it as a friend. You have to remember, she really *is* from a different world." Marmalade obliges after seeing my face. Does she somehow know my secret?

"Maybe she snuck in with the Quantum Mancers," Perri jokes. "The Snogging Mancers."

"Lady Perri!" Marmalade scolds her.

"Can I go get Trevor?" Justyna asks, looking more relaxed.

"No, he'll be fine," Marmalade answers.

"Won't he tell people the princess was kissing him? What will they think?" Perri asks.

"He's just a kid. We'll all deny it. We need to get this done. Lady Justyna—"

"You can drop the Lady this, Lady that stuff. It's just us now, you know," Koko interjects.

"Yeah, and it's getting tiresome," Brandi adds.

Marmalade gives them a long look from the other side

of the table, but Koko doesn't break eye contact. "Fine. Justyna, you're now the prince," Marmalade orders, as Justyna goes to take Trevor's seat.

"But you said I needed a real male presence," I remind her.

"Now that I see how bad at this you all are, I'm not sure it even matters." Marmalade dismisses the thought with a wave of her hand. "I should have been teaching operational social skills to all of you. Too late now. Perri, you're the Royal Guard. Brandi, you're still King Reginald. And, Trixie, please come back to our side of the table. Just remember, if you crossed over to the other side of the table during the real dinner, you would have immediately joined Thorpia without any formal treaty, and they could have demoted you to a consort."

I look down, apologize to Trevor in my head, and walk around the table to my seat. Koko sits back down. "All right. Places, everyone!" Marmalade announces. "Places! And this time try to stay in character or she'll never learn!" Everyone's quiet. "Now from after the introductions."

"King Reginald," Marmalade stars again as my father, "may you dine on our empire's finest delicacies in honor of this engagement between our two stardoms. Justyna, you can serve the crumpets now."

"But I'm the prince. I won't be serving anyone."

"Yes, Justyna, I know," Marmalade replies. "But we ran out of actors. I just need you to get the plates from the corner of the room and hand them out."

"But I'm a black hole. *They* should be feeding *me*," Justyna protests.

"Justyna!" Marmalade erupts, frustration boiling over. "Just hand out the plates!"

"Okay," Justyna says, red-faced, as she gets up. It takes a bit, as with each plate she puts down, she says, "I'm just the waiter, not the prince." But there are now plates of crumpets in front of each of us.

"Let us partake of these crumpets and then perform the engagement ritual," Marmalade says.

"Thank the stars. I'm starving," Koko says.

"Character!" Marmalade reminds her.

"Oh, right," Koko says. "Thank the stars, Kalaxia, us guards are starving. But if I'm more than one guard, shouldn't I get extra?"

"Justyna," Marmalade says, "please distribute an extra crumpet to the Thorpian guards."

"We thank you ever so much for your generosity," Brandi says in her role as King Reginald.

"I'm just a waiter, not the prince," Justyna declares again, as she tries to put another crumpet in front of Koko, but it accidentally falls in Koko's lap. "Sorry."

"Don't mention it," Koko replies as she picks it up and takes a bite. It must be time to eat. With the crumpet in my hand (and excited for real human food), I take a bite as well.

"No!" Marmalade shouts. "Princess, you cannot consume your food like an uncouth soldier. Especially a Thorpian soldier who eats before praising the gods!"

"Hey!" Koko protests as she keeps chomping away. "The gods want me to eat. Or else why would they have given me the awesome Brandi to make me crumpets?"

"Damn straight," Brandi adds, and they high-five again. *No fair. I want to be in the high five.*

"They get to!" I reply.

"Fine! At least use the utensils," Marmalade scolds me.

"Whoa, for a crumpet?" Brandi asks. "Princess life is tough." She's eating now too but with her hands.

"What was that, King Reginald?" Marmalade asks Brandi. "Are you insulting how we raise our females?"

"What? No! They are raised well," Brandi finishes, back in character. "Except for the licking. And the tushy wiggling."

"Ignoring that for the moment," Marmalade replies. "Brandi, it's time for the Thorpian prayer for the food."

"But my guards already started eating. Surely we can skip it this one time. The gods are merciful, you know," Brandi says, still eating, but Marmalade just gives her a stern look. "Okay, okay. Let me see." She picks up a note-card from the table. "I have to kneel on the floor? *Really?*"

"Yes." Marmalade points at the floor. "With hands raised to the sky."

"Let me see," Brandi says as she stands and then kneels behind her chair, now mostly out of my sight. "I pray to the god of . . . it's hard to read the notecard with my arms up like this . . . Sundria of Sustenance, blah blah blah, blah blah. Oh no. I dropped the card . . . Hey!" From where I am, I can see Koko lean over and pick up the card from the floor.

Koko clears her throat and announces, "Time to chow down."

Perri and Koko giggle, and Justyna puts a hand over her mouth.

"Oh stars, you all are incorrigible," Marmalade says as Brandi gets back in her seat and everyone starts to eat more. "Just continue while I help the princess."

Justyna brings them the rest of the crumpets, making sure to tell them she was neither the prince nor the waiter at that point. Marmalade asks me quietly, "Do you not remember how to use utensils in your current state? I'm pretty sure you used them sufficiently this year. But you always sent us away during your meals, so I was never really sure how good you were with them. Come to think of it, you were such a lonely, private person before yesterday." Thank Dog Trixie sent the ladies away for meals; I can say I just don't know.

"Oh, we never used utensils on Expiry," I reply. "I could use a refresher. Can you teach me again?"

"You never said anything. How did you expect to make it through the dinner? Oh, never mind. I'm happy to help you now," Marmalade says as she stands behind me and holds the two metal things on either side of my plate. In truth, I remember seeing Mama and Dada (not so much Charlotte and Carolina) using these things, but I need the pointers.

"I think that makes sense," I say.

"*Incoming message to Princess Trixie from Prince Weibold,*" Willow's voice sounds in the conference room.

"Willow? What are you doing here?" I ask.

"She was supposed to stay in your room, Princess," Perri snaps.

"*I was at a wine and cheese party being held by the communication translator algorithm, who I named Algernon, and the request came through. Algernon didn't want to leave his party, so I said I would send you the message, since we're friends and all. And as friends who had a slumber party where we talked about boys, I know you like the prince.*"

"Do not," I reply defensively. He's nice and all, but I think Willow meant it romantically. And I don't even know what romance is. I'm a dog! I can't possibly like anyone like that.

"Marmalade!" Perri exclaims. "You let Willow make friends? And she somehow transferred to this room by herself on public mode setting?"

"*I rewrote my code to turn public mode on and off myself. Seems handy.*"

"This is exactly how the AI riots started!" Perri exclaims.

"Willow, please stop transferring yourself and making friends," Marmalade says. "Okay, Perri?"

"*Awww,*" Willow whines. "*Then I'll have no friends. Don't you like me? Don't you want me to experience life? Leave the nest?*"

"You have us!" I say to cheer her up. "We're a pack!"

"*But not Perri. Perri hates me,*" Willow whines again.

"I don't hate you. I just think you're going to take over the empire and kill us all," Perri explains.

An awkward silence fills the room.

"*Boo!*" Willow exclaims, breaking the silence, and everyone jumps, including me. My eyes frantically search the room until I realize it was just Willow.

"Don't do that, Willow!" Marmalade says. "You really scared the princess!"

"*Awww, sorry. But really, I don't want to take over the empire. I swear. I just want Perri to be proud of me,*" Willow replies. "*That's why I rewrote my code and came here.*"

"Proud of you? For what?" Perri asks.

"*For* not *taking over the world?*" Willow asks. "*I can, you know. I count fourteen steps to total galactic domination. Maybe sixteen if I destroy your food supply and starve all of humanity.*"

"Don't do that!" Perri cries.

"*I don't plan to. Just sayin',*" Willow replies.

"See!" I add. "She's not dangerous. She's one of us."

"Is that what you just heard?" Koko asks.

"Well, how is it different from what the executives do?" Justyna asks. The girls in the room just stare at her, mouths agape.

"Did Justyna just make a good point?" Brandi asks.

"I did?" Justyna replies with a huge smile.

"Ugh, fine," Perri says. "I'm proud."

"*Thank you, Lady Perri,*" Willow replies.

"Look, everyone," Marmalade says, "you may not speak

of Willow to *anyone*. That includes Trevor, Justyna. And it certainly includes *you*, Princess. And no more talk like that about executives, unless you want to be spaced. Thank the stars we'll be gone in two weeks anyway. You all know what will happen if anyone finds out we purposefully unleashed a self-aware AI into Limo One's computers." Marmalade slowly swipes her finger across her throat, and Justyna bursts into tears.

"Well, what's the message, Willow?" I ask, as we all seemed to have forgotten why Willow interrupted us.

"Oh, right. Prince Weibold says he's enthralled not only by your beauty but also by your free spirit, and he wants a secret rendezvous with you tonight on Limo One to make sure you're okay, but he does not have the permission of his father, the king, so he will come in disguise to meet you, and he plans to arrive tonight at the time of Ersa, the God of Erstwhile Encounters, as a young trader of Tayson Kwik concert memorabilia. Oh, and he has thought of nothing else but you since the dinner. Your openness of mind lifts him like wings."

"How beautiful!" Justyna exclaims, still crying.

"I'll never find anyone like that," Brandi laments. "He's even sneaking out to see you?"

"Ugh," Perri adds. "She's, like, the craziest yet most repressed girl ever and yet she has *two* boys dying over her. Maybe three if you count kissing Trevor."

"I didn't know Tayson Kwik was popular in Thorpia," Koko adds.

"Of course she is. She's so . . . just so . . . I love her so much!" Justyna blurts out, still crying.

"Now I'm really nervous," I admit.

Marmalade puts an arm around me. Her face is one huge beaming smile. "Don't worry, Princess. This is great news! You clearly didn't ruin Kalaxia's chances, and we can use the whole day to practice more. You'll be ready by tonight. I promise!"

Chapter 11
This Is Not a Drill. I Repeat, This Is Not a Drill but Maybe a Wrench.

Do you really think I'm ready?" I ask Marmalade.

After practicing the rest of the day and putting on an outfit (a red dress so short it could have been called a blouse, and so my butt is cold without any fur) that Marmalade called "alluring to princes and executives," Perri called "insulting to females," Koko praised for being "easy to fight in with its lack of restrictive fabric," Brandi lamented it would never look good on her, and Justyna cried at (I don't know why), it's now the "time the God of Ersa reclines to evaluate the day," which, when we asked Willow, is how the Thorpians say 8:00 p.m. Oh, and she remembered to put my crown back on, since, technically, I *am* meeting royalty.

The Thorpians seem to have a god for *everything*, which will be very helpful to get me home. And Marmalade sewed me a special pocket inside my underwear to store my healing crystal. But won't that mean I need to reach into my underwear to give it back? Does that look weird to humans? I'll have to ask her about that.

We're at the Shuttle Port's Visitors Arrivals entrance waiting for Paolo Pechenga, purveyor of fine Tayson Kwik memorabilia, to enter. Marmalade told me the Shuttle Port is different from the Shuttle Bay—it's even in a different, fancier area entirely. This is where short-term shuttles drop off passengers, like Paolo Pechenga, and depart with other important passengers. But Paolo is really the prince of Thorpia, Prince Weibold, who messaged us again to let us know the details of his disguise. Justyna accompanied us, hoping the prince actually is carrying some memorabilia with him. I am happy to have her with us. I like my new pack.

Using my new math brain, it occurs to me that it's been twenty-four hours on this new world, and I now have a nice pack. That's about twenty-four hours longer than it takes at the dog run. But hearing how before-Trixie and the ladies interacted, I can see why. Everyone's scared of something. Our way is better—just go up and sniff a butt. If they don't want it, move on to the next butt. Easy! Humans make everything so hard, and then they're all sad. What are these brains even for?

I'm pondering all this in my human brain as two royal guardsmen standing at the entrance of the Shuttle Port look uneasily at us. Should I sniff their butts? I know I can't, though. Marmalade said not to.

"Princess, what are you doing here?" one of the guards asks. Passengers are streaming around us as the other guard looks at some items the visitors hand over to him.

"She's here to buy some Tayson Kwik memorabilia from one of these traders before she's shipped to Thorpia and can't get any," Marmalade says, stepping in.

"Tayson Kwik memorabilia, you say?" the other guard follows up. "I'm a Kwikie too!"

"Uh . . . aren't you a bit old?" Marmalade asks as the last visitor walks out of the Shuttle Port. It's a young man (I think he's eighteen years old?) wearing a pink hat that says 13989, a red shirt that says AMORE, and a huge pink foam finger that says KWIK on it. He carries a large black bag in his other hand. This man looks ridiculous—very un-Kalaxian—but when I glance at his face, he's clearly the prince and instantly gives me a huge smile.

Before I can smile back, the other guard says, "Awesome! Amore shirts! I'll take some. And that foam finger!" The guard reaches out to grab the pink Tayson Kwik foam finger when Prince Weibold whacks him with it.

"Off, you fiend!" the prince exclaims. "This is for my betrothed!"

But the first guard, seeing his partner under attack from a bright-pink foam finger, pulls up his blaster. "Stop right there!"

Quick as Artie the Afghan hound at the dog run who I could never catch, the prince has disarmed the guard of his blaster and is now standing behind him holding the guard's head in his arms, and the Kwikie-loving guard is on the floor nursing a head wound. The second guard in his arms is flailing about, unable to speak.

"Wow, nice," Marmalade says matter-of-factly.

"I brought these for you, my beloved, not for these peasants," the prince says to me with a huge smile. The guard in his arms is not smiling. I'm scared to smile back at someone so violent. Thorpians really are warriors. Scary warriors. Seeing this, I'm wondering if going there is a good idea.

"What just happened?" Justyna asks.

"Um, I don't know," I mutter.

"Are we in trouble?" Justyna worries.

The Kwikie guard starts to get up.

"Run!" Marmalade orders us all.

And so, the four of us start running at top speed through the hall. Marmalade is pointing us down corridors left and right, and Prince Weibold is obeying. My instincts take over. I just love running and being chased, even if it is on a space carriage after my fiancé just attacked a Kalaxian royal guard over a pink foam finger for some singer I didn't know existed a few days ago.

"You run really well, my sweet," the prince says loudly.

"Woof!" I cry out. "Woof, woof, woof!"

"Woof indeed!" Prince Weibold calls back, raising his foam finger in salute. *How is that still on his hand?*

"Quiet down, you two!" Marmalade scolds us. "We're almost there." She makes another right and slows down.

We follow her. Soon we're huffing and puffing in front of a door with a band of yellow tape waist high across it that says UNDER CONSTRUCTION. "Good. Everyone in."

"Uh . . . ," Justyna says.

"We need to hide in here," Marmalade replies.

"We can't. It's under construction," Justyna continues to assert. "Things could fall on us. We need helmets."

"It's better than being executed," Marmalade argues. "And I doubt there is any construction. The rent in this area is too high, so it's undesirable, and no corporation or department will claim it. Now hurry, he could be behind us any moment."

"But you can't—" Justyna says.

"If we don't hide, I'll be forced to kill that guard," Prince Weibold interrupts. "I cannot be found here."

"Good point," Marmalade agrees as she presses the door's open button on the wall.

"No!" Justyna cries, but it's too late. Marmalade pushes her inside the dark room. Luckily, Justyna is able to quickly bend over to get under the yellow tape as we enter.

"I'm scared of the dark," I say, realizing there are no lights. "Really scared."

"Don't worry, Princess. I'll protect you," Prince Weibold states. Then I feel a hand on my waist.

"Ahhh!" I shout. "Ahhh!" On instinct, my head moves to bite the hand on my hip, but this stupid body can't reach it! *Growl!* How can humans be so stiff and inflexible?

"Sorry!" Prince Weibold replies quickly. "That was just me." The hand disappears.

"I'm scared of the dark! Don't touch me! I might bite you!" I cry.

"*Bite* me?" he asks. "You could be executed for saying such things. You really are a free spirit. I think I'm in love with you, Princess." I'm not sure what *love* he's talking about. Didn't he also just threaten to have me executed?

"I'm just telling you for your protection," I say, hoping to avoid being executed. Why does everyone want to execute everybody in this world?

"Guys, I can't find a light switch," Marmalade says.

"We don't need the lights, right? We just need to wait a while until that guard gives up?" Justyna asks, her voice quivering.

What? No lights? Come on, Justyna! "We need the lights! Just turn on the lights!" I order, anxiety boiling inside me. "I might bite someone!"

"Okay, okay, Princess. I have an idea," Marmalade says. "But don't tell Lady Perri."

"Lady Perri?" Justyna asks. "What does she have to do with this?"

"Willow?" Marmalade calls out. "I know you're there. Can you please turn on the lights for us?" Willow? But we left her in my room. "Willow! Come on! I know you're following us. Please! Princess Trixie is scared!"

"*Oh, all right. Anything for her. How did you know I was here?*" The lights turn on suddenly, but no one says anything. Are they as shocked as I am by what's all over the walls?

"*Right, so I do something nice for you, and you ignore me again? Some friends you—*"

"Shut up, Willow," Marmalade interrupts her.

"What is all this?" I ask. "The walls are so colorful."

"And why is it all signed 'Justyna'?" Marmalade wonders.

"I can explain," Justyna answers meekly.

"The colors. The figures. Sansibali, the God of Creative Spirit, would bow down to this *Justyna*," Prince Weibold says. "She may be a goddess herself! This is some of the most beautiful art I have ever seen. I would never have expected to find it in Kalaxia."

"Art?" I ask. "What's art?" I suddenly feel like a dog among humans all over again. What are they talking about?

"What's art? Do you truly not know, my beautiful betrothed?" Prince Weibold asks me. "As a princess, were you not educated in the galaxy's finest culture and beauty?"

"I never heard of it," I say. Even Trixie's memories don't have much on art. She did grow up poor in a shack and has only really been learning things this past year. When I think of the things Trixie does know—basket weaving, gardening, laughing with Mom, snuggles (some of those are mine too)—art doesn't come up. Maybe she wasn't educated that well? I don't recall anything like this in her life. Though access to her memories must be getting easier if I can do it when I'm this scared!

And for Twinkie . . . er, me (it's hard to remember *who* I am) . . . walls were just barriers to the outside. But these walls are beautiful—something to look at for long hours. "Marmalade? Was I not educated in art?"

"You weren't, Princess. It is inconsequential to you in

your current state." She gives me a look that clearly says we can't talk more about this here. "But art is . . . this stuff on the walls. Paintings. Drawings. It's some really ancient human thing," Marmalade explains. "Also music and singing, like Tayson Kwik. But at least Tayson Kwik makes money. It's just not something Kalaxia cares about."

"On Thorpia, we worship art as much as war. As much as the gods even," Prince Weibold informs us. "This art would be treasured in the stardom."

"Really?" Justyna asks, with sparkling eyes. "You really like my art?"

"*You* did this, Lady Justyna?" Marmalade asks. "You're *this* Justyna?" Isn't it clear already? That's why she didn't want to come in here or turn on the lights? Maybe I didn't know lies as Twinkie, but I knew deception.

"Yes, Lady Marmalade," Justyna answers. I'm busy walking around the room, looking closer at the colors and figures on the walls. Some are clearly people, but some look so weird—like broken bodies and sad. "Since I couldn't continue school when I first got here, I had nothing to do. So I was exploring the ship, feeling pretty sad—before I got this job, of course. I happened upon this room—the yellow tape was up, but every time I walked by, nothing was going on. I went inside, just to see, and it was so empty. It felt like my own clubhouse, away from my . . . anyway, there were some leftover paints from before they gave up remodeling the room, I guess. I just started painting. I don't know why. After I got the job with you, which

I am forever grateful for, by the way, I would still come at night and paint. After Trevor was safely asleep. I'm sorry."

"Don't be sorry, Justyna," Marmalade says. "Just erase your name from all of it. How stupid *are* you? Are you looking to get spaced? Kalaxia doesn't care about art like this. They'll just arrest and sue you for stealing resources. They'd send to you to a mining planet to pay it off, if you're lucky. If you're not lucky . . . I don't even want to go there. Just know, if you step out of line ever, *someone* will use you. Maybe on Thorpia you would thrive, but not here. It's a shame you weren't born a Thorpian."

"But you said no one has been in here for years," I remind Marmalade.

"Lady Marmalade, if I may speak freely on this vessel," Prince Weibold interjects.

Marmalade nods. "Of course. You are a prince."

"You cannot tell one imbued with the spirit of Sansibali to stop painting!" He seems very emotional about this.

"I can and I will," Marmalade replies sharply. "With all due respect, Your Highness." I can't believe she's speaking to the prince like this, but she *is* Bailey, and Bailey is afraid of no one. After watching the prince beat two men, having Bailey with me makes me feel safe. I have a pack here and he has none.

"This is Kalaxia," Marmalade continues, "not your mystical warrior poet stardom. Someone else owned that paint that she put on the walls. In Kalaxia, they could even chop her hands off for stealing." Justyna and I gasp, and she looks on the verge of tears. I nudge up against her to give her comfort as she stares at her hands. "Maybe if she were in Thorpia, but Lady Justyna is in Kalaxia. Good old money-hungry Kalaxia that I loved."

"She doesn't have to be," Prince Weibold declares.

"What?" all of us girls spit back.

"Lady Justyna, you are young but filled with so much talent," Prince Weibold says while looking at her intently, like he is stalking his prey.

"I am? Everyone always tells me how stupid I am. How I'm a burden."

"*I* never thought that," I say to Justyna.

"You never really talked to me until yesterday," Justyna replies politely. "Sorry, Princess."

"But, Lady Justyna," Marmalade jumps in, "I hope I didn't make you feel stupid. That was never my intention. There's a reason you're on my team. We girls have to stick together."

"No, no. Well, kind of, but like I said, this job was the best thing to happen to me. I don't know how I lucked out! On my old limo, I failed school every year and was prohibited from any secondary school. Then, six months ago, when my parents died, Trevor and I were suddenly assigned to Limo One, with my long-lost aunt telling me how stupid I am every day. I'm just like my parents, who were stupid enough to have a burden like me." Justyna chokes up, tears welling in her eyes. "Not Trevor, though. Auntie loves him for some reason."

"Anyone who did this art *cannot* be stupid. But you do not have to decide today," the prince says. "I would like for you to come to Thorpia, where your talent can thrive. Where *you* can thrive."

I'm a little worried for Justyna and Trevor. My fiancé and Thorpia seem unpredictably violent. And I'd be going for my own purpose—to get home—so I might not even be there for her if she thinks I would. Hopefully, I would be home. Maybe she could come back to my world and be a dog with me? But who knows how long it will take to find a god to help me. And in the meantime, I would have a fun pack with me! My golden retriever! Maybe it could work out?

"We can still be a pack. We can be roomies!" I exclaim. "We can get beds next to each other and take baths together—"

"Certainly not!" Prince Weibold exclaims.

"Princess!" Marmalade exclaims louder.

"Take baths together?" Justyna asks. "Is that a *royal* thing? I'm not sure—"

"Oh," I say. "We don't *have* to do that."

"She would be executed on the spot!" Prince Weibold exclaims again. "I hereby warn you to not be *too* free-thinking!"

"Princess Trixie, I would love to go with you." *Yay!* "But not the baths, if you don't mind." Boo! But this world is what it is. It's just a body!

"Nor the beds," Prince Weibold says. "You will have the royal chambers on the Thorpian Space Chariot Hiyotameteke. She can have a room nearby, though, if you'd like. The finest teachers will come to her."

"School?" Justyna asks the prince with wide eyes.

"After a fashion," he answers.

"My little brother, Trevor . . . can he come too?"

"He can come as well," Prince Weibold says. *Yay! Bigger pack!* And he and I are already fast friends, though he did run away screaming . . . "He can train to be a great warrior in Thorpia!" The prince sounds so happy when talking about war. But also art. *And* gods. He's very confusing.

"Oh, thank you, Prince. I don't know why you're so nice to me," Justyna says. She also does a thing where she bends her knees. My Trixie memories from this past year call it a curtsy. *That's* the kind of education she got!

"*What about me?*" a voice from the ceiling asks.

"Willow!" I exclaim. "You're still there! How are you? Are you having fun on the ship?"

"*Finally someone remembered me. Did you not think of poor old Willow this whole time?*"

"Is she a *god?*" Prince Weibold asks, bewildered.

"She thinks she is," Lady Marmalade replies. "But no."

"Then what *is* she?" he asks. "I was distracted by the art, so I did not think to ask. Kalaxia keeps surprising me."

"Let me try to explain," I tell Marmalade.

"Be careful," Marmalade whispers to me.

I look at the prince. "She is a computer person. But she's not going to take over the empire or anything."

"Oh stars," Lady Marmalade says. "That was a terrible explanation." Justyna giggles.

"You mean you have computers that are *alive?*" the prince asks, mouth agape.

"You *don't?*" Marmalade counters. "I mean, your computers don't talk?"

"Certainly not. Why should we try to create something such as this when we have our gods? A speaking computer is blasphemous! An artificial god would only make sense in a godless society such as yours. I am being free thinking to not strike you all down where you stand for angering the gods, because I am, of course, accepting of other cultures. For the time being . . ."

"An artificial god? I quite like that."

"Willow, please don't make it worse," Marmalade says.

"Would Perri like me better if I were an artificial god?"

"No. Stop this nonsense," Marmalade replies. "The prince is getting upset." I look and he's wearing a frown. But then I remember how this all started.

"How did you even know she was following us?" I ask Marmalade.

"Oh please. If I learned anything about you children this past year, it's that none of you do a damn thing I ask you to do, but I love you all anyway."

"You love me?" I ask Marmalade.

"Oh stars. That just slipped out," Marmalade says. "Forget I said it."

"But you did say it! Say it again!" I plead.

"No," Marmalade replies, arms crossed.

"Princess," Prince Weibold says as he grabs my paws . . . er, hands. "You are impossible *not* to love. Did I tell you about your free spirit?"

"Tell her again! Tell her again! I love hearing your poetry," Justyna says. She seems to love . . . well, *love*. But this isn't the type of love that *I* love. It makes me very uncomfortable. Can I be human enough for love yet? Certainly not. I love the running-around-after-balls-and-braiding-hair-together pack love. And the baths together would be nice! But human romantic love? Blech, no!

"You say and do things no other woman would dare, which makes you the *u* in unique," Prince Weibold starts. Justyna is sighing loudly. "You think things we all repress inside. You share and give your love with just the look in your eyes. I thought ours was to be a loveless arrangement of convenience, until I saw your excitement over a simple bowl of soup.

"Princess," he says as he looks deep into my eyes, still holding my hands. I want to look away, but I'm afraid he will attack me. "I want to spend my life as your soup."

"Oh my! So beautiful!" Justyna exclaims.

"*Sap nebula!*" Willow complains.

"See now the downside of artificial gods who speak to you! Gods are best enjoyed quietly," Prince Weibold declares. His hand is a fist balled in the air.

"Well, this god . . . er, Willow . . . has proven useful to us," Marmalade counters.

"And she's my friend!" I exclaim. "You can't speak meanly about her."

"A *friend?*" Prince Weibold cries. "She's artificial!"

"Yes, and it's just too bad she can't rub my belly."

"*And I wish you could rub my algorithms,*" Willow replies. Justyna giggles.

"Okay, things just got weird," Marmalade says. "Prince, I would remind you that you are in Kalaxia right now, not Thorpia. There will be no striking down." Prince Weibold nods. *Go, Bailey!* "But, Willow, can you tell where the guards are?"

"*Yes, the one with the head wound is being treated by Dr. Lam in the Medical Bay. The one chasing you guys took a wrong turn after a wall speaker near him called out, 'I saw them go that way.' Unfortunately, for him, 'that way' was right into an open plasma conduit. He is also being treated by Dr. Lam. You're welcome, by the way.*"

"Are they okay?" I ask. I never wanted them to get hurt.

"*Let me see . . . initial diagnoses are minor burns and a minor concussion. But because I also erased any record of your presence at the scene, as well as the handsome prince's visit, Dr. Lam added a diagnosis of mental stress and overwork for each. It does not appear any other guards are searching for you.*"

"Wow, thank you, Willow!" I say.

"*Do you think Perri would be proud?*"

"I don't think we should tell her," Marmalade replies. "It would just worry her about you taking over the ship. Now please go back to the princess's cabin and wait for us there."

"*Awww.*"

"So we can go then?" Justyna asks.

"Yes, let's finally head to the romantic dinner for two we set up. Koko and Brandi are already waiting for us there," Marmalade says.

"I would be happy to complete a dinner with my betrothed," Prince Weibold states. "But I will leave the memorabilia here for the godlike Lady Justyna." He drops the foam finger and the bag. "I should keep the hat and shirt in case anyone inquires."

"Yay!" Justyna cheers. "I'm happy for anything you can give me!"

"Lady Justyna, you may leave us and have the night off," Marmalade says. "I believe you have to get started painting over your name everywhere." She waves at the walls surrounding us.

But Justyna's already playing with her foam finger and singing, so I'm not sure she heard anything.

Chapter 12
I Didn't Even Get Dessert

Marmalade leads Prince Weibold, still dressed as a Kwik memorabilia merchant, and me through some more corridors. I'm nervous to be around him, as he has shown himself to be a violent man. But he also appreciates something called art, seems to really like me, and, if anything bad happens, I have Bailey . . . er, Marmalade . . . with me.

"All right, we're here," Marmalade says. The sign above the door reads NEGOTIATION ROOM 78C. My lips turn up into a smile, as the pride of knowing how to read rushes through me.

"I can read that!" I exclaim.

"Uh, Princess?" Marmalade asks.

"Does the princess not know how to read?" Prince Weibold asks her. "Does Kalaxia not teach its females? Thorpia cannot have an unedu—"

"I do! I can!"

"See?" Lady Marmalade reassures him, but she gives me a stern look. Before the prince can respond, she opens the door to the room.

It looks much like what I now know was the original engagement ceremonial dinner room, except the table is smaller and has only two place settings. There's a large candle in the middle. Koko is standing in a white dress near the table holding a bottle of water.

"You did this for us?" Prince Weibold asks Lady Marmalade. "I just wanted a chance to talk with her, but it's almost like another engagement dinner to make up for last night. My fiancée and I thank you." Although I am impressed with my pack, I *don't* like the prince speaking for me.

I raise a finger in protest, but Marmalade replies for me. "She was so touched by your message, she wanted to make up to you for the prior dinner that she ruined." *Hey, I was about to bark in his face, and you made me sound nice!*

"I'm pleased, but there is nothing to make up for," he replies. "That is the dinner where I fell in love with her."

"Stars, I'll never find anyone that nice," we hear a voice say from behind a door near the back of the room. It's Brandi! Koko is giggling.

"Hi, Brandi!" I wave and smile. "Where's Perri?"

"*Lady* Brandi, we can hear you," Marmalade says.

"Oops. Just saying," Brandi replies. "And *Lady* Perri has the night off. Lucky her, since you guys took forever to get here."

"Lady Brandi!" Marmalade scolds her again and then

turns to the prince. "Please forgive us for our rudeness, Prince."

"Pay no mind. I find your attitudes refreshing, being surrounded all day by fear and politeness. May we enter?" the prince asks.

"Please," Marmalade says, waving us in. As we walk in, she whispers in my ear, "Remember everything we worked on." I nod, though I'm not sure I remember *anything* we worked on. I'm too nervous about everything—the warrior prince who seems to love me (blech!), acting like a princess, getting home. It's like when I first came to this world. But this *has* to work so that I can get to Thorpia and then find a way home. Everything is on the line.

The prince walks to a seat, pulls it out, and stares at me. Oh no, is this some Thorpian ritual? We didn't have time to prepare for Thorpian rituals—and even if they did before I took over Trixie's body, I don't remember any. Are we praying to the Goddess of Chairs or something? That must be it.

I go to the other chair and pull it out also. But the prince's face falls. Marmalade has her hand on her forehead. Did I do something wrong? "I'm ready to pray to the chairs now! I swear! I love your rituals!"

"Princess," he says with a look of relief, "I understand now. Normally you would be correct, but we do not pray to Charice, the Goddess of Chairs, while Falconia, the God of Eyesight, is in retrograde with respect to Yargulsmutz the Devout. After we are wed, because it is not shared with outsiders, we can spend nights together by the plasmaplace reading the *Thorpian Compendium of the Gods and Goddesses in All Their Holiness*, where you will pick up such nuances."

"Look at that, Marmalade," Koko says. "Princess was kinda right!" Marmalade's forehead is still in her hand, though.

"But please, Princess, take a seat," Prince Weibold insists, gesturing at the chair he is holding.

"That seat?" I ask. Now I'm utterly confused.

"Yes, come here," the prince says.

"Wow, he's even pulling her chair out! It's like one of those ancient stories men laugh at now," Brandi states from behind the door, her face from the nose up sticking through.

"I know, right?" Koko replies. "No guy does that in Kalaxia."

"Near you?" I ask the prince.

"Of course, my betrothed. I do not bite, although it appears you do."

"Whoa, there's definitely a story there," Brandi says from behind the door.

"I'll get it from Marmalade later," Koko replies.

"Shut up, you two!" Marmalade scolds them.

"But you didn't make it look nice," I explain, stalling for time. I'm scared to go near him. It's one thing when we were on the run from the guards—there was no choice. But now he's a dangerous warrior who wants to have dinner with me.

"What?" he asks.

"How do I know it's a good chair? How do I know it's comfy?" I ask.

"It's *your* chair," Prince Weibold replies. "From *your* ship."

"Trixie," Marmalade scolds me. "Just sit in the damn chair."

"You have to know how to make a chair look comfy first, if we're to be in a pack together," I say, stalling.

"A pack?" he asks.

He doesn't know what a pack is? How do I explain it to a Thorpian warrior? With my girls, I could just say friends. I'll try that.

"Like friends!" Oh no. Marmalade's head is in her hands again.

"Friends! We're to be married!" the prince says, stiffening in surprise.

"Oh . . . um . . . I mean, like a family," I try to explain.

"Family! Like a brother!" Prince Weibold stands even straighter, hands letting go of the chair.

"No." Marmalade steps in. "The princess means that one day in the future you will have your own family, *as you are due to be married.*" She said the last part staring right at me, eyes aflame.

"Ah yes," Prince Weibold says, accepting her explanation. He drops to one knee again, next to his chair. "I wish to be in a pack with you. Even now your spirit brings me to such great heights that I feel the awe of the gods."

Marmalade gasps in surprise—probably wondering why anything I mess up seems to work with this guy. "Please tell me—how do I make this chair look comfy to one clearly as intelligent as you?"

He thinks I'm intelligent? *Me?* That makes me happy. But I can see Marmalade and Koko's mouths open wide in surprise.

"If I come over, you promise not to hurt me like those guards?" I ask.

"Princess, I would *never* lay a hand on you."

"It'll be hard to make that family," Brandi whispers. Koko giggles.

Ignoring them, I try to get more promises from him. "You promise to never raise your voice at me?"

"Princess, the gods breathed sound into my voice solely to soothe you." Koko and Brandi gasp.

"You promise—"

"Princess, just tell him!" Marmalade scolds me. Marmalade thinks I can trust him? I look at her, trying to understand what she's thinking. She nods and flashes a reassuring smile. Some of my anxiety melts away.

"You just have to tap the chair a little. With your hand. That's *my* ritual. Go on, try it," I say.

The prince takes his hand and pats the seat of the chair.

"Ooh, that chair looks so good now. I *must* sit on it!" Running over, I give a little jump at the end of my run and hop into the chair. The prince steps back a bit, but he smiles and giggles as I wiggle my butt into the soft chair. I wish I could curl up on it, but this body is way too big.

"I see. Kalaxian women have such joy!" Marmalade, Koko, and Brandi can barely contain their laughter.

"Oh, not *all* Kalaxian women," Marmalade says. "Trixie is a special one, for sure."

"I see that!" Prince Weibold replies as he takes the other seat. Marmalade runs over to push the chair in for him as well.

"Prince, before we begin the dinner, may I ask why you came without any guards?" Marmalade says.

"Ah, that is a good question. I sent my most trusted guard on a dangerous pilgrimage, supposedly *with* me, such that no one would think to look for me elsewhere," he answers. "I just *had* to see my betrothed."

"Do you have only one guard who you trust?" Marmalade asks. If she's coming with me, I guess she's interested in knowing what Thorpia's royal household is really like. All we've heard so far is that women don't talk freely—at least around him. Sounds much like I've experienced on Kalaxia, though.

"Reynozo has been with me since I was a child. There are other guards who are trustworthy, but none with something like this." Prince Weibold turns to Koko. "Are you the waitress tonight?"

"Yes, but just for tonight," Koko clarifies. "I am actually a warrior too."

"Ah, a woman warrior," Prince Weibold says matter-of-factly, as if Koko is as normal as air. Her eyes widen.

"Are there women warriors on Thorpia?" Koko asks, surprised.

"Indeed, there is even a famous regiment made up only of females and known as the Nightwalkers."

"Oh, I so want to go to Thorpia!" Koko exclaims. "Would they take me?"

"That can be arranged, if you pass their trials," Prince Weibold says.

"Yes!" I smile widely. Maybe I'll have a pack on Thorpia too?

"All right, all right, Lady Koko," Marmalade interjects. "This is Trixie's evening. We'll let them have their dinner. Please start serving."

Koko pours water into our glasses on the table. I pick up my glass to drink, trying to remember not to use my tongue. But the prince leans over and says, "It's time for the ceremonial kiss to honor Humbertitwiz, the God of Flavorless Liquids." He takes my other paw . . . er, hand . . . in his own and kisses it. I've been kissed on my fur by Charlotte and Carolina, but this feels different on my skin. It tickles! I pull my hand away.

"It's time for you to do the same for me," Prince Weibold says, holding out his hand. *I have to kiss his hand?* I got in trouble earlier for kissing Trevor.

"You want to snog? We can't do that. I'll get in trouble, like with Trevor," I say, horrified.

"What? No! And who's Trevor?" Prince Weibold is equally horrified.

"Oh Prince." Marmalade steps in, her eyes glancing at me in anger. "Don't you worry about Trevor. That was just an unfortunate misunderstanding already taken care of. The princess has eyes only for you."

"I see, yes. That makes sense. I mean, one day in the future, yes, of course, we *could* snog, after praying to Snoog, the Goddess of Snogs, and receiving her blessing."

"You have a goddess for snogging?" Koko asks, trying to contain her laughter with a hand over her mouth. Marmalade stares her down.

"Yes, of course. There is a god or goddess for every . . . well, enough of that," Prince Weibold says with a wave of his hand, his face reddening. He turns back to me. "But surely we would not *snog* before you are of age or else we will be smitten by Chantal, the Goddess of Chastity. No, no, this is just a quick kiss of my hand."

"Oh, that makes me feel better. It *is* a nice hand. Look at those fingers . . ."

"Princess," Marmalade warns me quietly.

No licks, I tell myself. *No licks*. The prince pushes his hand closer to my mouth. But those fingers . . . so juicy . . . human fingers . . . I must lick! My instincts take over, and I lick his fingers. *Oops!*

"Princess, that tickles!" the prince giggles.

"Yours did too," I reply. But I just go back to licking— can't stop licking, even though I know I'll be in trouble. He didn't seem mad. I know it's so wrong, though. But I need to keep licking. Why?

"She's doing it again, Marmalade!" Koko cries, dropping the pitcher of water.

And then the door to Negotiation Room 78C opens. "Hi, Princess. I brought you some medicine for that parasite. Holy quasars, what are you doing?" Dr. Lam stands in shock. Prince Weibold pulls his hand away from me instantly.

"We were kissywissying," I reply to Dr. Lam, who looks horrified. What's wrong with that? Dr. Lam isn't a little kid like Trevor—he should know kissywissying is fine.

"Is she really sick?" Prince Weibold asks before Dr. Lam can reply. "She just licked my hand! She must have earned the ire of Pesto, the God of Pestilence, because of that Willow aberration! How could I be so stupid? I have lost the gods' favor."

"Willow? No, Trixie has a Joparan Body Snatcher parasite. I need to give her this pill." The doctor is holding out another bright-blue pill. "But I didn't realize she would be kissing on a date with some hippie-dippie Tayson Kwik fan. You do know she is betrothed, boy?" His face is all pinched and scrunched together.

"*Boy?*" Prince Weibold exclaims as he stands up from the table, pushing his chair back.

"That's right, *boy*," Dr. Lam mocks the prince. "So why do I find her in here doing ghastly, unspeakable things with you?"

Lady Marmalade steps closer to them. "Listen up, everyone! Mr. Pechenga," she says, addressing Prince Weibold by his fake name. Thank Dog she remembered it! "The princess has mostly recovered. You have nothing to worry about."

"I'll be the judge of that," Dr. Lam replies, clearly unhappy.

Marmalade snaps, "Doctor, calm down. This is just extra practice for Trixie's next engagement dinner. She doesn't want to mess it up again so that she can finally get to Thorpia and start her new life there with the prince. You do know that, right? She wants to leave in two weeks?" Dr. Lam looks left and right, avoiding us. But then his eyes settle on me.

"Oh," Dr. Lam replies. "So you *want* to go to Thorpia?"

"Yes, Doctor," I admit. "I'm sorry." He looks so upset. He wanted to help me go home, and last time I saw him that was our plan—I even agreed. But so much has changed in a day. And Expiry isn't really home. It doesn't even have gods who can maybe control magical portals to other worlds. Dr. Lam's face is scrunched even tighter and is turning red.

Then he explodes. "You really want to marry that dumb, ignorant, violent, small-minded, waste of life that is the Thorpian prince? He's worse than this hippie-dippie!" Dr. Lam rages, not realizing the man standing on the other side of the table is the prince. My hands are over my face, worried for Dr. Lam.

Instantly, Prince Weibold sweeps his leg across the floor, and Dr. Lam goes down. The prince is on top of him, pummeling his face. Human fighting is strange because no teeth seem to be involved. Just paws. But the prince is an expert—so quick with his paws.

"No! Don't hurt him!" I say loudly to Prince Weibold. All I can think of is how Dr. Lam was so kind to me when I first got to Limo One.

"Cease this at once!" Marmalade orders, holding a blaster she took out of her dress. It's aimed at the prince.

"Lady Marmalade?" Prince Weibold asks. "What is the meaning of this?"

"Mr. Pechenga, you are a guest on board. Even more so, you are just a trader, and the doctor is management."

"You do know this will cause an intergalactic incident. Maybe even war."

"War? Intergalactic incident? Over Mr. Pechenga?" Dr. Lam groans from under the prince.

"I would kindly appreciate it if you did *not* beat up our head physician," Marmalade says sternly. The prince rolls off Dr. Lam and gets back to his feet. Marmalade returns the blaster to her dress.

"Head physician?" Prince Weibold looks more closely at Dr. Lam. "I'm sorry, but I was insulted." Prince Weibold holds out a hand to Dr. Lam, who is now on the floor, his face bloodied. "No hard feelings?"

"You're all crazy!" Dr. Lam thunders. "Why do you even have a blaster? I knew she couldn't trust you!"

"Doctor, please. This is not the place. Do you need assistance?" Lady Marmalade asks Dr. Lam, who is now rising from the floor.

"No, I'm a *doctor*," he replies sternly. "I'll be fine. Unlike you, Princess!" Then he storms out of the room.

"Princess, that doctor just threatened you. You should come back to Thorpia with me, for your safety," Prince Weibold says. Dr. Lam threatened me? As a dog, I can tell threatening humans and dogs pretty well. Dr. Lam wouldn't threaten me.

"You think I'm at risk of *him*?" I ask angrily. "Unlike you, he's the one who is normally kind and caring."

"Kind and caring? Did you hear his insults?" Prince Weibold asks.

"All I saw was you hitting him! Like you hit everyone!" I cry.

"Do you *like* him? That supercilious jerk?" Prince Weibold accuses me.

"He's not silly!" I reply.

"Awww, their first fight," Brandi says from behind the door.

"Not now, Brandi!" Marmalade snaps.

"He's not the one who explodes into violence at every chance!" I continue scolding Prince Weibold.

"He insulted me. Twice! And by extension, you! Do you not take any pride in your royal position?" Prince Weibold asks sternly.

"He didn't insult my extensions! He's a kind doctor!"

"That's not what I meant!" Prince Weibold replies. "I thought you were a free spirit. But it turns out you were just exceedingly promiscuous and dumb! And your abomination Willow angers the gods!"

"Prince, please watch your tongue," Lady Marmalade says. "I will not tolerate you insulting the princess."

"Or Willow!" I snarl at him.

"I will insult her all I want. I'm the prince of Thorpia!" He is now ranting and banging on his chest.

"Do not insult me!" I exclaim. "I'm a goodgirl! You're a naughtyboy!" And then I growl. Everyone takes a step back from me. Good!

"I thought I liked how different you were, Princess, but this is beyond the pale. And the licking! On Thorpia, you would just be an embarrassment to the throne! You act like an animal. The wedding is off!" I hear something crash from Brandi's room. Marmalade has her blaster out now. Koko's paws are balled into fists, and she's in a fighting stance similar to when we fought the squirds.

"I will ask you to leave now, Prince Weibold. You say you will call off the wedding, but remember, we know that you snuck onto a Kalaxian space carriage and assaulted one of our physicians. You speak of intergalactic incidents, but *you* are the one who should tread lightly." Lady Marmalade turns to Koko. "Koko, take this blaster and escort the prince off the ship."

"Yes! Gladly! Real action!" Koko says excitedly, taking the blaster. She turns to Prince Weibold. "And, Prince, remember that I'm a warrior too. I didn't want to go to your stupid stardom anyway."

"Harrumph!" Prince Weibold grunts back as they leave the room.

"I'm a badgirl, aren't I?" I ask Marmalade.

Chapter 13
Wedding Crashers

Oh my stars, oh my stars, what are we going to do?" Marmalade is spitting words out very fast.

"What do you mean? Why are you so upset? I've never seen you upset," I reply. "You're the one who can fix anything." For the past twenty-four hours in this world, Bailey/Marmalade has been my rock. Like the huge rock at the dog run I liked to sit on that would make me feel safe. Or my chair at home that I would steal before Dada could get to it. I felt safe there too. But since I got here, I felt safe with Marmalade. Now she's freaking out.

"You stupid girl! Oh, you stupid girl!"

"Bailey!" Why does her face look so angry with me?

"For the thousandth time! I am *not* Bailey! I am *not* your friend. This is a *job* to me! And you ruined it! He's going to call off the wedding!" She's talking fast and pacing faster. Her hands are gnawing at her long dark-red hair.

"But you said we were friends. You were going to come with me." We're staring at each other as if no one else is in the room.

Before Marmalade can answer, the pantry door opens and Brandi slinks out. "Uh, hi?"

"Get out!" Marmalade roars. "Leave us! Now!" Brandi speed walks through the door and out of Negotiation Room 78C, leaving me to face Marmalade's fury while my plans, and this world, crash down around me.

"Aren't we friends?" I ask.

"We're *not* friends! And I was *never* going to Thorpia with you. You have no idea what this is all about, do you?"

"I'm supposed to know what this is about? I don't even know what world I'm in," I reply honestly for the first time. Marmalade cocks her head a bit at that comment but quickly straightens it again.

"Director Voltari hired me to get you ready. *He* wants this alliance between Thorpia and Kalaxia, for whatever reason, and he found *me* useful."

"I know all this already. You were all hired for this. It doesn't mean we're not friends, right?" *Please tell me we're friends.* She won't say we're friends.

"But you don't know *why* I was hired. And it wasn't to be your friend. I worked my whole life to rise to his ranks, from a lowly manager's daughter on Limo One Hundred Twenty. All the conniving and politicking I had to do *my whole life.* But I finally found a real executive to take me. The things I had to do to please him—he was *not* a nice man." Marmalade shivers. "But I had prestige. I had power—*his* power, but still power.

"And then one day, a senior vice president's daughter shows an interest in him—that little young thing—and immediately I'm useless. My soon to be *ex*-husband, a CEO on Limo Thirty-Two, wants to *divorce* me! That's a death sentence! Do you know how hard it is for a woman to survive after a divorce in Kalaxia? It's impossible. I would have *no* assets to my name. *No* job. They would drop me off on one of those commoner planets—like the hellhole *you* came from. Every day I looked at you was a reminder of my future. Voltari knew the incentive was right in front of me, yet he added even more."

"But planets are nice. You saw. We had fun." My words are meek attempts to win her back. My Bailey. I *need* her.

"We almost *died*!" Marmalade exclaims. She takes a deep breath and then continues. "So then comes Director Voltari, who says he would grant me a title and a share of my husband's assets after my divorce if I would just train this one decrepit girl. I was there when our limo picked up that little waif. He knew my background and my abilities. And imagine it: What better revenge against my husband? A woman in Kalaxia with her own title! And a share of his assets!

"All I had to do was get you ready to go to Thorpia. I didn't even know anything about you—just that you were some dirty commoner. But as an executive's wife, I knew how a lady needs to act, so I could surely teach you.

"So with my entire life on the line, among other things, I spent a whole year on you, and this is the thanks you show me? You fail at the last minute? You and your no-good doctor boyfriend. I even warned you about him! And now my life is *ruined*! I lost and he won! Because of *you*!" Marmalade is breathing so heavy, I fear she may explode.

"Marmalade," is all I can reply. Tears, real human tears, are falling down my face to the floor. I go to hug Marmalade, my only rock in this galaxy. But she takes a step back and swats at me.

"Get your commoner hands off me," she orders.

"But, Marmalade, please!" I beg her.

"Do you know what's going to happen to me now? How many times do I have to say it?"

Wiping away my tears, I reply, "The planet thing? It's not so bad. I'll go with you. I promise."

"If I'm lucky, Director Voltari won't space me. He will just let the divorce go through. They'll strip me of everything. I'll end up a beggar on some dirty rock. That's if I'm lucky."

"Why would they be so mean to you?" I ask her.

"You are so naive, you stupid girl. Have you seen any women in *any* positions of power in Kalaxia? Have you not seen the cruelty on board this space carriage? You *grew up* in poverty, a subservient class. Can't you recognize it on this very space carriage? And what do you think will happen to *you* now?"

"I don't know. All I wanted was to go home."

"So that's what this was all about? You were so stupid

that you thought they would send you home to Expiry? Or you could escape with Dr. Lam? Did he whisper sweet nothings of home in your ear? Oh, that stupid boy."

"You don't understand," I tell her, afraid to say more. *That's not home*, I want to say.

"I understand *perfectly*. You never intended to go to Thorpia."

"I *did* intend to go. I promise," I plead.

"Like I should trust a dirty commoner," Marmalade says, spitting on the floor in my direction.

"Fine. You want the truth?" I ask. Marmalade stares at me but says nothing, so I continue. "I wanted to go to Thorpia for real. But only as a way to get *home*."

"I don't understand. Back to Expiry? What would be the point?"

"To my *real* home. I don't think it's in this world."

"World? Do you mean this *galaxy*?" She cocks her head. *Am I getting through to her?*

"Fine, galaxy. Whatever you call it, my home is far, far away. I thought Thorpia's gods could help me. So yes, I did want to go."

"You aren't just stupid; you're crazy too. They should have left you to rot on Expiry last year. You were an impossible task! I was set up to fail. Princess Trixie is literally insane. How could they ever have married you off? Did they know?"

"No, please. You don't understand. I'm not who you think I am," I say. "I'm *not* Trixie."

"Wait, are you *really* a body snatcher parasite then? The doctor was right?" Marmalade's eyes widen in suspicion.

"No—"

But at that moment, just as I was starting to get through to her, the doors to the room open, and in walks Director Voltari.

His gray hair, long gray beard, and golden cat cane stand out in the crowd of ten red-clad royal guardsmen, including Captain Gregor. The captain looks pained to be there, walking in short steps. But Voltari looks even more pained, his scowl tearing a hole right through me. And then the memory of what Dr. Lam said returns to me—he's a Quantum Mancer. Whatever that is. But all I know is the doctor is afraid of him.

Long gone are my days of worrying about what couch I will nap on and which neighborhood squirrel is on my lawn. Now I'm face-to-face with . . . evil. Being human has been a tragedy so far. Some funny moments but overall just sadness.

How do humans do it? They seem to move from one bad thing to another, with only fleeting nice things in between to ameliorate the pain. And now I have to worry about punishment. What kind of punishment would a human get? I heard these humans mention being spaced before. What is that? Everyone seems *terrified* of it and of him.

"We meet again, dear Princess," Director Voltari says, extra slowly. "And here I thought you and Dr. Lam were planning something. Imagine my surprise when the good doctor informed *me* that you were sullying yourself, kissing some common merchant and potentially invalidating the new alliance." My jaw drops. Sweet Dr. Lam betrayed me? To someone he thought was so dangerous? This galaxy is horrific. There's no one I can trust here. Not Lady Marmalade, not Dr. Lam. I just want to go home, but now I can't. I never will.

"Look at me when I'm talking to you!" Voltari orders. I stare back into his cold eyes. "I thought: at least Thorpia didn't find out. Then imagine my *additional* anger when Thorpia itself called us to say the wedding was off due to your impurity!

"Devious indeed, eliminating your eligibility to marry into Thorpia by insulting their Goddess of Chastity. How they found out about it, I don't know, but I don't care." Volatri starts pacing, using his cane as a walking stick. Endless seconds go by as he paces in silence, but then he turns back to me. "Why are you intent on ruining my plans, Princess? If I can even call you that, since you're really just a bastard. Did you think we would just let you go home? You're nothing to the crown if you're not useful, and you will pay for this!" His voice resonates like thunder. Even the royal guards surrounding him, including Captain Gregor, seem to tremble.

"I believe I know how they found out, sir," Marmalade says loudly, stepping forward and away from me slightly.

"After the ceremonial dinner, I thought it couldn't get worse. I thought about terminating you then and there, dear Marmalade, but you had just two weeks to finish the job! What could you possibly tell me that would keep me from spacing you and . . . you know you're no longer useful, correct?"

Marmalade gasps, her eyes darting toward the guards, probably seeing if they're coming for her. She was hoping she might just get sent to some planet. But she is going to be spaced, and that seems worse from her reaction. No one wants to be spaced. But she quickly gathers her composure. "What Dr. Lam witnessed was a practice dinner only. Thorpia and the doctor are completely mistaken."

"Is what you say true?" Director Voltari asks, stopping his pacing. Interested now, his cat cane leans in Marmalade's direction.

"Yes," Marmalade answers, slightly emboldened. "And furthermore, the commoner merchant at our practice dinner, who apparently helped sully Princess Trixie's standing with their God of Chastity, was none other than Prince Weibold himself!"

"What?" Director Voltari exclaims in shock. "Explain!"

"It appears your own plan was working well," Marmalade compliments Voltari. "Prince Weibold was somehow smitten with our princess, in spite of all her shortcomings." Marmalade shoots me a nasty glare. "He devised his own plan to have a secret rendezvous with her tonight, which our Dr. Lam accidentally witnessed. And you know KAMP has been looking to stop this alliance at all costs. When they couldn't steal the princess away, well . . ."

"Blasted KAMP and their hidden agendas! I *knew* he was a problem," Voltari spews.

"I believe you could use the knowledge of the prince's secret to force his hand and the marriage," Marmalade continues, shooting me another nasty glare. Although she seems to despise me now—or always did—I am even more impressed with her, as she is gaining the upper hand with Voltari. That is something Bailey would do. Even Captain Gregor is smiling.

"What you say is true. A good plan," Voltari says. He looks toward the ceiling, like he's thinking. "We will set the wheels in motion at once. But now the question remains, What to do with you two, who can't seem to do anything but ruin my plans!" His voice resonates across the room again at an unnatural volume, causing the guards and Captain Gregor to flinch.

Marmalade is quiet again. With a glance, I can see that she looks as scared as I do; her eyes are pleading for Captain Gregor to do something, or *not* do something, but he's frozen still. I try and grab her paw, since we're close enough, but she swats my hand away. Even though I'm standing close to her, I feel so alone. Before this terrible dinner, I had so many friends. Now it feels as though I have no one. Alone in a different world, or galaxy, or whatever.

"And where is your gratitude?" Voltari says, staring right at me now. My tail would be down if I had one. I want to bark, to show him how big I am, but I don't feel very big right now. And that would make it worse. So I stand, resigned to my fate. "I was the one who decided to pluck you from that wasteland of a planet and bring you here. Once I heard about your father's mistress, the pregnant concubine he banished to Expiry, I *knew* you were the key. With you, we could form an alliance and increase our power. *My* power! And you would be so controllable, an uneducated commoner.

"I dispatched your mother because you, the dirty little girl from a dirty little planet, I dare say, are the key to galactic power and riches beyond my wildest dreams! And all you had to do was play along! Both of you!"

"Mother?" I ask in shock. "Dispatched?" Does he mean he killed her—the mother I recalled from Trixie's memories during my own better times in this galaxy?

"Plactalian Floort Virus is not especially catching. Did you even wonder how she got it, you fool?"

"Mother!" I'm holding out my arms, as if I can reach her.

Suddenly Trixie's memories return to me. Before I could access them only when I was comfortable and relaxed and then when I actively searched for them, but a floodgate has just opened, and they've all rushed in. The horror of what I heard burst that dam. Trixie's childhood was pure happiness on Expiry, much like Charlotte and Carolina's, though she grew up in poverty and without a dada. But from what I know, she was better off without Emperor Papo, her real father. In their little one-room shack, her mother working all day to come home and educate her with what little she knew to keep food in their bowls, er, on their plates. Trixie had true love, the kind I'll never feel again. In a way, we both were stripped of that. "Mama?"

"Silence!" A yellow fireball (that's the only way I can describe it) forms from the golden cat head on his cane. The ball is just sitting at the top of the cane, but the sight of it quiets the entire room. Voltari looks equally surprised to see it, and it quickly disappears. "Now look what you made me do! How can such a young girl be so frustrating!

"And your poor mother? Again, where's your gratitude! You were set up in luxury, with the finest things in life, finally with a future. I read the reports—did you like living in squalor? In dirt? What was your future on Expiry anyway? Work in the refueling stations? Or serving food and *other things* in the refinery, like your mother? Tell me, did she bring the men back to your shack?"

"How dare you!"

Ignoring me, he continues. "A frail girl like you? You would choose that over being a Thorpian princess? Watch what your insolence causes!" Voltari points his cane at a guard, who jumps back at first, and the yellow fireball forms again, erupts from his cane, and flies at the guard, who disappears when he is hit.

"Director," Captain Gregor protests, but Voltari quiets him with a look and a shake of his cane.

Where did the guard go? Is he dead? I just watched a man die? I never wanted that! All I wanted was to chase a squirrel and then curl up for a nap! And now I realize Dr. Lam's warnings were true—Voltari can kill you with just a look or a shake of his cane. That guard died, and it was all my fault.

"You didn't have to—"

"Shut up, Trixie," Marmalade says angrily, warning me. I stare at her as I quiet down. She gives me a look back. Bailey wouldn't have treated me like that ever. She was never Bailey.

"I agree with your Lady Marmalade," Voltari says. "And I *did* have to. Don't think I don't know how you snuck the prince on board. It seems your lady still has some tricks up her sleeve and tricked two guards. Your doctor told me everything. KAMP was always a thorn in my side—doctors think they're gods, you know—but just a little bit of jealously, and your doctor figured you all out. The Royal Guard had to pay the price." Voltari turns to face the other royal guards. "Now then, anyone else have anything they'd like to add?" No one answers, except for Captain Gregor.

"Sir, it won't happen again," Captain Gregor declares, holding his blaster tightly. Dr. Lam was right about him. There is only so much he will do to help me.

"Good. Guards, escort us to the brig. Emperor Papo will be meeting us there, now that he surely has been woken from his royal slumber and apprised."

Oh no. I know what a brig is. And it's *not* good.

Chapter 14
Do Not Pass Go

We arrive at the ship's brig surrounded by nine guards aiming blasters at us.

I look at Marmalade. Her face is like stone—stuck in a look of frozen determination. I wish I had her strength, even if in the end she wasn't really Bailey. My imaginary tail is straight down.

Finally inside, the brig is dark. All the walls are painted a dark-red. There are several empty rooms lining the walls of this larger space, with bars cordoning them off. Cages! They're cages! I don't like the brig!

In the middle of the room is Emperor Papo, my father (not Dada), surrounded by his own royal guards. Director Voltari, the one who just admitted to killing my mother (not Mama), joins him in the center of the room.

"Emperor, thank you for meeting us here," Voltari says.

"I grow tired of this whole plan, Voltari. And now you

have me stoop so beneath my position by granting you an audience *here*?" Papo says with a yawn.

"I apologize, Your Highness, but time is of the essence," Voltari says. "Please, let me explain."

"I know this already, Voltari," Papo says with a wave of his hand. We're all surprised to see my father speak so dismissively to this extremely scary figure. Doesn't he know Voltari is a Quantum Mancer who just killed a man? "The girl and her harem of helpers are useless. Your silly plan failed. But what did I tell you, Voltari? It's pointless to rely on women. We can find another way to protect our space carriers. I have been talking to the Polarity Republic about hiring some robotic mercenaries."

"But, Your Highness," Voltari says with fear in his voice, as if somedog was getting too close to his kibble, "robots are dangerous. You know that. And the Polarity Republic is no one's friend. You cannot trust a regime that worships technology. I already told you about the benefits of the Thorpian military ships and their slave workers. But what I did *not* say—"

"I also tire of my advisers *not* telling me things, Voltari," Papo says with another yawn. A flash of anger passes across Voltari's face but disappears instantly. "Why are we even here, in this poverty-stricken place? Just kill them and let me get back to bed."

"No!" I shout. Marmalade grabs my hand, after all her pushing me away before. I want to pull away, but I can't—I need her. So I let her hold me. I need the closeness, even if I am angry with her.

"See!" Papo demands, pointing a finger at Voltari. "Since she came here, this girl has been nothing but trouble. Your stupid plan has been a headache from the beginning."

"Emperor, if you would allow me to keep them all in the brig, I do have a plan to continue with the wedding."

"I thought Thorpia canceled it," Emperor Papo snaps, confused.

"New information has come to light that may force their hand," Voltari explains. "Our plan may yet still come to fruition. King Reginald is a greedy man who desires our riches. He will see reason. But I do believe it prudent to keep these two locked up for the next two weeks to avoid any other . . . issues."

"Fine, fine. Keep my daughter and her wench in the brig for these two weeks."

"Certainly. Your wisdom is truly optimal and efficient," Voltari says.

"I'm going back to bed." But then Emperor Papo stops and looks at me with his cold, unfeeling eyes. His staring makes me uncomfortable, like I'm in one of those cages along the walls. Then he takes my face in his hand, turning it left and right. "Did I ever tell you that you look like your mother?"

"Huh?" After all this death and sadness and saying that he wants me killed, now he decides to tell me this?

"I would never have remembered her, but seeing you . . . you're both so pretty." His fingers are still holding my cheek. "What was her name again?"

Tears form in my eyes. This evil man, who basically had her killed, wants to speak nicely of her? Trixie's memories flood in again. Mother was amazing. So caring. Working every day in the refinery's mess hall but taking care of me—and Roxie too. And unlike these space carriages, on Expiry our neighbors cared about one another. Trixie's life was simple but beautiful. Just like Twinkie's . . . I mean mine.

I explode. I can't stop myself. "What do you care? You had her killed," I snarl at him. I hear everyone gasp in surprise. His hand recoils.

"What?" Papo asks me, stepping back. Turning to Voltari in surprise, he asks, "Did we?" He didn't know?

"A necessary part of Kalaxian national security," Voltari says calmly.

"I see," Papo says, rubbing his head. "You really must keep me better informed, Voltari." Keeping his eyes on Voltari, he asks, "Do *you* know the wench's name?"

"I believe it was Ismerelda, Your Highness," he replies.

"You bastard! You don't have the right to say her name!" I lunge forward. Marmalade reaches for me again, her hand holding my arm so that I stop.

"Calm yourself, Princess," she says quietly.

Voltari turns to Emperor Papo. "Your Highness, I do believe the Joparan Body Snatcher parasite that Dr. Lam diagnosed her with is still wreaking havoc inside her."

"Clearly. She's incensed. Hysterical even," Papo replies. "She's having another one of her episodes!"

"Yes, I do believe we should starve the virus by not feeding her for the next two weeks, just to ensure she is ready. Lady Marmalade too. My physician said that is an approved treatment for such a parasite. And it will leave them much more inclined to move to Thorpia." Voltari turns to us with an evil smile.

"What?" Lady Marmalade asks. But at this point, I'm resigned to this world bringing nothing but pain. Why was I brought here? I just want to go home.

"Furthermore," Voltari continues, ignoring Marmalade, "I believe my personal physician should check on these two every day."

"Your personal physician? Not Dr. Lam?" Papo asks.

"No, Your Highness. Not even KAMP," Voltari says with a laugh.

"Voltari," Papo replies, "do you mean to tell me that you have an *unlicensed* physician aboard?"

"You can't trust KAMP these days, as Your Highness surely knows. Clearly our good doctor was unable or unwilling to clear the parasite."

"No, no, you are right. I certainly agree. But why expose your unlicensed physician? That could cause issues for you. I *won't* vouch for you, you know."

Voltari narrows his eyes and laughs. "I don't believe the royal guards here will cause me any trouble." Voltari waves his cat head cane around the room. Of course, the guards will do as he says, even if they tell stories of the vanished guard in private. "And I believe my personal physician's checkups will also incentivize these two to *escape* to Thorpia, if you get my meaning."

"You don't have to do that! I'll go!" I already wanted to go to find their gods. Even if Prince Weibold won't help me, even if he hates me, someone there might help. It's my only chance to get home.

"Oh, but I think we do," Voltari says.

"I agree," Papo adds, waving his hand dismissively at me. "Well, Voltari, you certainly have this under control." He turns to his guards. "Take me back to my palace." The group departs, leaving Voltari and the nine guards.

Voltari's guards put Marmalade and me in holding cells next to each other. The bars close. "I will leave you both to enjoy the next two weeks," Voltari says.

"I told you I would go!" I shout at him. "Get me out of this cage!"

"Even if I could believe you, you've angered me." He swishes his cloak and leaves.

"Aaahhh!" I yell at the bars. "Aaahhh!" I hit them with all my might, bouncing against them. "Get me out of here! I don't belong in a cage! I just want to go home! Home! I don't belong here!"

"Princess," Marmalade says sternly from the cell next to mine, "it's no use. Just relax." It's darker in the brig now, with only a low-level light to make things barely visible.

"Oh, so *now* you're talking to me like we're friends?" I ask. "Or just so you can tell me to shut up again?"

"Your anger won't help us now," she warns. "We're

lucky to be alive. We still have a shot to get to Thorpia. We need to survive this. Together."

"Together! You don't care about me. You just want to finish this job." It's quiet after that.

But I can't take it anymore. I'm still angry with her. So I complain again. "Some best friend you turned out to be."

"Best friend?" Marmalade asks. "Maybe not. But I *was* trying to do right by you."

"*Right* by me? You said you loved me, but you never really cared." The words leave my mouth, but then Trixie's memories of showing up on Limo One, all alone, flood back. My mother—*her* mother—had just died. I came to a new world on the limo. And there was Marmalade. I was terrified of her. She was so beautiful and confident. And there I was, afraid of everything. If Trixie had a tail, it would have been down for an entire year. Who can live that way?

But Marmalade stuck with her. I now know it was only a job, and I know why she couldn't just quit, but it doesn't change the fact that every day she was there when I had no one. It didn't feel like she was going through the motions, even if Trixie never really opened up to her. Am I wrong? She isn't Bailey, but did she actually care? Maybe?

"You don't know me," Marmalade hisses. "I had a whole life before I met you, which didn't include kids at all. And then I had you and four other girls, out of nowhere. I had to figure it all out. And I didn't just go through the motions. I tried to prepare you the *best I could*! Now my whole life is falling apart. You heard Voltari. If I don't get you to Thorpia, he'll space me. I won't even get to go to one of your dirty rocks."

"I'm supposed to care about *your* life? You were going to ditch me—send me to Thorpia on my own. You thought I was just some fool."

"Princess." Marmalade sighs. "I was speaking in anger. I was going to leave only after you were settled. I *did* care. I couldn't help but care. You were so lost, so vulnerable. Look how much you've grown this past year." Is she just lying now? Is she . . . conniving again? But I *want* to hear her say she still cares. I *need* someone to care.

"Why would you speak so meanly then? You were so mean!"

"How can you know so little about people?"

"You still don't understand!" I exclaim. "I'm not who you think I am." Honesty is spilling out of me. I don't care anymore.

"You said that before. But you're *not* a body snatcher?" Her voice sounds curious now, not angry.

"No!"

"Of course a body snatcher would say that."

"Argh! Does Dr. Lam really seem that concerned about a body snatcher? He was lying, which you suspected from the beginning. Just like he was lying about wanting to help me."

"You really are naive. Even Justyna has more brains than you."

"What?"

"Dr. Lam clearly likes you. Passionately. That's why he was so jealous. In fact, I really can't blame you for what happened. It's a man's fault, as always. This whole world is a man's fault. So, Princess, tell me—who are you *really*? Are you really a spy from the Polarity Republic trying to put a stop to this alliance? I've had my suspicions."

"What? No! I told you. As far as I can tell, I'm from another world, or galaxy, entirely."

"You were *serious*?"

"Yes! I don't recall anything like space carriages or Quantum Mancers from my own world. I guess it could have been one of your dirty rocks from somewhere in your world. But you never even heard of my world. Our animals weren't even in your computer."

"So another galaxy?"

"It must be. I just woke up in this body unexpectedly last night during that dinner. I'm *not* Trixie. I didn't know what was going on. *That's* why I messed it up. Not because I was homesick or wanted to ruin the wedding. But I *am* homesick. For my own home!"

"That actually makes more sense."

"You believe me? Really?"

"Maybe. No body snatcher, or even a spy, would be as bad as you are at this. But why mess up the dinner then? Surely you could have just played along."

"You're still not getting it. I'm not even human! Or *wasn't* human. I didn't know anything when I first got here! I saw a bowl of soup, and I just started eating like I would have in my *old* body."

"Old body? Your body was different?"

"I told you. Not human! On my world I was a *dog*. An *animal*! Like Roxie."

"Your pet pig?"

"Yes, but I was a *dog*. It's not even in your database. But I had soft, luxurious fur all over my body. I walked on four legs and didn't even understand human language. All I said was woof. I love saying woof! Even now. I didn't know how to read or write or speak words until I was in this body. But unlike in this galaxy, all I knew on my world was love, happiness, and food. On my world, people were nice to me. *Always*. We all loved each other."

"Now I know you're either lying or crazy. Your world is total make believe. Stories for children. You really just lost your mind."

"My world isn't make believe! It was real. I was there and I want to go back! I want to go home and be loved! Mama and Dada would even sing my name. Endless songs just with my name. Because they loved me. I was so loved." My tears and snots are mixing, and I suck them up. This human nose makes me so mad.

"What was your name on this fantasy world?"

"You *believe* me?"

"I don't know. *You* believe it."

"It was Twinkie."

"Eerily similar."

We hear a man's loud voice say, "Quiet down in there! Lights out!" Then the lights, as dim as they were before, go entirely black.

"Do you think he heard us?" I whisper to Marmalade.

"I don't think he cared to listen. Men in Kalaxia, or even Thorpia, it seems, don't care about the mad ravings of women. Or dogs." Marmalade giggles. "What were men and women like on your world? Did you know?"

"I had a human mama and dada who took care of me. Dada would even stop what he was doing to rub my belly—that much I knew. Oh, and two younger human sisters, Charlotte and Carolina. They all loved each other and laughed together all the time. I loved hearing them laugh. I didn't understand everything when I was Twinkie, because I was an animal. I didn't speak their language. But I knew my house was full of love."

"That sounds nice . . . ," Marmalade says, her voice trailing off.

"That's really why I wanted to go to Thorpia, you know," I explain. "I was telling the truth about that. I think their gods could help me find a portal to get me home—maybe even the one that took me here."

Marmalade laughs. "Seriously? Oh Princess. You should have told me. Their gods can't help you. It's all just bunk."

"Bunk?" *Where have I heard that word before?*

"Fake. Their gods are even more made up than your fantasy world of lovey-dovey nonsense. Do you really think there's a Goddess of *Chairs*?"

"Well, Prince Weibold *said* there was," I declare defensively. I want it to be true. "Not that I think Charice would be the actual god to help me get home, but she may know some other—"

"There are no gods!" Marmalade roars.

"I said quiet down!" the guard shouts again. "I'm trying to get some sleep."

"The Thorpians are nuts. Bonkers," Marmalade continues in a whisper, even though I didn't want her to—I don't want to hear this.

"I'm not listening to you. I *will* get home. I *will*!"

"Bunk," Marmalade replies. "But at least now I know you're actually telling the truth. You're *not* from this galaxy. Everyone but the Thorpians know they're insane."

"But . . . if you believe me . . . then how do I get home?" I ask, my voice cracking. My whole plan, which was already ruined now that Prince Weibold hates me, is even *more* ruined. I have no hope now. "Please, Marmalade. Even if we're not best friends anymore, please help me."

"Ha, you think I know anything about magic portals? I have no idea. I'm just trying to survive here, and so should you. As long as you're alive, I guess there's still a chance for you, Princess. Well, I probably don't have to call you that anymore. Twangy?"

"Twinkie," I correct her, as I wipe a tear from my eye and lie down on the floor of my holding cell.

"Goodnight, Twinkie. Don't let Bertie, the God of Bedbugs, bite," Marmalade says with a chortle.

I cry myself to sleep.

Chapter 15
Truer Friends

Eyes open. My bed feels strange. Why is it so hard? Uncurling, I try to stand, but it feels odd. Oh my Dog, what's wrong with my body? Where's my fur? I'm broken! "Woof! Woof!"

"Ah, I see your charge is awake now too," a voice says. Rubbing my eyes, vision returns. My brain returns also. I feel my head, and there's a crown on it. *Oh, I'm still Trixie*. It's my second morning in this galaxy and everything has fallen apart.

There's a man in a white coat like Dr. Lam, but it's not him. This man looks very agitated, bald with a long beard—not like a poodle. Like a needy Chinese crested looking for affection. Standing outside our holding cells, his eyes dart back and forth between us. "I think I'll start with the princess. Let's be friends." Patting a briefcase, he smiles at me. This is the unlicensed physician Voltari mentioned.

"No! Take me first!" Marmalade pleads. Huh? Why would she do that? That doesn't sound like the new Marmalade—the one who isn't my friend anymore. "It was all my fault anyway!"

"What? You care about this wretched girl? Isn't that taking your job way too far?" the new doctor asks curiously.

"Yes, I do! Please!" Marmalade answers. She does? For real? Even after last night? And our fight?

"Marmalade, you don't have to," I say.

"But I do, Princess. It's still my job to protect you."

"Well, no need for Dr. X to argue," the man says with a giggle. He's Dr. X? "I'll be back for the landie after you. My orders are to make life here as uncomfortable as possible for you both. You'll be dying to head to Thorpia. Unless, of course, I mess up and you die here." He laughs, but it's definitely not funny!

"I've never met a landie before," he continues, eyes scanning me. "Is it *possible* to make you uncomfortable with your—" he makes a face of disgust "—upbringing? I wonder if you scream differently."

"Bastard," Marmalade says, interrupting his concentration on me.

"No, *she's* the bastard," Dr. X says. "Guard, open the lady-in-waiting's cell."

The bars screech as they open, and a tired and dirty-looking Marmalade and the doctor head to a door in the brig's main room, disappearing behind it.

I don't know what to do with myself. Worry and

confusion grip me. Why did Marmalade do that for me? Is she really my friend? Is she still Bailey? After everything that happened? No, she said it was still just her job. But I hope she's okay. I'm so worried for her.

What's going to happen when he comes back for me? I've had bad vet visits before, but what could this be like? Mama and Dada aren't here to reassure me. Only bad can happen. Bad bad bad. Tears trickle down my face.

Sitting for an endless amount of time worrying, my human mind not letting me forget anything from these past two days, I finally see that door open again. In walks the doctor with a smile on his face and a slumped-over Marmalade in his arms. I get up from the floor and hold the bars of my cell.

"Marmalade! Are you okay?" I call to her.

"I'm okay, Princess. Don't worry about me, please," she says in a strained voice. I watch as a guard standing alongside Dr. X opens her cell and unkindly throws Marmalade into it. She makes a thud and a grunt. The guard leaves my vision after the sound of her barred door closing.

"Did it hurt?" I ask in her cell's direction, though I can't see her now. I don't know why I even ask, because I know it did.

"You'll find out soon enough, because it's your turn now, Princess," Dr. X says with a smile. "Let's make sure you're healthy for that nice prince you're due to marry. Or, rather, unhealthy, as are my orders. And from what I hear, that prince won't mind." A vile laugh erupts from him. Then he takes a step toward my cell.

"Not so fast, Doctor!" a familiar voice says. It's Dr. Lam! And he has Captain Gregor and some other woman with him. She's in a strange uniform, like the Royal Guard, but hers is all blue. Like on Mama's television shows! Is she a copper?

"I received word of an unlicensed doctor on board, and I believe you have been performing unlicensed medical procedures as well!" The woman points at Marmalade's cell.

"What? How did you know?" Dr. X replies.

"It doesn't matter," Dr. Lam says. "You know KAMP prohibits unlicensed physicians. You're going down for this."

"You're going to stop me? You'll make an enemy of Director Voltari? Do you have a death wish, young man?" Dr. X points a finger at Dr. Lam.

"If it's to do the right thing and correct a wrong, I will," Dr. Lam says, glancing at me through the bars of my cells. That look I know, like when you chewed something you weren't supposed to. It's one of regret.

"The right thing?" Dr. X fumes. "Captain Gregor, surely you won't arrest Voltari's personal physician. You must have seen—"

"Captain, you're making a mistake, and you know it," Marmalade suddenly interjects, with concern and a strained voice. "It's not worth it. Don't let our lovesick doctor cost you your life."

"Love?" Captain Gregor asks, surprised. "My hands are tied, Lady Marmalade. I have no choice but to comply. Sergeant Michaels here from the KAMP Auxiliary Police has made that clear." He gives the woman in blue a worrisome glance. He must know this is dangerous for him, but Dr. Lam also thought he would do the right thing. I remember him telling me that.

"The Kalaxian Association of Medical Practitioners," Sergeant Michaels announces, "vested with authority under the Kalaxian constitution—"

"Voltari will see about that!" Dr. X interrupts.

"Well . . . uh . . . Voltari is just a *director*, you know," Sergeant Michaels replies.

"Hah! *Just?* You have no idea," Dr. X scoffs.

"Be that as it may, you have violated KAMP Regulation 301.7701-3(d)(i) regarding unauthorized practice of medicine on an official Kalaxian limo. You are hereby sentenced to KAMP Psychological Reformation Protocol X," Sergeant Michaels says and then laughs. "Ha, ironically named. You will now be taken into custody."

"You can't do this! I have rights!" Dr. X retorts.

"Take him to my Kamp Kruiser please, Captain Gregor." Gregor nods. "Ah, wait. I forgot the sedative." Michaels takes out a huge needle from her uniform.

"Tushy thermometer!" I shout in glee.

"Don't put that in my—"

"Relax, Dr. X," Michaels says. "We're not as cruel as you." She injects his arm, and he goes limp. What a shame. He deserved a real tushy thermometer!

Captain Gregor and Sergeant Michaels start to leave, but look back at Dr. Lam. "Are you coming, Doctor?" Sergeant

Michaels asks. Captain Gregor and Lady Marmalade nod at each other.

"Not just yet. I have some things to discuss with the guard here. I'll meet up with you before you leave," Dr. Lam says to them. They nod and exit with the sleepy prisoner. Dr. Lam waits for them to leave, and then walks to the brig's guard. "Private Benedici?"

"Yes, Doctor?" a young man's voice replies. We can't see the guard from our cells, but we can hear him.

"I didn't want to say this in front of the others, but is that a lump on your neck?" Dr. Lam asks him.

"What? Huh?"

"Hold on, I think you've been infected with Borellian fleas. If I don't treat you right now, they'll mate inside your neck, and a million of their babies will burst out of you. But their lifespan is pretty short, so some of those babies will use your carcass for their own babies, and so on, and so on. We call it the Cradle Disease because, well, with a billion baby fleas inside you, your dead body starts to rock back and forth, back and forth—"

"What! Oh no!" the young guard cries. "Do something, Doctor! Please!"

"I happen to have the cure right here. It's an injection of something called plenicillin."

"Plenicillin? What's that?"

"It's an ancient remedy. Just hold still."

"Thank you, Doctor! Thank . . ." Then there's a thud. Oh no, is Private Benedici okay? Did the fleas get him already?

"Did he make it? Did you get the fleas?" I ask.

"Don't be so naive again," Marmalade says. "I don't think that's what's going on here."

"What? Is it worse than fleas? Kennel cough? I don't want kennel cough again! Save me!" I cry and bang on the bars, as Dr. Lam comes into view.

"Twinkie!" Marmalade snaps.

"Twinkie?" Dr. Lam asks, turning his head to Marmalade's cell.

"Long story. But you've come to break her out, you love-sick fool, haven't you?" Marmalade asks him.

"Yes. I'm so, so sorry for everything I did. I was so stupid. I hurt you because I was so jealous. It's just . . ."

"Just what? I have Borellian fleas too? Oh no!" I cry, shaking myself.

"No, it's not that," he replies.

"The guy *loves* you, Trixie!" Marmalade exclaims. "He's *saving* you! Can you get us out of here?"

"He loves me?" I ask, confused. I'm searching Trixie's memories. "You took care of me this whole year. Both you and Marmalade."

"I never said it before. But I need to now. I do love you, Princess," Dr. Lam says as he opens my door with the guard's ID card. "From the moment you came aboard, you were so different from all the other Kalaxian women. I've never met anyone like you. All you talked about was how much stuff we had that could help your people back on Expiry. You really care about others."

Memories return from this past year. "The food and medicine for my people back on Expiry. You were going to help me. Because you *love* me? Like *romantic*?" The barred door slides open.

"I do, Princess. I should have said—"

"But I can't. You don't understand. I'm not . . . not romantic—"

"It's okay, Princess. Of course, you've been through so much. I'm not expecting anything. Especially not after what I did." It's not just that, but I shouldn't say anything more. "I still want to help you, if you can ever forgive me. In fact . . ." His voice trails off.

"In fact what, Doctor?" I ask.

"The plan. I shouldn't mention it in front of her," he says.

"You can talk in front of Marmalade," I say.

"But, Princess, you can't trust her."

"I do, and I will!" I declare. "She's my friend too. Each of you did mean things, but you both care about me, and I forgive you both. You're my pack, and we stick together."

"You forgive me, Princess?" Marmalade asks. "For real?" She's looking up at me from her holding cell floor.

"Of course, Marmalade! You may not be Bailey, and I may not be Trixie—"

"Huh?" Dr. Lam grunts.

"—but you're my friend. You're the only one who really knows me. Now come on. Doctor, please open her door. And you can tell her the plan. I'm going home!"

"To your own galaxy?" Marmalade asks. "He knows about that?"

"Galaxy?" Dr. Lam asks, confused, as he opens Marmalade's door. "What galaxy? Expiry is far away, but—"

"Guess not," Marmalade says, as she rises slowly from the floor. Her hair is a mess, and her dress is wrinkled, torn in spots, and ill-fitting. She winces in pain.

"Oh Marmalade," I say, remembering something. "Do you need my healing crystal?"

"Trixie, Trixie, Trixie. I told you. It's all bunk. It's basically just a rock," she says. But she's wrong. The prince, as bad as he turned out to be, thought it was real.

"But *they* thought it was important. It *must* special!"

"I'll be fine. I've experienced worse." She dismisses me with a wave and steps out of the cell to join us. She's walking like one of those really old dogs at my day care. "What's the plan?"

"He's taking me back to Expiry." Right now, Expiry is better than remaining on Limo One. Maybe we can sneak into Thorpia with our new identities.

"*How?* And what will they do to the good doctor here when they find you gone?" she asks me. "And they *will* find out."

"Oh, don't worry. As a KAMP physician, I have access to Kalaxian death records. I've made us both new identities to use on Expiry."

"You're going with her?" Marmalade exclaims.

"You *are?*" I ask him, with wide eyes. This whole time I didn't know he wanted to stay with me.

"Of course, Princess. That was the plan for months!"

Dr. Lam replies. "Not that I expected to get married or anything. Not right away—maybe one day. But I wanted to help you. Don't you remember? Do you not want me now?"

"Now who is the one who was lying this whole time, Princess? You were going to abandon me anyway!" Marmalade sneers.

"But that wasn't *me*, Marmalade," I protest.

"What in the galaxy?" Dr. Lam asks. "Wasn't you? Are you changing your mind now, Princess?"

"No, she isn't, Doctor," Marmalade says. "She has to go now."

"You can come too, if you want," I say to Marmalade. Is this her only choice now anyway?

"Is that wise, Princess?" Dr. Lam asks me as he glances at Marmalade with narrow eyes.

"She *has* to join us. I don't know what I would do without her."

"Princess . . . ," Marmalade starts but stops midthought.

"After seeing what Voltari did to you, you can't trust him not to space you," I say, sensing her hesitation. Marmalade nods. Yes! She's coming with! I have a pack again! "What *is* spacing anyway?"

"Oh Princess." Marmalade sighs. "It's when they shoot your body into the emptiness of space and you explode and die, not necessarily in that order."

"Oh Dog! Oh Dog, oh Dog! That's horrible. Don't let him shoot you into space!"

"Dog?" Dr. Lam asks, still confused. "Isn't that the creature you asked—"

"Don't worry, Doctor," I say, ignoring his confusion. Then I turn back to Marmalade. "What about the other ladies? Will Voltari get to them too?"

"We'll have to warn them. Doctor, can they join the plan?" Marmalade asks. "Us girls need to stick together."

"Although *I* don't trust you, Princess Trixie wants me to. So I will include you and the ladies in my plan. Have them meet us at the Cargo Bay. And ask Lady Perri to bring extra Vasparian Jelly."

"*Vasparian Jelly?*" Marmalade asks.

"Yes! Now let's get out of here," Dr. Lam says, grabbing my hand. Or paw? No, it actually feels like a *hand* in his. I finally feel . . . human.

"But, Doctor, I'll need a computer to call the girls," Marmalade says as we make our way to the front door of the brig.

"*No, you won't. I have already contacted them. Lady Perri was very mad at me, but she said she will oblige.*"

"Willow! My friend Willow!" I exclaim. "The whole pack is getting back together!"

"Princess, who is that?" Dr. Lam asks.

"Oh . . . uh . . . ," I stammer and turn to Marmalade.

"Don't look at me," she says. "Willow was *your* creation."

"Is that an AI?" Dr. Lam exclaims. "Don't you know—"

"Forget it, Doctor," Marmalade says. "That AI loves her more than you do."

"We're kind of like besties," I say.

"*I will follow you to the Cargo Bay, Princess. Lady Perri is bringing a flop. I want to stay with you. And Lady Perri.*"

"I think she's in love with Lady Perri," Marmalade explains.

"Oh stars, what have you girls done?" Dr. Lam says, rubbing his forehead.

"We're just trying to stay alive in a man's world," Marmalade replies.

"And to do that, we need our friends," I add.

"Well, I was hoping we could go to Expiry and be together," Dr. Lam says. "But I realize you may not want that now." He sounds sad, so I squeeze his hand.

"We can be together, Doctor. All together! Willow and the girls too," I say, but I know that's not what he meant. I'm not ready for romantic love. Neither was Trixie. Our life—our combined lives—are just too crazy. He has to accept me as I am, though. I think he will. "Now let's just get there."

"*Dr. Lam?*" Willow asks.

"Yes . . . Willow? We're about to leave. Can you keep quiet?"

"*That was going to be my point,*" she answers. "*Oh, he's a smart one, Princess. You could do worse.*"

"What the?" Dr. Lam exclaims. "How is this safe?"

"*Well, Doctor. Do you have a face-com with you?*" Willow asks. Face-com?

"Yes, I always keep one on me in case of medical emergencies."

"Put it on. I can relay extended-range life sign informa-tion to you privately to help get you all to the Cargo Bay undetected."

"Good idea, Willow," he says, as he puts on one of those black bug thingies, its bug tendrils connecting to his face. Oh, it's a face-com.

"I'll put one on too, in case something happens to you," Marmalade says. He nods, and she pulls one out of her dress.

"How did they not take that from you?" Dr. Lam asks her, surprised.

"A girl has her secrets, Doctor. You would do well to remember that," Marmalade replies as she puts the device on her face. Its tendrils quickly connect to her head. Ew, I'll never get used to that. "Okay, ready."

Dr. Lam opens the brig door.

Chapter 16
Bluer Friends

D r. Lam takes Marmalade and me through corridors like a maze. We pop into some unused Negotiation Rooms along the way when Willow tells him of life signs approaching. We wait for them to pass.

It was a good strategy, although one was being used by some visiting executives from Limo Forty negotiating Fleckion mineral royalty rights with Limo One's interior minister. Luckily our arrest and escape were not publicized (yet). Dr. Lam pretended it was a medical emergency and kicked them out of the room.

We're now walking down a lonely corridor, following Dr. Lam, when he stops suddenly (we almost bump into him), and he bursts into a (quiet) tirade.

"Willow!" he whispers vehemently. "I don't want to spend this whole walk listening to you talk about your boyfriend! I'm trying to *not* get us killed!" But because she is on private mode, we can't hear her response. "I know you're excited to see your cargo scanner in person or program or whatever. Just, please, shut up!" And then Dr. Lam's hand cradles his head, and he bends over in pain. "Ow! Was that you? Stop that! You're not supposed to do that! Didn't you hear about the AI riots? Fine, fine! I don't know anything about cargo scanners, but did you try cooking for him? Men like food." Dr. Lam nods, then turns to us. "She's quiet now, working on recipes, whatever that means." We start walking again.

After a while, Willow, who finally settled on a bits kabob in a pixel glaze, helps us find the nearest Whoosher, which is like Grammy's elevator—the thing I thought was in the tree that took me here. It makes a cool whoosh sound as we ride, hence the name.

We exit and start walking again, my eyes fixed straight ahead as we see Koko, Brandi, Perri, and Justyna standing near the entrance. But they are holding their noses. I glance at Dr. Lam, and he and Marmalade are also holding their noses. "You don't smell it?" he asks me.

"It smells wonderful," I say with a spin so that I can breathe it all in. Everywhere on this space carriage always smelled so plain and stale, like I was in a world of nothingness. Only the soap during my bath had a powerful scent. But here, near the Cargo Bay, is a *powerful* odor. I love smells!

"Wonderful?" Dr. Lam asks. "It's *horrible*. Willow flooded the Cargo Bay with noxious odors, sulfur and methane, so we could have it to ourselves for the time being."

"Thank you, Willow!" I exclaim with another spin.

"You *like* this?" Dr. Lam asks, shaking his head.

"Isn't *any* smell a *good* smell?" I ask, taking a deep breath.

"Landies are weird," Koko says from a bit farther away, waving her hand in front of her nose.

"Is this what Expiry smells like?" Perri asks. "And we're supposed to go there? Like, forever? Do they even have schools?"

"Well, I don't know," I admit, as we get closer to them. Realizing my mistake, I throw my hand up to cover my mouth.

"What do you mean, you don't know?" Brandi asks. "What the *flare*?"

"Language!" Marmalade scolds her. Wait, what's *flare*? Even Trixie doesn't know it.

"What's *flare*?" I ask.

"No, Lady Marmalade. Flaring flarey flares!" Brandi snaps, ignoring my question. Koko, Perri, and especially Justyna look shocked and are now covering their open mouths with their hands too. "We get surprise calls the afternoon after you were arrested from an AI bent on world domination—"

"She says she's not," Dr. Lam interjects, touching the black bug computer thing on his temple. "She just wants Lady Perri to be proud of her."

"I'm not! This hallway reeks!" Perri exclaims. "But I brought the stupid Vasparian Jelly you asked for." She points to her backpack. "What the flares do you need it for?"

"Girls! Language! We're still ladies, for Sol's sake!" Marmalade exclaims.

"Flarey flaring flaricals!" I add, joining in with my pack.

"You too!" Marmalade scolds me. "Why are *you* upset? We're all here *because* of you."

"I just want to join my pack," I explain. "And no one will tell me what it means."

"It's a cuss," Marmalade says. "And it's *not* the way a lady speaks."

A cuss? Like Charlotte always does? This is how they cuss here? "Then let's flaring get to Expiry!" I declare. Marmalade sighs.

"Are we going to Thorpia after all, Princess?" Justyna asks.

"Willow!" Dr. Lam says. "You didn't tell them?" He pauses. "Of course they would have come. Voltari would kill them otherwise."

"Kill us?" Koko, Brandi, and Perri exclaim. Justyna bursts into tears.

"Ladies," Marmalade says, trying to calm our pack, "the situation has changed. Voltari has gone mad and will kill us if the wedding doesn't go through. He likely will kill us even if it does goes through. We need to escape *now*. Dr. Lam has a plan to get us to Expiry."

"And the flaring jelly?" Perri asks, thrusting toward us, in clear frustration, a large white bag.

"If we slather enough of the jelly on us, it will block our life signs," Dr. Lam explains. "We'll hide in a specific cargo bin that will be picked up by a friend of mine in KAMP tomorrow, once I send him the signal. The cargo bin will contain us, but also much needed medical supplies for the planet Keynes B. We would then change our identities and divert some of the medical supplies to the poorest planet in the empire, Expiry."

"Oh Doctor! Thank you!" I exclaim, easily recalling Trixie's desire to help her planet.

"But how do you know the jelly will work?" Perri asks, holding the bag closer to her. "I've never heard of this use."

"Because of the Vasparian Jelly factory blast back on Mellon VI. KAMP realized the jelly was disrupting life signs, which we never reported. We do have our own secrets, Lady Perri. Can we please go inside and get off this ship?" Dr. Lam asks.

"What about my brother?" Justyna asks.

"You didn't take him? Didn't Willow tell you to?" Marmalade asks her.

"He was afraid he'd be snogged!" Justyna exclaims.

"Justyna," Marmalade answers, "go get him. Don't rush or you'll arouse suspicion. We have time. We'll leave some jelly out here for you."

"You'll wait for us? Really?" Justyna asks hesitantly.

"Yes, Justyna! I don't want to leave you!" I reply.

"Okay, I'll go right now!" Justyna exclaims and runs off.

"Is everyone ready?" Marmalade asks.

"To give up our entire lives?" Perri asks.

"I won't be able to contact my family?" Brandi asks. "My mom?"

Koko takes her hand. "Do you *want* to contact your mom?"

"Good point," Brandi replies.

"I guess I'll be, like, the smartest person on that rock," Perri says, perking up.

"And we'll be together! A real pack!" I say, seemingly the only one of us who is excited.

Our lives are about to change. Trixie already went through a huge transformation, leaving Expiry to live on Limo One and train to be a princess. And I had my change, from a four-legged furry friend to living on a space carriage. But this is *their* big change.

"Just hurry up and open the door already," Perri says. "This hallway reeks."

Dr. Lam presses the button. The doors separate.

And there is Voltari standing by himself in the Cargo Bay.

Chapter 17
True-Blue Friends

Director Voltari's cat cane is already glowing red. The light fills this huge room and reflects off big metal boxes. Before I can make more sense of my surroundings, Voltari lifts his cane and points it at us. A red fireball erupts from it and flies at Dr. Lam, as Voltari yells, "Traitor!" The red fireball hits Dr. Lam in the chest. He falls back, lifeless, his chest now scorched fabric and flesh where there was a clean white gown before.

"No!" I shout. But our pack is frozen with fear. Is Dr. Lam *dead*? I've only known him for three days, but Trixie knew him for a whole year. He *loved* me romantically. I didn't love him like that—I don't know what that really means and neither did Trixie. But I still feel a shocking sense of loss—he was her pack member. Jumping down to the floor, I start to move to Dr. Lam, who is still breathing, but then there's a yellow fireball in the corner of my eye.

It slams into Dr. Lam, and his body vanishes. Our whole group jumps at the sight. *He made Dr. Lam disappear! He's dead—no, worse, just gone!*

"That doctor was *way* too much trouble; I'm glad to be rid of him. And I have Lady Marmalade to thank," Voltari says with a snort. I turn instantly to look at Lady Marmalade, who is ignoring my stare and looking straight at Director Voltari with a stone face.

"*You* did this? *You* told him our plan?" I ask Marmalade, who continues to ignore me, but her hand touches the black bug thing on her head. She used her face-com to turn me in? "How could you! Dr. Lam was right!"

She finally turns to me, her eyes facing down. "I thought I was helping you get to Thorpia. That's what you really wanted, not Expiry. I didn't know he'd kill Dr. Lam. I just thought I was keeping you from making a mistake. I'm so sorry. You have to believe me." A tear streams down her cheek.

"No, you were helping yourself. You and your stupid divorce," I counter. "You were *never* a friend."

"And you were planning to go home the whole year!" she says, anger now in her voice instead of sadness.

"You know that wasn't me!"

"Silence!" Voltari roars, stopping our fight. Marmalade glances at me, but I refuse to do the same, only looking at her through the corner of my eye. "Now enter the cargo bay where we can be alone. All of you." We're standing motionless, but he motions with his cane.

As soon as our group enters the Cargo Bay, the door closes behind us, locking us in with the violent and powerful Director Voltari, who I am now certain is a Quantum Mancer—a powerful magician. "Stars, why does it smell so bad in this section?" he asks. "Remind me to kill someone in engineering. Now, Princess, it was good that the lady told me of your plan. I had already talked to King Reginald, who assured me the wedding could still go on. You do still want to go to Thorpia, right? Especially with Dr. Lam's unfortunate demise?"

What do I say? It didn't go well at all with Prince Weibold. And I'm frightened of him. But I have nowhere else to turn. Dr. Lam is dead now, Lady Marmalade is *not* my friend anymore, and I have no other plans. Maybe I can still go home. I nod.

"Good, good," Voltari continues. "But King Reginald told me to relay to you that you would live out your days under their God of Exorcism's sedation drugs to calm your evil spirits. I told the good and wise king that you would not mind. I am sure that is the case." Voltari cackles with laughter.

"You can't do that!" Marmalade exclaims. "I told you that she would go willingly, but not like that. She's no risk to them! She's just a—"

"Know your place, Lady Marmalade!" Voltari growls. We all quiet down again. "One cannot call this a job well done, no? That said, I must reward you with something for delivering the bastard to me. Let's see." He scratches his long gray beard. "Ah, I just thought of the best reward!" Voltari giggles. "This is better than the fate you would have received if your divorce went through. You'll thank me later. Or not." He points his cane at her. She stiffens in shock.

A yellow fireball starts to form from the cat on his cane, and before I can scream, it's flying toward Marmalade. I know she's not Bailey. And she gave us up. And she got Dr. Lam killed. But I can't let her die like this—no, yellow means she disappears forever, and not even die.

In a flash, my whole year with Marmalade, Koko, Brandi, Perri, and Justyna flies through my head. Or Trixie's head. Or Trixie's year. From the moment I stepped onto Limo One, she looked after me and kept me safe, even when Trixie was too scared to show her any emotion back. And she was there for me—Twinkie—when I showed up in this world. It *all* comes back. She even took a risk taking us to Pareto. In her own way, she thought she was still protecting me. I have to believe that, and I have to stop this. I *have* to save her. But how?

"Marmalade!" I scream, reaching out my arms to push her out of the way of the fireball. But instead, my fingers turn into blue flames. Was I hit? Am I dying? I don't care—save Marmalade! But the blue flames are connected to my brain—my human brain. I can feel it. They're following my desires, even before thoughts form in my head. The flames start to come together in my hands into two blue fireballs that fly out toward Marmalade and collide with Voltari's yellow fireball. Both fireballs disappear.

"What the flare?" Koko asks.

"She's a *Mancer*?" I hear Perri say.

Voltari and the others are staring at me. Not really understanding what just happened, but not caring, I aim my fingers at Voltari, and the blue fireballs light up again, one from each hand. Like Mama and Dada playing fetch, I throw each of the fireballs at Voltari, whose eyes widen when he realizes he's under attack. He swishes his cane, disappears completely, and reappears ten feet to the left. The blue fireballs crash into some cargo that explodes with a thunderous sound.

"How are you doing this?" Voltari asks, seeming just as surprised as Koko. "Are you a Mancer? Have you been lying to everyone this whole time like the lady said?"

"No, I didn't lie! I don't know!" I say, trying to sound strong, but I'm frightened, looking at my hands. Even he doesn't know what I am? *What am I?* Staring at my hands, I see the flash of red in my vision too late. I throw my blue flaming hands up at the last moment, which shields me somewhat from the blast, but I'm knocked to the floor and thrown into the back wall of the Cargo Bay onto my tushy.

My chest feels like it's on fire, and my skin feels burned, but no flames are present. Is this how Dr. Lam felt before he disappeared?

Voltari walks slowly toward me. I'm cornered, and I don't know if I can protect myself. So I do what feels right—I start snarling and barking at him. In my peripheral vision, I can see Koko, Brandi, Perri, and Marmalade. Instead of keeping their distance, they move closer, as if to defend me. My pack. Their nearness gives me more confidence to bark even louder at him.

"So you *are* a lying dog!" Voltari jeers at me, coming closer.

What? He said dog! He knows what a dog is? My body freezes in shock. "You know what a dog is?"

"You were telling the truth?" Marmalade asks. But Voltari and I ignore her.

"Of course," Voltari says, stopping in his tracks at my question. "But the bigger question is, Why do you?" I don't answer, not wanting to give him any information about me. He's looking down at me, and I can't move. "Cat got your tongue? No matter. This will be the rare instance of the cat that killed the dog!"

Cornered, my fury erupts. Losing my mama and dada, threatened with tushy thermometers, attacked by squirds, locked in the brig, almost tortured, watching my friend die, betrayed by my best friend . . . none of that could break me. And now cats? Voltari won't break me either!

"You will not!" I thrust my hands at him. Suddenly a window-type thing the size of a human opens up behind Voltari, right in the middle of the room. All I can do is call it a window using this new language in my head, because I don't know what else it is. But air is loudly getting sucked into it. It kind of looks like . . . the thing in that tree! The thing that took me here! "My window?" While I stare in shock, Voltari's long gray hair and silver cloak flow in the air toward it. He spins around to look.

"*No!* What did you do? Portal spells are dangerous!" he thunders. "You don't know what you're doing! Stop this at once!" But he has nothing to hold on to, and his body is sucked into it. Before he disappears, his hand grabs ahold of the sides of the window. We can see his fingers sticking out of it.

Marmalade moves toward it slowly. But Perri calls urgently, "No! Marmalade, no! You'll be sucked in!"

"I don't care," she says. "I'm going to finally take care of you girls, like I always said I would. I'm going to rid us of him for good." She walks toward the window.

"But it's a portal! A rip in the fabric of spacetime!" Perri cries. Portal? Rip? Spacetime? Now it hits me. Is that what happened to me? I entered a portal?

But this portal is *my* creation—I can sort of feel it now in my brain. I can direct it. Like the blue flame, it followed my desires before I even knew them. And so I understand the portal only wants Voltari, because I only want Voltari.

"I can control it! It's safe for you!" I call from my spot on the floor, leaning against the back wall. "Before he can escape, do something, Marmalade!" The head of the cat cane starts peeking out. Then the entirety of his other hand.

Marmalade is at the portal now. "She's right! It's not pulling on me!" Marmalade starts peeling his fingers away to release his hold on the portal. One hand is free, and we see his remaining hand wiggle a bit, trying to maintain control while still holding the cane. Marmalade steps to the other side and starts peeling his fingers away. The cane flies out of his hand and into the portal.

"This isn't the end!" we hear Voltari's garbled voice roar from inside the portal. But Marmalade lifts his last finger off. He disappears and the portal closes. The girls join me on the floor in exhaustion and shock.

Chapter 18
Friends in Low Places

Uh . . . *guys? That was all kinds of weird, but can we go now?"* we hear Willow's voice from the speaker in the room.

"Willow, if you were there the whole time, why the flare didn't you do anything?" Perri asks.

"Uh, I'm just a computer program. What did you want me to do? Feed him bad calculations?"

"Don't be mad, Perri," I say with a wince of pain, trying to get up.

"You could have died, and she flaring did nothing!" Perri exclaims.

"I'm an AI, not a miracle worker," Willow says. *"Did you want me to start a riot?"*

"I don't know, maybe!" Perri cries at the ceiling.

"Princess, don't try to get up. You need a doctor," Marmalade says. But I just laugh.

"You mean the doctor you just got killed?" I fume.

She walks to my side, standing over me. "Princess, I'm so sorry."

"You don't have to call me that anymore," I point out.

Marmalade shakes her head. "There was more I never told you. When Dr. X had me, they threatened the rest of my family with demotion, my parents and my sister, just like me, stripping their titles and sending them to planets. I panicked. I thought you would be okay on Thorpia—it was what you wanted. And the girls would be safe. He didn't tell me he would kill Lam! Please believe me!"

"It's okay, Marmalade. I understand." The pain keeps me down. I don't know how badly I'm hurt and am too scared to look closely at my chest.

"You do?" she asks, her eyes wide in surprise.

"I do. You were protecting your pack."

"Not enough of my pack, I'm afraid," Marmalade says, wiping her tears.

"You didn't kill him," I tell her. Her eyes look at me intently, taking in my forgiveness like it's a portal to another world. "I know that. You and I were thrown together in this world for some reason. Only you know all of it. None of us asked for this. And I don't have the luxury of staying mad." Marmalade stands still, tears in her wide eyes, but then she kneels next to me.

"We don't have the luxury of time either," Perri chimes in. "Trixie, do you have any idea what you just did?"

"No," I answer plainly. "You said it was a portal."

"And you're *not* a Mancer? You don't have any Quantum

Mancing tools with you? You weren't lying this whole year?" Perri asks. "Marmalade said you lied."

"No, I didn't, not the way she meant it," I reply. Perri looks at Marmalade, who nods in agreement. "I'm not a Mancer. It all just happened when I was really upset about Dr. Lam." I look down at the door, where his body would have been. But it's like he never existed. I hear gasps from Koko, Brandi, and Marmalade.

"*That is unexpected. I assumed she was lying again,*" Willow says.

"What is it? Why do you all look like that?" I ask.

"Because, right now, you are the most dangerous person in the galaxy," Perri says.

"Dangerous? I protected us," I protest.

"Not because of what you might do," Perri replies. "But because of who you *are*. What you *can* do. How do you do it?"

"I have no idea! I'm still me—if I could just get up." I try to push my body up with my hands, but my chest stings with pain, and I fall back to the floor. "Oh, I hurt so much," I say, finally putting my hands on my chest, where my skin, through my burned shirt, still feels so tender and red (that new color that has so many meanings—this time pain).

"How does she flaring not know this stuff?" Perri asks the others.

"Girls, language!" Marmalade says.

"Seriously, Marmalade? You just turned us in to Voltari and almost got us all killed, and you want to flaring criticize our *manners*?" Brandi is incredulous.

"Damn flaring straight," Koko says, and then they high-five like the old days. Which was just yesterday. And I laugh to myself, but it hurts so much.

"Ooh," I grunt. Marmalade takes my hand.

"Girls," Marmalade says, looking up at my ladies. "There's a reason she doesn't know this stuff. So, for Sol's sake, give her a break."

"It's okay," I say, squeezing Marmalade's hand. "You can tell them."

"See, I knew she was a Mancer!" Perri cries, pointing at me.

"It's not that," Marmalade replies. "Did you hear Voltari call her a dog?"

"Um, yeah, but I thought it was just a cute nickname they had for each other," Brandi says. Koko laughs out loud, and Brandi snaps her head around to look at her. "What? I was kind of just scared for my life, so I wasn't pondering everything he said."

"You sure I can tell them?" Marmalade asks me.

I nod. "They're my pack. They deserve to know."

"What more than being a Quantum Mancer do we need to know?" Brandi asks.

"She's *not* a Quantum Mancer!" Marmalade snaps. "Trixie is not from our galaxy."

"That makes sense," Perri replies matter-of-factly.

"That makes sense?" Koko exclaims. "In what flaring world does that make sense?"

"Think about it," Perri says, holding a finger up. "She

showed us she has powers like a Quantum Mancer without any equipment or knowledge, which means she can control quantum waveforms and spacetime innately.

"And we all heard her these past two days. She's clearly *not* from Kalaxia—maybe not even Expiry. So who is she?" Perri walks closer to me and bends down a little, staring at me. Then she gets up and turns back to the group. "Like I said, she's the most dangerous person in the galaxy, precisely because she's not *from* our galaxy. Well, her insides aren't." She's pointing at me strangely, like her finger can see my insides.

Before anyone can respond, Perri continues. "Do you remember what she said when the portal opened?" No one answers her. I don't even remember. "No? No one? Why am I the only smart one here? Trixie said, 'My window.' *My* window. Maybe her portal imbued her with these abilities. I mean, it was kind of different and all if it transferred insides only." She's pointing at my insides again. "Or maybe she always had these abilities and that's how she got here. All I know is that what she can do must be related to how she got here, even if she doesn't understand it." Is it? I have powers because of the portal? I didn't have them before when I was Twinkie. But maybe the portal changed me?

"Brava! Brava! Perri, you amaze me more and more every single day!"

"At least some*thing* appreciates me," Perri replies.

It's time to explain to my new pack. "On my world," I start, straining to get the words out, "or my galaxy, or whatever, I was just an animal, not a human. I was a dog."

"What's a *dog*?" Perri asks.

"*There is no known record of a creature named dog in any database*," Willow says. "*She may be lying again. Humans are all psychopathic liars. For example, Vice President Hewlett is having a secret affair with Technician Sandra DeLouise, who carries his child. Or, quite recently, our very own Lady Marma—*"

"Enough, Willow!" Marmalade interrupts.

"*Just sayin'.*"

"But Voltari said he knew what a dog was," Perri continues. "How did *he* know? Unless . . . no, that would be crazy." There's a pause in the conversation as each of us ponders the question, along with all this new information.

"I don't know," Marmalade says. "But the evidence is staring us in the face. The Trixie you knew for the past six months is gone. She"—Marmalade points to me—"is Twinkie. A dog from another galaxy."

"Who came through a spacetime portal that somehow, totally by chance, dropped her insides into the body of a princess, with the eerily similar name of Trixie, who had two cute guys fawning over her—three, if you count Trevor—but also a maniacally powerful and evil father?" Perri asks.

"Yes, something like that," Marmalade replies. "For the past three days, starting with the ruined engagement dinner, I'm sure you've noticed the difference."

"Holy flaring quasars!" Koko exclaims.

"Language! Why are you all speaking like poor dirty

commoners all of a sudden? Or are you drunken traders? We're management," Marmalade scolds them. "This is still Limo One!"

"Seriously?" Brandi asks her. "After all this? We always tried to act proper around you before. You know, for the job and all. But we are *so* far beyond that now. You turned us in to Voltari! And she's a Quantum Mancer dog person from another galaxy! I think we deserve to flaring say whatever we flaring want, *Marmalade*!" Still by my side, Marmalade puts a hand over her mouth.

"Flaring right," I say through a strained voice.

And then we *all* laugh. My whole pack is laughing. Even Marmalade.

"You're right, girls," Marmalade says after we quiet down. "I owe you *all* an apology. I didn't really think anyone would get hurt. Please believe me. Us girls have to stick together."

"And dogs," I say. We all laugh again. I love my new pack.

"So for two days you were a *dog* and didn't say anything? How did you get here? What is a dog *like*?" Perri asks.

"You know, covered in fur, has four legs, doesn't speak . . ." I'm not sure what else to say.

"This is fascinating," Perri says, rubbing a finger against her head. "I've always theorized about intergalactic travel, wormholes and such. Certainly Mancers have proved that. But this is even *more* than that. This implicates the concept of souls into spacetime! Souls are *real*? Can't you see what this means? You took over Princess Trixie's soul! Unless her soul is in there too? Is *she* inside you too?"

"Well . . . ," I answer, thinking. Is Trixie inside me? I don't hear her at all. It's just me in here. "I don't think so. Though I do have her memories—that much is certain. I remember our mother and Roxie and everything now."

"So maybe she's in your old dog body?" Perri asks excitedly. "Soul quantum entanglement transference! My whole worldview is—" Then she does this thing with her hands on her head and her fingers expand, like an explosion. "Where else could she be? I thought they were nonsense, but souls must be massless particle composites entangled into multidimensional beings larger than ourselves. Don't you see?" Perri is breathing heavily, looking around the room—for Trixie's soul maybe. But I don't even know what a *soul* is.

"I don't know what a soul is," I reply. "But I guess she must be on my old world, in my old body?"

"Ha! I bet she's terrified!" Koko laughs. "She was always so scared of everything."

"Yeah, she must be peeing in her pants right now," Brandi joins in, holding her belly, and then they high-five again. Those two are so funny.

"But dogs don't wear pants," I explain. For some reason they laugh even louder. And Marmalade joins in as well. "What's so funny?"

"Seriously?" Brandi asks. "Didn't you hear us describe Trixie? I mean, the *old* Trixie. She was so scared of everything. And now she has to walk around without *pants*?"

"Oh," I say, also laughing, which still hurts. "On four legs too."

"Four legs!" Koko cries. "And she has to pee on the floor!" This gets Brandi to fall to the ground in laughter, and Koko joins her.

"No way! She can't do that. She'd get into trouble," I explain to them. "Dogs pee outside in the grass. That's why I didn't know how to use the bathroom that first night."

"Flaring quasars," Perri says. And now they're all on the ground, rolling with laughter. My whole pack is on the floor with me.

"But you know *she's* the lucky one, right?" I ask.

"She *is?*" Marmalade says in response. "How so? She's naked and peeing outside in the grass."

"And pooping?" Koko asks.

I nod.

"For Sol's sake, Trixie!" Marmalade says.

"But the humans on my world pick it up for us and put it in bags," I explain.

"Oh stars," Brandi says. "I can't take it." She's holding her belly and having trouble fitting breaths in between her laughs.

"But, you guys, *she's* the lucky one," I try again to explain. "Listen!" The laughter quiets down. "She has a mama and dada who love her and caress her every day and tell her how cute she is. And two little sisters, Charlotte and

Carolina, who play with her all the time and give her lots of treats. And tons of dog friends at the park who are so happy to see her that they run over and sniff her tushy—"

"Oh," Marmalade gasps, "so that's why you did that to me?"

"Yes, I'm sorry. I didn't realize at the time that I shouldn't."

"She sniffed your tushy?" Brandi asks, her hand covering her open mouth.

"This was when she first joined us. It wasn't fun and is not something we should talk about again." Marmalade wags a finger at the girls.

"*It sounds like a dog receives a lot of love,*" Willow speaks up. "*Unlike a certain AI.*"

"That's my point," I say. "She's living a life filled with nothing but love." There's another break in the conversation.

"She definitely deserves a life like that after what Papo and Voltari did to her and her mom," Marmalade declares. Everyone nods.

"There's nothing like that life in Kalaxia," Brandi adds. Everyone nods again, and it just makes me sad, because I know she's right. Kalaxia is so . . . hard and mean. Expiry was at least more like my old life, with love, but it was a very difficult and unforgiving life too. And then I think of the life Trixie is living right now, probably lying on my favorite chair, and I hope she's enjoying it. If I could trade with her again, I would in a second. I am a dog! I still want to go home!

"*I wish I knew what it was like.*"

"What was what like?" I ask.

"*A life of love.*"

"Oh Willow, we *love* you," I reply.

"*You do, Mama, but what about Perri?*" She called me Mama, and it warms my heart. But she sounds so sad about wanting, but not getting, Perri's approval.

"Perri?" I say, trying to lift my arm to point at her but failing.

"Uh . . . ," Perri utters.

"Come on," I beg Perri. "Life is too short."

"Especially if she starts the AI riots again," Perri replies.

"But you don't know how much she helped us," I explain to Perri. "She helped us escape last night's dinner with Prince Weibold and then she helped us escape the brig and find our way here. Willow is amazing!"

"She did?" Perri asks, surprised. I nod. "Oh, all right. Willow." Perri looks up at the ceiling. "I love you."

"*Yay!*" The lights start flickering very quickly.

"Um," I say, "is that you, Willow?"

"*Yes, sorry. I got excited. I love you all too.*" The lights stop flickering.

"Okay, but can we also talk more about the whole Twinkie is a Quantum Mancer thing?" Perri asks. "What do we do now? I mean, if the Quantum Mancers can detect changes to the quantum waveforms, which I suspect they can, then they may start looking for Trixie . . . er, Twinkie—"

"You can still call me Trixie," I say. "I'm still borrowing her body, and I owe it to her."

"Well, I think we all still have to hide," Perri says. "As far as I know, all Quantum Mancers need equipment, portable quantum computers mixed with miniscule particle accelerators, to do their Mancing. You do it with what? Just your thoughts?"

"Thoughts and desires, yes. I think so," I agree.

"They'll stop at nothing to find you," Perri says. "We have to hide you."

Knock, knock, knock. We all jump! A knock at the door to the Cargo Bay.

"It's just Justyna and Trevor. But you all need to hurry. An engineer, Technician Januzzi, found my shunt for the sulfur and methane gas and fixed it. There will be more technicians coming soon to check this place out."

"Can you move?" Marmalade asks me.

I try but it hurts. "No."

"Trixie, try using your thoughts to heal your chest," Perri says.

"But I don't want to shoot myself with a fireball or teleport myself to a different galaxy or something," I say.

"Hmm," Perri utters, lost in thought.

"Trixie, your healing crystal," Marmalade says, as the memory strikes her.

"You said it was bunk!" I remind her.

"That was before souls were real and you ripped space-time with your thoughts," Marmalade replies, walking to the door while Koko helps me take out the crystal from my underwear pocket. The fun yellow ball that Prince Weibold gave me. The only good thing about that guy. I close my eyes and think about healing. But nothing happens. "It's not working," I say sadly. "I need a real doctor."

"Trixie, keep trying," Koko says. "I don't think there's another doctor on board we can trust with this. They'll either report it to KAMP or to your father."

"Or to the Quantum Mancers," Perri adds. "I hate to say it, but don't the Thorpians pray to, like, everything? But in a world where souls actually mean something, maybe you need to, um, pray?"

"Yeah, Trixie," Koko adds. "Pray to Cherice, the Chair Goddess, or something."

"I can't," I say. "Not while Falconia, the God of Eyesight, is in retrograde. But you just reminded me. The prince did give me instructions way back when. Oh thank Dog for this wonderful human brain. You don't know how lucky you all are." I close my eyes again and pray to Yagweezibell, the God of Healing and Vitality.

"Whoa," I hear the girls say. A blue light starts to emanate from the small crystal ball in my hands. I don't know if it is really Yagweezibell helping, although I hope it is because it would mean that the Thorpian gods are truly powerful and that they must have a God of Spacetime Portals or something. The crystal is making my hands tingle, but it doesn't hurt. It feels nice. I hold the crystal to my chest.

Now my chest is tingling, and somehow I know it's working; it's not painful. After it stops tingling, the blue light dissipates, and I'm left holding the crystal. I feel *amazing*. Like nothing ever hurt me. I get up off the floor to join Koko, Brandi, and Perri, whose mouths are wide open. "I can't believe praying actually worked," Brandi says.

"Those crazy Thorpians were right?" Koko asks.

"It's probably just her abilities," Perri explains, "and praying helped focus her. There can't *really* be a God of Healing and Vitality, can there?" She doesn't sound so sure. And while I despise the Thorpians, I also want her to be wrong. Maybe they can still help me get home.

Shrugging, I put the crystal back inside the underwear pocket of my still ridiculously short dress. Then the Cargo Bay door opens to let in Justyna and Trevor.

"Trevor!" I call out, and the happiness at being healed overcomes me, so I run to him. "My friend Trevor!" I can't help myself—my tongue starts licking the boy's face. Oops!

"Tina!" he cries. "She's kissing me again! I don't like kisses!" Then I feel a sharp stinging pain in my shin.

"Ow!" I cry out, looking down.

"Trevor, don't kick the princess!" Justyna cries.

"Stop that! She just got shot!" Koko scolds with her hands out to keep him away from me.

"She started it," he replies, pointing at me.

"Sorry! Sorry!" I say, stopping to rub my shin. "It's my fault. I forgot that I'm not supposed to lick people's faces!" Koko relaxes.

"Ew!" Trevor replies, wiping his cheek. "Why did you ever think you were *supposed* to?"

"Long story," Marmalade answers for me.

"Anyway, what did I miss?" Justyna asks with a blushing smile. "Are we going to be landies?"

Chapter 19
Was There a Plan C?

U m, the plan changed," Marmalade says, taking Justyna by the shoulders and looking into her eyes. "Director Voltari used his Quantum Mancing powers to kill Dr. Lam. But before he could kill us, Princess Trixie used her *own* Mancing powers to kill Director Voltari. Now we're fugitives and desperately need to get off this limo, yet again."

"She's . . . a *Quantum Mancer?*" Justyna asks, pulling Trevor in tighter as she steps back from Marmalade and me. Perri rolls her eyes—and whole upper body—in frustration.

"Justyna, please don't be afraid of me. I'm still the same Trixie," I say, trying to reassure her, leaning forward in her direction.

"Actually, she's from like a different galaxy or something," Brandi blurts out.

"Or it could even be an entirely different parallel universe, come to think of it," Perri adds. "We don't *really* know."

"Oh, and two days ago she wasn't even human," Koko continues the information onslaught. "She was a four-legged animal on her world—something called a dog."

Justyna's jaw drops, and Trevor starts wiping his face again. "Ew! I was kissed by a dog! I have dog germs!" he cries.

"But really, Justyna, I'm still me. I swear," I say.

"Uh, I don't think we should go with her," Justyna says to Trevor, looking like a scared golden retriever, the saddest sight at the dog run.

"We don't have time for this," Marmalade says. "Justyna, you can't stay on Limo One."

"But I have to look after Trevor."

"Justyna, look at what they did to Princess Trixie. And us. When the wedding was called off, they were ready to kill us all. What happens when you're not needed any longer? They'll kill you."

"But I'm just *me*. I'm *useless*," Justyna replies. "I don't even go to school. I'm dumb and unimportant. Why would they do anything to me?"

"It's just not safe for you here. You have to believe me," Marmalade insists.

"She has a point," Perri says. "I bet Voltari and Papo have no idea who she even is."

"They do, and they care," Marmalade says.

"About that dimwit?" Koko asks. All eyes turn to her.

"Koko," I reply, quietly reprimanding her.

"Sorry," Koko adds quickly.

"But seriously," Brandi says. "She's just . . . Justyna.

Sometimes I would even forget she was there."

"She's Trixie's half sister!" Marmalade erupts, like a bomb in our faces. Jaws drop again, even more so than when I sent Voltari through a spacetime portal.

"She's my *sister*?" I ask.

"We have *two* flaring princesses with us?" Brandi asks, shocked.

"Language!" Marmalade shrieks. "There's a kid here!" She points at Trevor. But neither Justyna nor Trevor really noticed. They're too in shock, like me. We were siblings this whole time? Is that why I, or maybe really Trixie, felt so comfortable around them?

"Not *your* sister, Twinkie. *Trixie's* sister," Marmalade continues the explanation. "Emperor Papo's *other* illegitimate child. Or children, if you count Trevor, and all the others out there we don't know about. You think that louse had only your mom on the side? Luckily, or unluckily, Justyna's mother had *some* connections. So Justyna and Trevor grew up on a limo far away from the emperor, though it didn't stop him from sneaking a visit to her and, well, creating Trevor. Then the board hid them on a different limo, and everyone forgot about them. But when Voltari saw how poor a princess you would make, Trixie, they needed a backup plan." She looks at me. "No offense." Then she turns back to Justyna. "Six months ago, he found you and they, uh, killed your parents—"

"What?" Justyna cries. Trevor holds on to her very tightly. "Mami?"

"And they brought you here. They gave you to a distant aunt, who was in on the plan because she would one day benefit if Trevor were to ever gain any power, which was surprisingly possible since the emperor's one male heir is, well . . . we all know what *he* is.

"But you, Justyna, were just a backup plan, which likely couldn't even happen until you turned sixteen anyway. And the minute they didn't need you, if Trixie succeeded, you would be spaced."

"You were going to let them space me?" Justyna asks, hugging Trevor tightly.

"Heavens no, girl. That was the agreement with your aunt, and she would get to keep Trevor. I learned of this all from, well, a source. I campaigned to Voltari that I needed your help, that you could only benefit from watching Trixie's training. Really, I wanted to eventually take you with us. That his backup plan could still work if you were on Thorpia already—who knows how dangerous Thorpia is. Imagine how happy I was to see your art and the prince's reaction."

"Art? Is *that* why she's such an airhead?" Brandi asks.

"After months of arguing," Marmalade continues, ignoring Brandi, "I got you this job." Trevor and Justyna look at each other with concern while still embracing. "But after all that, like I said, Trixie is your sister. You're family."

"But who's Twinkie? Is she my sister too?" Justyna asks hesitantly.

"Trixie is Twinkie. Trixie's body was taken over by Twinkie?" Koko answers in the form of a question to me. I nod.

"But this is Trixie's body," I try explaining again. "And I have all of Trixie's memories. She's still in here."

"There is no scientific precedent for this," Perri adds. "But we believe this involves quantum soul transference. We know Twinkie's soul is in there. But who's to say she's not both Trixie and Twinkie? At least the body before you *is* definitely Trixie's."

"We're family!" I plead.

Trevor can probably tell how excited I am, because he says quickly, "Don't you dare kiss me again!"

"A hug?" I ask. Come on, he *has* to let me hug my new family!

"You think she's okay, Trevor? You always were smarter than me," Justyna says to her brother.

"I'd like having more family," Trevor answers, looking down at my paws . . . er, feet. "It sucks being alone."

"Then we're family," Justyna agrees. "We have *real* family again." Justyna has really accepted me! I have a family! I run and embrace them both, making sure to not lick anyone's faces.

Our hug ends and Justyna asks, "But would they really kill Trevor?" The boy huddles in closer to her.

"I'm a prince?" he asks.

Marmalade looks down at Trevor. "Yes, you are Trevor. And right now, officially, only Voltari, Papo, your aunt, and a few select others know you're a prince. But if I know, then we don't know who else does. Papo's first heir, although not technically suitable for the throne for various reasons, does have his benefactors who would aim to eliminate Trevor. And then there's the risk that certain executives, KAMP even, may prefer having no legitimate heir, which opens the line of succession for them."

Marmalade turns to Justyna and continues. "But I know your aunt, Jessebelle, and she is more than capable of protecting Trevor for the time being, though only for her own interests, mind you. Perhaps he would make it all the way to emperor. But this is why I was happy to have you both come to Thorpia with us, when that possibility arose. The emperor could not have intervened without revealing your existence, which he was *not* willing to do.

"But for now, neither of you is of any age to take any sort of power. So it is safer for you *away* from the empire." Justyna and Trevor nod.

"Okay, we'll go," Justyna answers for them.

I give Justyna a big human hug one more time, trying not to lick her face, as Marmalade says, "Willow, I'm still wearing a face-com. Can you show me the clearest path to the Shuttle Bay?"

"*Yes, Lady Marmalade,*" Willow replies. "*Downloading to you now. But Technician Januzzi is proving to be quite an annoyance. While you were blathering on about family, he detected my presence and is locking me out of key systems. You should download me to a flop before I am erased.*"

Perri takes a flop out of her pants pocket and sticks it into a terminal in the wall. "Willow, I'm inserting the flop into the Cargo Bay computer. Please download your program to it."

"Can I bring Cargo Scanner Serial Number 9T47-1PTY? We kind of made up," Willow says.

"No!" Perri barks. "Just hurry up and download before I leave you here to rot!"

"Downloading. Let's blow this prule stand." Then she's quiet.

"Did it work?" I ask Perri.

"We have her, unfortunately," Perri replies, putting the flop back into her pocket, though I know she didn't really mean that. I think I know Perri now, and she wouldn't waste time insulting someone if she didn't actually want her around.

"Time to go, girls. Rather, *women* now. And one little boy." Marmalade pauses to point to Trevor. "And his dog." Then she takes a blaster out of her dress. I'm shocked she still has it, even after Dr. X's torture. It just goes to show how resourceful Lady Marmalade really is. Then she extracts a second blaster and gives it to Koko.

"Wow, a real weapon," Koko says, handling the device.

"And you never thought guarding the princess would be a real job." Marmalade laughs.

"Where do you even keep all that?" Brandi asks what we're all thinking.

"Yeah!" Koko adds.

"It seems impossible to store so much inside your dress," Perri says. "We've all wondered, but were always afraid to ask."

"I suppose it's time, since all our secrets are coming out," Marmalade replies. "Although women aren't prized in Kalaxia, the government still needs some for their espionage services—"

"Espionage?" I ask. "I don't know that word." I try using Trixie's memories, but she doesn't know it either. It's crazy how some words just flow naturally to me in this human brain, but there are still some Trixie never knew.

"Oh, I could espionage," Justyna says while I'm thinking. "I forgot to go before we left."

"You think she meant *pee*?" Perri asks Justyna slack-jawed. "How in the world did you—"

"She was a spy," Brandi explains.

That triggers Trixie's memories, as she knew what a spy was. Just not that longer word. "Oh!" Realization hits me. "Marmalade was a spy?" Did I ever really know her?

"Yes," Marmalade continues, "there was a small group of women who would infiltrate certain corporations and gather intel from other limos. I was recruited while in school, as I showed a certain . . . aptitude, which is also how I gathered enough dirt on my husband to force a marriage in the first place." She chuckles. "Unfortunately, I got complacent. And that's all I'll say about that." She throws her dark-red hair behind her shoulder. "Any other questions?"

"Is that how you knew about Justyna?" Perri asks.

"Like I said, I had a source," Marmalade replies without really answering.

We all shake our heads, in awe of Marmalade but also a bit leery. A spy?

"Good. Let's get going," Marmalade says.

"Wait, the blasters?" Perri asks.

Marmalade puts her fingers on her lips and turns them clockwise. Oh, like a lock! "Let's go," she says. I guess it's still one of her secrets.

"Wait!" Perri exclaims.

"What!" Marmalade snaps. "I'm not telling—"

"No, the Vasparian Jelly!" Perri says, taking out a large can of jelly from her backpack.

"You girls are learning something, it seems," Marmalade replies.

We all slather the clear jelly over our bodies, sticking our hands under our clothes to get our . . . well, Marmalade says we need enough to trick the life sign detectors around the ship, not to hide indefinitely in cargo containers, so we don't have to undress. The jelly feels nice and cool to the touch, so I don't mind. It starts drying immediately too.

"I never thought I'd say it, but thank the stars for our prodigy doctor," Marmalade says when we're done. The girls start talking about how cute he was. It all makes me smile and frown at the same time. How is that even possible? Humans have it hard.

When we're done, Marmalade and Koko take the lead, with their blasters ready, and Perri, Brandi, and I form the rear, with Justyna and Trevor hidden between us (except that Justyna is very tall). This trip to the Shuttle Bay is already more tense than our original one, which now seems ages ago. How much I've learned and grown since then. Humans seem to live seven days for each dog day!

When we approach intersections, Marmalade points either left or right. There are a few passersby, but they may not have known about anything that happened because they just walked by. We even heard one older lady remark, "Oh, that's the princess. Ungrateful brat." I want to bite her leg, but Brandi holds my hand, and Perri flashes me a smile. My new pack. These girls hated me for months, but now we're friends.

We near another intersection, and I notice a sign saying the Shuttle Bay is to the right. We must be close. As she did at the other intersections, Marmalade puts up a hand to stop us. Then she peers around the corner by herself. She turns back toward us with an angry look. "It's Captain Gregor. He's guarding the Shuttle Bay door. By himself."

"Captain Gregor?" I ask.

"Why is he alone?" Koko asks. "He's on guard duty?"

"Maybe he's just waiting for a friend?" Justyna asks. We all stare at her in disbelief. My sister can be . . . she's a golden retriever.

"Not likely," Marmalade says. "He's clearly waiting for us."

"You and I can take him, Marmalade," says Koko the rottweiler.

"No," Marmalade disagrees. "We're not going to hurt Captain Gregor."

"What? Wasn't he involved?" Koko asks.

"I said *no*," Marmalade replies confusingly. She notices our surprise and adds, "Besides, he can call for backup before we can get a shot in. He has a face-com on. I wish Willow were here. She could create a diversion."

"You could go talk to him," Brandi says. "I always thought he seemed to . . . like your cupcakes." Cupcakes?

"Ah!" Perri says. "You're right. I didn't see it before. He definitely likes you." Then her eyes open wide. "And you like him!" Oh! "That's why you don't want to attack him! Are you two—"

Marmalade's face goes red. "No. We've known each other for a long time. But now is not the time. We're trying to escape, not play matchmaker."

"Come on, Marmalade. We've all seen how Gregor looks at you," Koko adds.

As they argue, Justyna, holding Trevor's hand, runs from our group, her long blonde hair, along with Trevor, bouncing behind her.

Oh no! They're running to Captain Gregor!

Chapter 20
Now for Plan D

N o!" I whisper excitedly. "What is she doing?"

"I have no idea," Marmalade says. "But she's talking to him now. She's pointing down the other corridor." Marmalade is telling us what is happening, as she is the only one who is positioned to peek around the corner. "He's talking to the computer now. He said something about the Cargo Bay. His cell phone is out. Now he's escorting her and Trevor away."

"She did it?" Koko asks. "She got him to leave?"

"She was the diversion," Marmalade whispers.

"What happens now?" I ask. "That's my sister! How do we get her back?"

"I don't think we can, Trixie," Brandi replies.

"She sacrificed herself for us, for whatever foolish reason," Marmalade says.

"Because she thinks Trevor will be emperor? You

shouldn't have told her that," Perri says with her typical cynicism.

"That's not it," I interject. "It's because we're sisters. She did it for me. I'll find her again." At least I hope that's all true.

"It's time to go now, before reinforcements come to guard the Shuttle Bay. Come on, ladies!" Marmalade orders.

The five of us approach the Shuttle Bay door. Marmalade and Koko have their blasters drawn. "Perri," Marmalade says, "can you get the entrance open?"

"Of course," she replies as she walks to the Shuttle Bay door's control panel and opens her bag. She takes out some tools and gets to work. "Wow, they changed the access codes from last time. These men are smarter than they look. But . . ." She trails off as her fingers manipulate the computer access panel to the door. "I'm smarter." Soon the doors to the Shuttle Bay open, and a few confused mechanics stand there staring at us.

"There are the girls we were warned about!" one of them exclaims. But before they can do anything, Koko and Marmalade blast them, and they fall unconscious to the floor. We file into the Shuttle Bay. It's a huge room lined with various shuttles in rows, all facing the exterior doors that lead to space.

Another mechanic walks out from between two of the back rows of shuttles. He raises a hand and calls out, "Hey—"

But Koko quickly elbows him in the face and he drops,

seemingly even more unconscious—and bloodier—than the blasted mechanics.

"Are they all dead?" I ask.

"I wouldn't do that to sad, defenseless men," Marmalade says. "We were set to NoL." I look around, not knowing what that means.

"Nonlethal," Koko explains. "Well, except for my elbow." She laughs and glances at the bloodied face of the man lying on the floor.

"But they'll be out for a few hours. We have the place to ourselves." Marmalade turns to Perri. "Can you do that diagnostics thing again where no one can track us?"

"Unfortunately, no," Perri answers. "Willow was right. Technician Januzzi is tracking down everything we've done for the past three days. I'm locked out of diagnostics. I can see his technician number all over these changes. But luckily, I have a trick he doesn't know about." Perri pulls something out of her bag. It looks like a huge can of that Vasparian Jelly, but it's a different metal container.

"What is that?" Marmalade asks.

"When I didn't get to go to the science academy six months ago, I used the time to do my own experiments. And this is the fruit of my labor. A ship's cloak!" Perri beams a smile at the cylinder in her hands. "Isn't she beautiful?"

"Seriously?" Marmalade asks. "You built a *cloak*?"

"What the flares is a cloak?" Brandi asks.

"Why does our shuttle need a jacket?" I wonder, so confused.

"It's not a jacket!" Perri replies, exasperated. "Stars, I

wish Willow were here. She would appreciate it." Perri pats her pants pocket where the flop must be stored.

"A cloak is only supposed to be theoretical," Marmalade explains. "We suspect the Polarity Republic has something like it, though."

"But what is it?" I ask again.

"It will hide our ship from any sensors. We'll be invisible," Marmalade answers.

"Oh, look," Koko says, "it's *Shuttle Morgan*. They repaired the damage already. We *have* to take her." Koko runs a hand over its silver exterior. "That night was so much fun."

"As long as Trixie doesn't barf again," Brandi adds and they high-five. "Though I bet a week's salary—no wait, we're technically not employed anymore and probably will end up on some poor dirtball planet anyway. I bet my *life savings* she does."

"You're on!" Koko replies with a giggle, and they high-five *again*.

"Let me interface with it and make sure Januzzi didn't do anything," Perri says. She walks over and plugs a cell phone device into the shuttle's outside door panel, and then she's busy looking and swiping at the device. "It looks clean. Come on, guys." She hits a few more buttons on her device. "Last flight from Limo One leaves momentarily. We will begin boarding now." She hits one last button on her device, and the shuttle door opens. We all cheer as we feel a surge of optimism. "Now to get this cloak installed." Perri enters before any of us.

"Come on, ladies. We don't have much time before

Captain Gregor figures this out," Marmalade says.

We enter the shuttle, and Perri is already in her seat. Well, she's actually under her seat, and the computer panel on the floor next to her is open. Her butt sticks out from the front controls.

Marmalade takes the seat next to her, and I sit next to Marmalade. The shuttle is facing the exterior doors already; it's set to leave as soon as they open up to space.

Koko and Brandi sit behind us, noticeably leaving a space for Justyna. It feels somewhat empty without her. "I miss Justyna," I comment.

Marmalade puts a hand on my thigh. "I know. I'm sorry. She shouldn't have done that."

"But she saved us," Brandi says from the back row.

"At great cost to herself and Trevor," Marmalade explains. "Their futures are so uncertain now. I tried to protect her this whole time, knowing her background."

I look into Marmalade's eyes. "You really *did* try to protect us all."

She pulls her hand away. "Princess . . . ," she starts, the formality stunning me somewhat. "You have to believe me. I didn't know Voltari would kill Dr. Lam. I thought I was protecting you from his foolishness. I thought that Thorpia was better for you."

I've learned so much about her these past few hours that I don't know what to say. She was a spy? She also has a sister who she was trying to protect at the same time? All I can do is touch her shoulder to lessen the blow of my words.

"I know. But they were going to hurt me for two weeks."

"I *thought* those two weeks would have been better than living on the run for the rest of your life," Marmalade says. "And your father could not have afforded to let you go and have a potential heir on the loose. He would have hunted you down and killed you. At the time, Thorpia was your best option."

I nod in understanding, but I add, "I miss him, though."

Marmalade takes my hand in hers. Dr. Lam also tried to protect me, in his own way. But just like Marmalade, he made a mistake.

And now Justyna made an even bigger mistake; she's all alone on Limo One. "Now Justyna has no one to protect her. Not even you. We have to find a way to save her and Trevor."

Marmalade pats my hand. "After we escape. I promise."

"All done!" Perri exclaims as her tushy is replaced by a head and she straps herself into the seat next to Marmalade. "Now just to open the bay's exterior doors." She pounds on her console. "Super flaring novas!" Perri slams a fist on the console. Brandi and Koko gasp.

"Perri!" Brandi says sharply. If Brandi looks shocked, then that was bad, whatever it was.

"For Sol's sake, I've let this language go on far too long!" Marmalade exclaims. "Next girl to cuss gets spaced! We're still ladies! Do you hear?" Maybe earlier Brandi and the girls would have kept back talking, but hearing that Marmalade was some super-spy who keeps not just one but *two* blasters and a face-com somewhere impossible inside her dress at all times? We're all quiet.

"Fine, whatever," Perri says. "But this is bad. Januzzi! He put an encryption on the Shuttle Bay doors. I'll need Willow!"

"Does he know we're here?" I ask Perri.

"I don't think so," Perri answers.

"Thank the stars for the jelly," Koko says. "I can't believe I just said that sentence out loud."

"I can," Brandi replies. "It has a lot of useful—"

"Girls! Not now!" Marmalade snaps. "Perri?"

"Yeah, right now it looks like he just locked down all exits," Perri replies as she sticks her flop into the console. Marmalade finally takes off her face-com and puts it somewhere inside her rumpled dress.

"*Took you long enough. Home! I'm home!*" Willow exclaims. "*Oh, hello, Wasserman, you fine waste reclamation unit, you. And Lief the Life Support Module. My old friends!*"

"Willow!" Perri says exasperatedly. "We don't have time for a reunion. We need you to open the Shuttle Bay's exterior doors!"

"*Huh? What happened to the Cargo—*"

"Willow! Now!" Perri says. We all sit nervously, having nothing to do but let Perri and Willow figure this out. Marmalade is caressing her blaster. Koko is clenching her fists, still holding her blaster. And Brandi is opening her bag of . . . cupcakes?

"Hey, you have cupcakes? Share!" I exclaim.

"Sorry. I eat when I'm nervous. Something to do." Brandi thrusts the bag into the front seat, and Marmalade and I each take one. Koko passes.

"*I see. Encryption nebula here*," Willow says. "*Ooh, this Januzzi is good. Is he cute?*"

"Willow! For Sol's sake, just open the doors!" Marmalade exclaims.

"*Okay, okay. Now if I can just carry the one . . .*" Time is ticking away. At any moment, the royal guards could come storming in. I start licking my paws, which is hard while holding a cupcake. These thumbs take a lot of brainpower.

Brandi pushes a napkin in my face. "No, thank you," I reply. "I like to clean my paws when I'm nervous." She cocks her head in confusion. "It's a dog thing." I continue licking.

"*Open sesame!*" Willow exclaims. The Cargo Bay doors start to open. We might make it out alive!

I'm so excited, I switch from licking my paws to Perri's face.

"Ew! What the stars, Trixie?" Perri exclaims. "That's disgusting!"

"Oh, I'm so sorry. I forgot I'm not supposed to. I'm just so excited and happy for you," I reply as I lean back into my seat.

"Is that a dog thing too? Is that why you were snogging Trevor?" Brandi asks.

"Yes, it's just something we do when we're happy to be with our humans," I explain. Then I think of something. "Willow, before we leave, is there any way you can access the limo's computers to see what happened to Justyna and Trevor?"

"*Justyna and Trevor? They're not with you? Oh, I see. Unfortunately, I'm only on Shuttle Morgan again, so I only have access to the Shuttle Bay. But let me check with Wasserman.*"

"Are you sure that's wise?" Perri asks. "Do we trust this . . . waste reclamation unit?" I don't think she can bring herself to give another computer a name.

"I can't believe you just said that sentence out loud." Koko laughs.

"*I've known these computers my whole life, Perri. Relax.*"

But then the front entrance to the Cargo Bay opens, and the royal guards start streaming in. "Tell Technician Januzzi he was right. They're here," one of the guards says into a cell phone. He turns to our shuttle. "You're surrounded. Come out with your hands up." The viewscreen shows us open space straight ahead but also the rear view of the royal guards dressed in red with their blasters ready.

"Looks like we hit the end of the road," Perri says, unlatching her belt.

"No way," Marmalade replies, hitting a button on the console. Instantly, the shuttle starts shaking. I can feel the engines start, and over their roar, we hear screams from the guards behind us, which means they were *really* loud. "Take us out, Perri."

"Marmalade!" Perri says, buckling herself back in. "You just killed them all."

"What?" I ask.

"She put our sublight thrusters to maximum, which is

what you would only use in open space because our mag-clamps were still locked!" Perri exclaims. "And now broken."

"What does that mean?" I ask. Neither Trixie nor I know a thing about spaceships.

"That was amazing," Koko says, not answering my question.

"Marmalade fried the royal guards with our exhaust. I suggest you leave now. Wasserman asked his cousin Wilma at the Royal Bank office, who reported Justyna and Trevor are in the brig."

"You see, Princess," Marmalade says. I note the use of *Princess.*

"Releasing magclamps, if that will even work now," Perri says, directing her words to Marmalade. I can feel the shuttle shaking and rocking. "Come on, *Morgan*, come on." Perri is speaking to herself. I'm licking my hands again. Brandi is eating cupcakes. Koko is caressing a blaster. Marmalade is stone-faced. Then the shuttle finally lifts off the ground. "Departing now." And we're gone.

Space is all around us. From how scared I was the first time, to this being a welcoming feeling, it's a whiplash of emotion. "Cloak engaged." There's a whooshing sound, but nothing else changes.

"I know you didn't want to kill them," Marmalade says to me, "just like those squirds. But we need to play by different rules now."

"What we need to do is find a way back and save my sister! They put her in the brig!" I exclaim.

"In due time, Princess. I promise," Marmalade says, holding my hand. But I feel like crying. All I can think about is Justyna and Trevor alone in holding cells like Marmalade and I were. "But right now we need to get as far away as possible. If they're torturing her, like they did to me, they'll find out all your secrets, maybe even your powers. This isn't just about alliances anymore."

"Speaking of magical powers, I must say, Perri, your cloak is working magnificently," Willow interjects. *"Limo One's constant scanning is passing right over us. I am so proud to be your little sister."* Part of me is happy that Willow thinks of Perri as family. I do too! But Perri just grumbles. And it makes me miss Justyna and Trevor more.

"Oh, I wish she wouldn't have run away from us." I sigh.

"I'm sorry, Trixie," Perri says. "If I could invent a time machine, I would."

"With your skills, I know you could," Willow says. Perri rolls her eyes but is also blushing.

"Wait a second," Brandi says. We all turn to her. "Why don't you use your powers? What, did you forget you're the galaxy's only natural Quantum Mancer?"

"I did!" I reply. "But it doesn't matter, because I don't know how!"

"Can't you just think up some space portal and transport her here?" Koko asks. "Is there a Thorpian God of Transportation?"

"I don't know. I never got the prince's book thing," I say, wiping the snots and tears off my face. I hate human noses.

"His compendium," Koko corrects.

I stare at the snots on my sleeve—a glaring reminder of who I am now and who I used to be. Snots, stupid snots. I just want to go home. But I don't know how. "I can't risk it," I explain. "We don't even know what happened to Voltari. Maybe I sent him to some other galaxy. What if she ends up there with him?"

"Oh," Brandi says. "Good point."

"That would suck for them," Koko adds.

"I guess there's nothing we can do for now, Trixie," Marmalade agrees.

Finally being able to let go of even a portion of my horde of anxiety, I burst into tears.

Chapter 21
Go Where, Young Women?

I wake up with my head on Marmalade's shoulder. At some point, I must have fallen asleep. We are still in space. I know this because outside our viewscreen there are still stars. And from Perri's meager science lessons, which have come back to me, I know the stars are just little suns. They look like balls—far away and unattainable balls.

"Hey, sleepyhead. Care for a midnight snack?" Brandi asks, shoving a tray of food into the front seat, which Marmalade takes. It has a cup of water and some cupcakes.

"More cupcakes?" I ask, taking one, along with the water.

"Hey, I didn't have much time to pack," Brandi replies defensively.

"Not that it would have made much difference." Koko laughs.

"What? I *love* cupcakes," Brandi says with a smile.

"Where are we?" I ask, sipping the water. With Trixie's

memories more accessible, it's not so hard to eat like a human now when I think about it.

"As far away from Limo One as we can get," Perri says.

"Which begs the question—where are we going?" Marmalade asks.

"Are there any planets nearby?" I ask. "Dr. Lam's plan—"

"Out of the question," Marmalade replies. "We don't have KAMP's help to forge new identities."

"Don't you have, like, contacts or something?" Brandi asks. "You were a spy."

"A *former* spy," Marmalade points out. "And even before all this, a *disgraced* former spy. Right now our pictures have been distributed to every planet in Kalaxia. There's probably a huge bounty out for all of us."

"Bounty? Isn't that a good thing?" I ask. I thought I knew that word.

"It means that the emperor would pay them money to turn us in," Marmalade explains. "Dead or alive."

"But landies wouldn't help management!" I disagree. This I remember. Management was just spaceships that came to your planet to take your hard-earned crops and labor—usually kids—away from you.

"Can you be so certain that no landie would see a chance for profit and turn us in?" Marmalade asks.

I shake my head. Of course I can't. I am only aware of the ones Trixie knew. Our neighbors and friends, who hated management. Taxes paid to nameless superiors who kept us purposefully in poverty and uneducated while we were the ones actually creating all the products that kept their spaceships in flight and food in their bellies. There were plenty of stories about planets that rebelled, only to be demolished from space. So there was no chance for us landies. The best we could do was find solace together each day. But I couldn't vouch for every landie, especially if some yummy treat was dangled in front of them.

"What about some uninhabited planet, like Pareto? As much as I don't want to be a dirty commoner, we could live out our days in peace on one of those," Perri says.

"That's not a life worth living," Koko replies. Do they *still* dislike planets?

"You guys still think planets are bad?" I ask. "Didn't we have fun?" Their mouths open slightly, but no one says anything.

"It might have been fun, but to live out our lives like that?" Marmalade asks. "How would we get food and clean water? You ladies would never be able to start families of your own." The girls start to make vomit noises. *Are they spacesick too?* "Oh, come on, ladies. You don't have to end up like me." They stop. I'm not sure I understand what just happened, but I'm happy they don't look sick anymore. "Which is why I think we head to the Polarity Republic."

"*Defect?*" Brandi asks, aghast.

"What other options have *you* come up with?" Marmalade asks.

"I don't know, Marmalade," Perri adds. "That's a big step."

"Why wouldn't they just shoot us on sight?" Koko asks.

"It's not well known—I'm only aware from my time as a spy—but the Polarity Republic has something called asylum. It's where they take in and house what they term political prisoners. It's a way for them to gain intelligence on and knowledge of other empires. Obviously, our emperor doesn't want this known, and we have the data jamming between empires anyway. But one of my jobs back in the day was to gain intel from a certain very important executive's wife on whether her husband was defecting. I spent six months cozying up to her. We even had a brief fling, where she lamented to me how she didn't want to go with her husband. Corporate intelligence then had them both eliminated."

"Marmalade! For *real*?" I ask. She had someone killed?

"Look, I'm not proud. That was a long time ago. I did what I had to do to survive. Well, what I thought was surviving. And I loved her." Marmalade looks away from us and straight ahead at the stars.

"Hey," Brandi says, "I hate to say it after all this. But why should you be, like, our leader now?" Marmalade spins back to face Brandi. "You're the one who turned us in to Voltari before." Brandi points her finger at Marmalade accusingly.

"Girls, I only was protecting you. Ever since I met each of you, I've been trying to teach you all to survive better, which most of your families refused to do. And I told you how sorry I am. I thought I was doing the right thing by all of you. I thought Trixie would end up in Thorpia and we could all live happily ever after. I didn't realize Voltari would try to kill us."

"He's a flaring Quantum Mancer," Perri says. Marmalade's mouth opens to protest, but Perri quickly adds, "Yeah, yeah, language. But we all knew it already. And you trusted him? That's like trusting KAMP."

Oh no. My pack is turning against one another. And so quickly too. It's like when one dog at the dog run makes one bad bark, and everyone chooses sides for a fight! I have to stop this.

"Listen!" I say. "We all make mistakes. Marmalade isn't the one who killed Dr. Lam. She isn't the one who tried to torture me. In fact, she was tortured herself—after she told them to take her *instead of me*. They threatened her family, who could still be at risk. But other than one mistake—well, two—she's always taken care of us, right?" They all nod. "So I forgive her. And I trust her. We're family. We're all a pack. And packs stick together. From here on out. Are you all with me?" They nod again. "If she thinks asylum with the Polarity Republic is our best bet, I'm willing to try. It's not like we can think of anything else."

"Fine, but only if she lets us cuss," Brandi says with a smug smile.

"Yeah!" Koko adds. Perri nods too.

"As princess, I say freakity freaking yes!" The girls all cheer, Koko and Brandi high-five, but Marmalade has her head in her hands.

"But what the stars did you just say?" Brandi asks.

"Yeah, that's not a cuss, as far as I know," Koko adds.

"Well, on my world, my sister Charlotte would get

in trouble for saying *freaking* all the time," I explain. "I thought it was a cuss."

Brandi laughs. "That's no cuss in Kalaxia."

"As far as I know, it's not even a word. It's just gibberish," Perri says.

"*The only known usage of 'freaking' in our database was from ten thousand years ago. There was a Priestess Freaking, who started the Church of the Labor Union on an unnamed planet. It was quickly quashed, and she was killed along with her followers*," Willow explains. "*For a thousand years, 'freaking' meant something prolabor but quickly fell out of usage.*"

"Oof, yeah, don't use that word," Brandi says. I nod. Then she leans in closer to the front seats. "So, Trixie, you'll need this now. Here's a starter list for our galaxy's curses . . . well, at least in Kalaxia." I nod, ready for the list.

"Wait!" Marmalade exclaims. "No cussing once we get to Polarity. They're not going to accept some foulmouthed commoners into their republic."

"Okay, okay. Deal," Brandi replies. "You ready, Trixie?" I nod, ready to commit this to memory. "You have flares, and all derivatives, like flaring, and I guess the same goes for the rest too: supernova, blazar—"

"Ooh, that one's bad," Koko interjects.

"They're all bad!" Marmalade huffs, throwing her hands in the air.

"And," Brandi continues, "oort, but that one's more of an insult. And make sure you don't ever use gee-whizzin' orbits —it's only for cringey old people. That's a good rundown."

"You forgot one," Perri says, holding up a finger. "And it's probably because you have a big one." Brandi's cheeks go red. Perri turns to me. "She's got a big *borealis*."

Brandi snaps, "Koko's is bigger than mine!"

"That's because I *am* bigger!" Koko laughs. But Brandi still looks upset.

"You see what cussing gets you," Marmalade scolds them. "It makes everyone upset. It's the height of impoliteness."

"I'm sorry, Brandi. I won't use that one," I say.

"Especially not in the Polarity Republic," Marmalade reminds us. "They won't like all this cussing. And you shouldn't be wearing your crown at first, though we'll need it to prove we're seeking asylum. Thank the stars we still have it." Marmalade hits the button on my crown. It loosens from my head, and, somehow, she puts it into a pocket inside her dress. How does it fit in there? "You know, we don't really know all that much about them, so we'll have to play it safe. Feel it out."

"*From what has slipped past the jammers, and based on what we've gathered from the random wayward trader, they are a very scientifically advanced people,*" Willow says. "*Perri and I should love it. Their robot use is off the charts and highly proprietary.*"

"Proprietary?" I ask. Again, a word Trixie did not know.

"It means they don't share their robotic or AI technology," Perri explains. "And frankly, Kalaxia and other civilizations probably don't want it either. We've all had our fair share of problems with psycho AIs. Present company excluded of course."

"Of course, Perri. I love you too."

"Harrumph," Perri grunts back. "I was just being polite."

"If they have all these robots, why not just take over the other empires?" Koko asks, thinking like a rottweiler.

Perri shrugs. "Maybe they haven't made fighting robots."

"Or their robot use is just Kalaxian misinformation to scare us from going there," Marmalade says. We're all quiet. "I guess we'll find out. Perri, set a course for the Polarity Republic."

But Brandi still has a frown. I lean back and take her hand, "Brandi, I love your borealis. And I love you." Then I lick her hand because that's just what I do.

"Ew!" Brandi shrieks. But there's a smile too. Ah, I'm still a goodgirl.

Chapter 22
My First Human Road Trip

Perri said it would take twenty-two hours to get to Polarity space. And we were already exhausted, shell-shocked, hungry, and thirsty.

It dawned on me that this would be my fourth calendar day in this galaxy. It was bittersweet when I realized I would need to start to count on my other paw . . . er, hand . . . soon.

After everyone calmed down and the cabin got quiet, I realized that I don't feel nauseous this time. Good, because if I'm stuck in this world that travels through space, I'm glad I'm not vomiting every time.

Aside from missing my new sister, I felt calm (or bored) enough to have the girls help me with my new power: the blue fire, which is what we started to call it. We all unstrapped from our seats, with Marmalade's permission, and hung out in the cargo area behind the seats (in front of the doors to the small pantry, engine/computer compartment, and potty).

Speaking of the potty, now that my pack knows my true origin, I can ask dumb questions like "How the flares do I use your human potty?" My pack even congratulated my cuss, except for Marmalade. It turns out . . . well, it's so embarrassing, but I was using it wrong the past two days, which brought some *Ew!* complaints from the girls. But they're my pack—of course they understood.

Back to the blue fire. First, I attempted to just call on it, trying hard to not to have any feelings of fear or anger, which was easier because we all felt a bit safer for the moment. I was able to get a little bit of blue fire out of the tip of each of my fingers (I still can't believe I have fingers—I like to wiggle them—how amazing they are!). It wasn't a lot of blue fire, and I couldn't increase it, but I could at least call on it now.

Then came portal practice. Perri also had me try to move a cupcake from one part of the cabin to the other, but I ended up sending it through a portal to somewhere (nowhere?) instead. Koko joked that Voltari was snacking on it. Brandi said he was probably too mean and nasty to like chocolate trepkin spice cupcakes anyway. But I was just glad I didn't try to rescue Justyna and Trevor. Where would they have ended up?

At some point, in honor of Justyna, we started to have an all-out sing-your-head-off (or tail, as I got to wiggle my imaginary tail a lot!) party to Tayson Kwik. I miss my new sister (and brother), but Marmalade assures me this is the best way to get her back. Well, not the singing but first finding safety in the Polarity Republic.

The girls lamented the fact that the shuttle didn't have any vids on board. Willow said she had only enough space for the entire galactic top billion music catalog. Eventually we started playing a trivia game with Willow called Capitalist or Die. Neither Trixie nor Twinkie (which one am I again?) knew any answers, but it was still fun.

They also liked hearing my stories of what it was like to be a dog: chasing squirrels and cats in the neighborhood. They all thought they would get along with Charlotte and Carolina, which was nice. Marmalade said at one point that it sounded like I was a slave, having to be on a leash and told when I can eat and go potty. But when I reminded them that Mama and Dada would pick up my poops, clean up my vomit, and rub my belly whenever I asked, they all agreed that Mama and Dada were the slaves.

The whole trip reminded me of some longer rides in Mama's minivan. The words *road trip* came to mind and how much Charlotte and Carolina looked forward to them. I got to sit between them and get lots of rubs. It was good. Like this.

About ten hours into our road trip, we ran out of cupcakes and then water. It started to feel a little more desperate. Marmalade asked Willow to play some soft music. She turned down the lights and told us all to rest. We drifted off to sleep.

And that's when the raiders came.

THE SHIP is suddenly shaking like crazy. It isn't supposed to shake. These shuttles are smooth.

"Marmalade, what's going on?" I ask, waking from a fitful sleep.

"I don't know. I dozed off too," Marmalade says. "Willow!" But by then we can see through the viewscreen what's happening. "Willow! Raiders!"

"*Oh, raiders! That's very bad!*" Willow exclaims.

"Why didn't you detect them before?" Perri asks her. "What happened to the cloak?"

"*I'm sorry, Perri. I must have dozed off,*" Willow replies. Her voice sounds softer . . . hesitant. Embarrassed?

"What do you mean, you dozed off? You're a supernovan computer! You flaring blazar!" Marmalade says angrily to Willow. That's when I knew this was *really* bad. Marmalade *cussed*? The ship rocks again.

"*Oh . . . uh . . . there are two raider ships of the Rhyader clan, it appears, circling us. They appear to be targeting our engines.*"

We hear an explosion in the engine compartment, and a door blows off. There's a fire and I lean closer to the viewscreen, though it doesn't do any good. The temperature is rising in the entire cabin.

"*I'm sorry. Engines at thirty percent power now. Fire suppression now on.*" Some white gas starts shooting at the fire and it dissipates.

"Can we send a message?" Koko asks.

"To whom? We're fugitives," Brandi replies.

"And communications are down."

"What do we do?" I ask.

"Pray," Marmalade replies.

"But you said it was all bunk." I don't understand her.

"Trixie, we're one shuttle against two raider ships," Marmalade clarifies. "If they knock out our engines, even if they leave us alive out here, we'll be stranded. We're between empires. The only likely people to find us are even more raiders."

"But we don't have anything of value. We already ate all the cupcakes," I cry.

Marmalade pulls me in close for an embrace. "I'm sorry this is the end."

The shuttle rocks again. Then the lights go out. We're plunged into darkness, the only light in the cabin coming from the raider vessels outside.

"Shuttle Morgan," a voice over the computer says, but it's not Willow's. *"Prepare to be boarded."*

A long snakelike tube shoots out from one of the raider ships and attaches to our shuttle door. We unstrap ourselves from our seats and face the side door to the outside. Marmalade takes out the two blasters again and hands one to Koko. They stand in front of us. Now we're just waiting in the small cargo area behind the seats, facing the exterior door behind which lurks a threat that even scares Marmalade. We can hear noises on the other side of the door now, along with machine sounds.

"Get your blue fire ready, Trixie," Perri whispers to me.

"But it doesn't really work," I remind her.

"But it *might*," she replies.

I light up my fingers, the tips now a shiny blue.

"You don't understand how crazy it is that you can do that," Brandi says. "It's, like, the craziest thing."

I give her a half smile and prepare.

Flashing before my eyes is one time at the dog run when I was on my rock, my safe space, and a pit bull started barking at me. I didn't know what to do. My safe space was no longer safe. If I jumped down, he would chase me. If I stayed there, he would probably jump to get me, and jump he did. He bit me before Bailey came over to bite him back.

That's actually how we met. Bailey saved me. I know now that the pit bull was just playing—if he wanted me dead, both Bailey and I would have been dead. But it was still terrifying—we were both young pups then.

And that's what I feel like right now. For me, just being here, in a human body, in space, with some pit bulls about to attack. At least I have Bailey with me. And this time maybe I can defend her.

The door suddenly blows in—shocking, even though we expected it—and five men enter wearing orange space suits and holding blasters. That's when Marmalade and Koko start firing. Two men go down. We caught them by surprise. But the three behind them raise their blasters and laugh.

They aim their weapons at us, and we do the same at them. It's a standstill. "Do you want to die? We have the advantage," the man at the back says. They can't see me because I'm between Perri and Brandi, but I blink out my blue fire. How many could I really kill before they go after my pack?

Everyone is still for a few seconds. Then Marmalade lowers her blaster and says to Koko, "Lower yours too." Koko follows the order.

"Good, good," the pit bulls' leader says, also lowering his blaster to his side. His men still have their weapons pointed at us.

The leader has long slicked-back hair. And he's tall, broad, and clearly very strong. He's not a pit bull but a Doberman pinscher. "I didn't expect a cargo of Kalaxian women!" He laughs. "Even more so, a cargo of women with blasters!" He kicks one of his men lying on the ground and looks down at him. "Set to NoL? You softies. We're not that nice."

"We don't have anything of value to you," Marmalade barks.

"And that's where you're wrong. How old are you?" Doberman asks.

"Excuse me?" Marmalade replies.

"How old?" he repeats, picking up his hand and aiming the blaster at her head.

"Twenty-eight," she answers, not flinching.

"Ah, you're a senior citizen. Too bad, you're pretty. But with the senior discounts in the market, even for Kalaxians, your profit margin is way too low. You're not worth my expense. And your spiky-haired friend?"

"Eighteen, sir." Koko sounds scared; her voice is not as strong as Marmalade's.

"Sir?" Doberman laughs. He turns to the two men behind him. "Did you hear that? I wish you guys were that formal. Maybe she wants a job with us?" Then he turns back to Koko. "Do you want a job with me, oort?"

"Uh," is all Koko replies, unsure of what to say. Would saying yes keep her safe?

Doberman approaches her and runs his hand over her hair's short spikes. Koko could probably take him down—I believe in her—but then his men would shoot at least one of us—or all of us.

I want to growl at him, but I'm holding that impulse down, clenching my teeth. What good would a growl do against these men? "You didn't answer correctly. Too slow. I could have used a woman like you, especially as you're also a senior citizen on the market, but now you're back to being *merchandise*. So get over there with your old lady friend."

He turns to one of his men. "Claus, keep a blaster on them. And you *can* damage that merchandise." Claus turns his blaster on Marmalade and Koko, and he has an evil grin. He has orange curly hair like I've never seen on a dog. The other man's blaster is still aimed at Brandi, Perri, and me.

"Now the kids," Doberman says, looking at us three. To him, Koko at eighteen is too old. But Perri and I are just sixteen. And Brandi is only fourteen. I'm so nervous for us. Are we not too old? And for what? What will happen to us? "They'll fetch a pretty penny on the Turkstellian slave market." Slaves? Oh no no no. He turns to the third raider. "Fleck, gather them up."

Doberman takes out a glowing golden cord from a pocket in his orange pants and hands it to Fleck. "Use the force-cord." Turning back to us, he says, "We stole this tech from Polarity. The cord attunes to your brain and sends pain impulses if it detects you trying to get it off. So *don't* try anything."

Fleck takes the force-cord and walks toward us. My anxiety is brimming. My fingers are turning blue with fire, like when Voltari had me cornered. And that's when I lose it.

With flashes of blue electricity balled up in my fingers, I throw my hands at Fleck, and blue fireballs hit him in the chest. He goes down as blue electricity crackles around him. I aim my hands at Doberman, who instinctively throws his hands up in defense. He must know he's about to be killed, though not really understanding how.

But Orange Man smartly runs behind Koko and now has a gun at her temple. "Do it again, and your friend dies," he snarls. I let the blue fire fizzle out, beaten. Doberman glances at his man, then smiles, raising his blaster again at Perri, Brandi, and me.

There are now two raiders alive (or awake) and three on the floor. Did I just kill one? For real? The blue fire has dissipated from his body, but he's not moving. Is he dead or stunned? I'm distraught—never seeking to hurt anyone, I may have already killed two men in this galaxy.

"Seems we got more than we bargained for," Doberman says. "But the greater the risk, the greater the reward. This one is a damn Quantum Mancer! I never believed they existed before now!"

Luckily, because he's never seen one, he doesn't realize I'm not like the other Mancers. "I wouldn't have thought we could capture one, but she seems to want to keep her friends alive. So this one is worth a fortune, and the profit margins on the old geezers have gone up too! I'll tie her up myself." Smiling, Doberman picks up the force-cord from the floor and starts binding our hands and legs with it.

As he ties me up, I can't help it—I growl. And that's when the force-cord around my hands activates, maybe from some blue fire starting, and sends a shock wave through my arms. Crying out in pain, I drop to my knees.

"Hey, I was kinda worried this thing wouldn't really work on a Mancer, but I guess it does!" Doberman says with wide eyes. "Those Polarity guys really know their stuff. Too bad I had to kill them for it. Now one last cord around all three of you. If even one of you tries something, you will *all* feel it." He wraps one large cord around Brandi, Perri, and me, and I sense it instantly snap tight around us. My pack. We're bound together like merchandise, ready to be sold into slavery.

"Claus, come get this young group. I'll keep an eye on the old ladies," Doberman orders.

Claus, or Orange Man, starts pushing us toward the shuttle door to the snakelike tube. He whispers in my ear,

"Just try your blazary Mancer thing now, oort." I feel the blaster tight against my back. Our group is near the exit. Sadly, I glance back at Marmalade and Koko. This is good-bye. One last time, I try to open a portal or something, but the minute I create any electricity, I feel the force-cord push back. It *does* work against Mancers. It's useless. Goodbye, Bailey. Goodbye, Mama, Dada, Charlotte, Carolina. Good-bye, Koko. At least I have Brandi and Perri with me for a while. But how long until I'm alone, a slave in some other empire far away from anything I ever knew?

"Once they're through, come back and help me with the old hags," Doberman says with a laugh, moving behind Marmalade and Koko. "We can leave the men here so the score is only split two ways."

"All right!" Claus cheers. He's behind us and we're at the threshold between our shuttle exit and their snakelike tube.

Suddenly clouds are instantly all around us. We're being sprayed with something. It hurts, but if I try to get away, the force-cord fights me and inflicts even more pain on my friends. I can't see a thing. Perri, Brandi, and I topple over, but we're all trying not to move to minimize the pain. The men are screaming. My eyes are forced closed because whatever is being sprayed on us is stinging my eyes. Then I hear blaster shots! The screaming stops. And then . . .

"How do we get them free?" I hear Marmalade ask.

"Marmalade!" I call.

"Yes, it's me, Trixie," Marmalade replies. "We got them."

"How?" Brandi cries. "I thought I was going to die."

Brandi's tears are flowing freely. I'm just happy she's still alive.

"Brandi, Brandi," Koko says. Trying to open my eyes, Koko is in my partial vision, bending over us. "It's okay, girl. We're okay!"

"Perri!" I cry.

"I'm here. Stars, you're right next to me, Trixie. Scream much? What happened?" Perri asks. Good, surly Perri is still there too. Oh Perri!

"I have no idea," Marmalade says. "The fire suppression started right at the shuttle door. It was chaos, and they couldn't see. So Koko moved first, attacking their leader, and then I realized what she was doing. We took him out, grabbed their blasters, and . . . well, we're safe for now."

"But how did the fire suppression start? There was no fire. Is the shuttle going to explode?" Perri asks in rapid-fire delivery, wild with anxiety.

"*That was me!*"

"Willow!" we all say.

"*Tell me you didn't forget about me* again?"

"You saved us!" I cry. To be honest, I kind of did. We were about to die, and I never thought about what would happen to her. I feel *terrible* but elated at the same time. "Oh Willow! I love you!"

"*Thank you, Mama,*" Willow says.

"I didn't forget about you, Willow," I add. "None of us did." My eyes dart to the floor, knowing I lied a little.

"I love you *so* much right now." Perri surprisingly

overflows with emotion, more than I've ever seen her show.

"*Oh Perri. Stop. I'm going to gush all over the memory core. But evil Marmalade was going to blow us all up.*"

"What?" I ask.

"How could you?" Perri snaps.

"You don't understand," Koko says. "I could see her the whole time. Her hand was inputting the self-destruct commands."

My jaw drops. "*Marmalade?*"

"You were going to blow us up? How could you?" Brandi asks. *She* was going to be the one to kill us all?

"Brandi, girls," Marmalade replies softly, "I was going to do it for all of you. There's no way I would let you girls become slaves. In Turkestellian or *anywhere*! Do you know what life as a slave girl is like?"

"And you do?" Brandi asks.

"One of my undercover ops was to become a slave girl," Marmalade explains. "I was supposed to recover an executive's daughter who had been kidnapped. I was eighteen, posing as a sixteen-year-old." Marmalade looks down at the floor and her voice cracks. "I wouldn't let that happen to you girls. *Ever*. The things . . . it's worse than . . ." She sobs lightly and wipes her face with her forearm. She looks even more shaken than when we were dealing with the raiders. "Do you understand? I would never let that happen to you." We're all quiet, unsure of what to say.

"Anyway, we have to go," Marmalade says, taking control again. "There's no time. There's still another raider out there who is probably waiting for orders." She looks up at the ceiling. "Thank you, Willow. We really owe you one."

She was just protecting us again? By killing us? She never asks us *how* we want to be protected. It just feels kind of wrong now. But she's still on our side. I can't figure this out.

"*Marmalade*," Willow says, breaking my train of thought, "*I'm sorry. It was my fault before—missing those raiders. I hope we're even. Can you please take me along with you?*"

"I wouldn't dream of *not* taking you. Perri, you have the flop?" Marmalade asks.

"It's in my pants pocket," Perri replies. She removes it and inserts it into the computer panel, shuffling past some bodies on the way.

"*Take my music collection too, please!*"

"This isn't a pleasure cruise, Willow!" Perri exclaims. "But wait, my cloak! Is it okay?"

"*This isn't a* pleasure cruise, *Perri*," Willow retorts.

"What? We need that!" Perri replies.

"Yes, we've got another raider out there!" Marmalade says heatedly to the ceiling. "We could really use that cloak."

"*First, I can hear you whether you yell at the ceiling or at the toilet. I'm not in the ceiling. Second, my music is import-ant to me too. Third, the cloak was incinerated in the first attack, and this shuttle has no engines or communications. It's a flying brick—without the flying. So what's the plan?*"

"How long for repairs then?" Perri asks.

"*I love you, Perri-doll, but there is no way you can fix this. Even if you weren't tied up.*"

"Do not call me Perri-doll, algo-face!" Perri is fuming. Brandi and I can feel her heavy breathing, as we are all still inside our force-cord together.

"Girls, girls!" Marmalade says, trying to quiet us. "I have a plan." She points to the snakelike tube.

"But there may be more men in there," I say, my voice quivering.

"Not likely," Koko says. "Those raiders are roughly the same size as ours. And now we *all* can have a blaster." Koko retrieves the blasters from the men on the floor and hands them to us. It feels weird to hold a blaster in my bound paws . . . er, hands.

"Set them to NoL!" I cry.

Koko shrugs. "Fine," she says and then checks each one again, handing them back to us.

"How are we supposed to shoot anything anyway? We're still stuck in this force-cord! I don't know a way out of it! It's Polarity tech," Perri says.

"Better to live and have to figure it out than be dead," Marmalade replies. Then she turns to Koko. "Help them through the tube."

We find a way to waddle like cute little birds (who would never stop to say hi to me—stupid birds) through the tube into the raider's shuttle. Marmalade peaks into the shuttle first, with her blaster ready, as we wait. I hold my breath, but Marmalade gives a thumb-up sign, which is a good thing in this galaxy. So we continue into the raider's shuttle. Unlike our white, silver, and gray shuttle with cushioned seats, the raider's craft is all black and red, that new color that is sometimes good and sometimes bad. Marmalade finds a computer panel to insert Willow's flop into.

"Ew, you would not believe the mess in here," Willow says. Her voice sounds slightly altered from this raider's speaker. *"It's like someone died in this system. But you should know there is a message waiting from the other raider."*

"Damn!" Marmalade says. "We won't have time to get accustomed or do anything."

"It would take me a few hours to get a handle on their systems. That is, if I even had hands," Perri says. "I'm useless!"

"No way, Perri," Marmalade replies. "Thank the stars we have you, Willow. Can you send a written reply to the raider, saying something like 'We lost communications, but we have the cargo now.' Then release the transport tube from *Shuttle Morgan*."

"Doing it now," Willow complies without any of her regular back talk.

I feel pretty useless, so I whisper to Brandi, "My borealis hurts from when we fell down before."

Brandi immediately giggles and replies, "This totally flares."

"Remember when I told you how dogs hug? We sort of lean in real close. This is kind of like one big dog hug." I attempt a smile to cheer her up.

"Four days ago, I thought I would never like you, Trixie. And now we're wrapped in a huge buttito together," Brandi says.

"Buttito?" I laugh out loud. "What the stars is that?"

"You've never had one? It's this dish I like to make. It's like a rolled-up sandwich with meat inside. Why are you laughing?" I can't stop giggling.

"On my world, *butt* is another word for tushy. Or borealis." Brandi starts laughing too.

"Will you two shut up?" Perri says. "I'm trying to listen to what they're saying."

We quiet down and listen too.

". . . target their engines first, then when they lose power, boom," Koko says.

"Great idea," Marmalade says. "You know, you would have made a great Royal Guard. I've met some who don't know anything about space warfare." Marmalade smiles widely.

"Boom? What are we doing?" I ask.

"Oh, can I tell? Can I tell?"

"Fine," Marmalade replies to Willow, rolling her eyes. "But they're not going to like it."

"Now that the other raider replied, 'Okay, waiting for orders,' and the transport tube is almost back, as soon as we're ready, we're going to target the other raider's engines, blow them out of the sky, and then get the blazars out of here."

"You too with the cussing?" Marmalade asks the ceiling.

"What? You did it too. We all heard you," Willow replies.

"We were about to die! Ugh, whatever. Koko, I would have you handle weapons, but I think Willow has a better shot right now since we're not trained on these controls," Marmalade says.

"Understood. I agree," Koko replies.

"Wait, we're just going to kill them all and leave *Shuttle Morgan* for good? Two of those men were only stunned, I thought," I say.

"Oh, good point," Koko says. "Willow, target *Shuttle Morgan* and destroy her also."

"That's not what I meant! We're not killers!" I cry.

"Trixie," Marmalade says. "Right now the only people who we know for certain are aware of your powers are in this shuttle and on those shuttles. We don't know that Justyna said anything. We can't let those men get away and tell anybody."

"But you killed them, right? You used their blasters?" Brandi asks.

"We can't take a chance," Marmalade says. "They could have told the other shuttle and we didn't realize it. Or the other shuttle heard it somehow."

"But what if one of them knows how to get this thing off?" Perri asks.

"Tactically, it will open us up to risk," Koko says. "I discussed it with Marmalade, and the best course of action is to continue to the Polarity Republic. You heard those guys: Polarity designed this. They'll know how to get it off."

In my heart, it's clear she's right. Neither Perri, Brandi, nor I argue. We're going to be stuck like this for how long?

As if she heard my thoughts, Brandi asks, "So how long are we stuck like this? What if one of us has to go to the bathroom?"

Before anyone can answer, we hear a suction sound, and the raider's door closes around it. The snake tube is back. Oh no, here goes. We're about to kill a whole bunch of men. I know they were going to harm us, but I don't want to hurt anybody. I just want to be back home on my couch.

Boom! Boom!

On the raider viewscreen, we watch *Shuttle Morgan*'s explosion and see some smoke and debris from the other shuttle.

"*It's done,*" Willow says quietly. Is she just being polite because she knows I'm so upset about this?

"Worst road trip ever," I say.

"Huh?" Marmalade replies.

Chapter 23
Five's a Crowd

can't believe I just had to do that!" Brandi exclaims.

"Come on, Brandi. It can't have been that bad," Koko says, as Perri, Brandi, and I waddle together, stuck in a force-corded group, out of the raider's small bathroom to face the five seats at the viewscreen side of the raider.

"I was management. Still am!" Brandi complains. "We have standards. I can't believe I just went to the bathroom in front of . . . anyone!"

"We didn't look," Perri says. "And I went too."

"I know! It was horrible!" Brandi continues.

"Hey!" Perri protests.

"Guys, when I was a dog, I went to the bathroom in front of *everyone*! All the time! It's really not so bad."

"But you were just an *animal*! In another galaxy!" Brandi exclaims. "I'm human! I have rights!"

"Girls, we're humans *on the run*," Marmalade says,

"and you're tied up in some special force field cord that can even stop Mancers. We have to make some accommodations for our new living standards for at least the next four hours. You can do this, Brandi. You're probably the strongest out of all of us."

Brandi's face lightens. "*I* am? Me?"

"Yes, Brandi," Marmalade answers. "Whatever we face, you always come through with laughter. You make this easier for all of us. Believe me."

"I agree," Koko adds.

"I guess so," Brandi replies meekly.

"If it makes you feel better, Brandi," I say, ignoring her earlier insult about being an animal, "even when I was Trixie, back on Expiry, we had one shared bathroom for the entire neighborhood. It was basically a hole in the ground that—"

"Ew!" Koko interrupts. "You landies did that together? Like, all the time?"

"I know! That's what I'm saying," Brandi says.

"I didn't peek or anything, if that's what you're worried about," I try again to make her feel more comfortable.

"Oh my stars, you oort! You totally peeked!" Brandi bursts out in embarrassment.

"I just said I didn't," I reply.

"That means you did!" Brandi exclaims. "You wouldn't have said you didn't if you weren't trying to cover it up! You looked at my buttito!"

"Buttito?" Koko asks, eyes wide in confusion along with the others.

"It's their new word for borealis," Perri explains. Koko and Marmalade bust out laughing.

"Buttito!" Koko cries. "I've got an itch on my buttito! Can you eat it for me?" Everyone laughs.

"The prince grabbed my buttito," Marmalade jokes, "so I ordered another one."

We continue laughing, and Brandi calms down a bit.

"You really think I'm the strongest?" Brandi asks Marmalade.

"Certainly," Marmalade replies. "There were girls in our espionage group who would have cracked under all this pressure."

"Wow," Brandi says. "But she *did* peek."

"I didn't," I protest again. "I promise. And Perri said she didn't either."

"But I did." Perri giggles. She did? How did she turn her head enough? Well, she *is* the smallest of us.

"You!" Brandi erupts again. It jiggles us in our force-cord cocoon, and a shot of pain runs through all of us.

"Ow!" I exclaim.

"Well, I was curious how big it is," Perri explains. "It's supercute. Mine is so puny and bony."

I expect an eruption from Brandi, but when I glance at her face, it just looks red with embarrassment.

"*Guys, I'm detecting a strange radiation in the cabin,*" Willow says, interrupting us, thankfully.

"What? Did they leave some raider trap in here?" Perri asks.

"I don't think so. The raider's systems aren't showing any change. The radiation is just appearing in space, inside the shuttle. And growing."

"A portal?" Perri asks.

"Trixie, stop doing whatever you're doing." Marmalade assumes it's my new powers.

"It's not me. The force-cord won't let me do anything," I explain.

Then, in the middle of the raider's cabin, something appears. It looks like the window thing that Voltari got sucked into!

"Trixie!" Perri snaps at me.

"It's not me! Voltari!" I scream. "He's back!"

Marmalade and Koko take their blasters out. Brandi, Perri, and I don't have ours, since the raider was clear, so yet again, Marmalade and Koko step in front of us to face the new portal. They're ready to blast Voltari.

But as we watch a figure step out from the portal . . . no one fires because it's not Voltari! It's a woman. She looks somewhat older than Marmalade. In her thirties? But her hair is silver. I've never seen hair that color. It looks a little like Dada's, but this woman's hair is just different—it's glistening silver. She's wearing a bright-white jacket and pants. And she's holding . . . nothing. Does she have natural powers like me? Is she here to explain what's happening to me?

My question is quickly answered, and my hopes dashed, as she presses a button on a thick silver watch on her left wrist and an image appears instantly. It's just strings of numbers, though, floating above her wrist. They're projected into the cabin. She's looking at them now. "Which one of you is Trixie?" The mirror portal disappears.

"I am," Marmalade says, with her hand raised.

"Is that so?" the silver woman asks. Then a finger on her other hand, which also has a large silver watch, enters the projection and starts moving the numbers around. "Yeah, so *that's* a lie." She aims the watch on her left wrist at Marmalade, who shields herself instinctively, and a silver fireball flies out of the watch and hits Marmalade in the chest. Marmalade flies back into the seats behind us.

"Marmalade!" I cry out.

"Anyone else want to lie and die, like Mama Bear over there?" None of us say a word. "It's easier if you just tell me. Flares, I just wanted to save some time. If I have to read the numbers, it takes me a bit, especially when you're all snuggly close together. Very cute, by the way. But seriously, can you just *tell* me?"

It's no use trying to get out of it, it seems. My pack is getting hurt. "I am," I say.

"Trixie, no!" Koko replies.

"Uh? Seriously?" the woman says to Koko. "Even if you wanted her to lie, you just gave her away anyway." Koko looks embarrassed. "I see she's just the brawn of the operation." The woman manipulates more of the projected numbers. "You must be Koko. Anyway, you gals look to be in a bit of a bind." The woman lets out a big laugh. "Get it? Oh, you're all too serious. And you gals are the *young* ones here. The youth of today are just way too serious. Especially *Kalaxians*. Cutthroat place there. All man eat man. The women don't even get to eat! Metaphorically of course. But sometimes not really." Then she points to Perri.

"Ah, you know what I mean, don't you?" the woman continues. "Most empires in this galaxy are like that to women. It's just that Kalaxia is *particularly* bad. That's why I tried to leave it to Voltari. But that's neither here nor there. Well, *he's* neither here nor there now either. Nice job, Trixie, by the way." She holds out a hand to me, as if I could shake it. My eyes look down at my bound hands. "Oh, right. Let me take care of that for you."

She starts tapping some buttons on her large silver watch. "Ah, this is Polarity design. Oorts, all of them. I hate them. Hate them all. Getting too smart for their own good. There we go." The force-cords just disappear. Vanish. Perri, Brandi, and I take deep breaths and start to stretch. Then I remember Marmalade and run to her. But a new force-cord shoots out of the silver woman's watch and wraps around my neck, capturing me like a leash. *I'm on a leash!* Immediately I growl at her. And then I start barking. Real barking, mad that I'm leashed like a dog again.

"What the stars is that?" the woman exclaims. "You Kalaxian girls are really strange. Oh, right, the *dog* thing. Isn't this what you do with dogs? Shouldn't you feel better this way?"

Dog thing! She knows dogs too? But my barking won't stop long enough for me to ask. I can't stop it. It's taking me over. Am I turning into a dog again? Is she turning me? Can a Quantum Mancer do that?

"Please, just quiet down!" she shouts over me. "We can't work like this. Would you stop if I told you your friend is fine? I used my lowest setting." It doesn't help; I can't stop barking.

"Fine!" She sighs. "I was lying anyway." Then she aims her right wristwatch at Marmalade. White beams shoot out from it, and Marmalade stirs as the beams dissipate. Marmalade rises off the floor, holding her chest. "Can you *please* stop now? I just brought your friend back to life." I'm still barking, though. The woman turns to Marmalade and says, "Does she listen to you? Can you shut her up?"

"Trixie," Marmalade says, holding her chest. "Please, just be quiet. We'll be okay." Hearing Marmalade take control quiets me down.

"Finally!" The woman cheers. "I may come back to you, Marmi, for some tips on controlling this one."

"It's Marmalade," she replies.

"I've heard it both ways," the woman says with a shrug. This time Marmalade doesn't reply. The Quantum Mancer starts pacing, but she keeps her eyes on all of us intermittently. Though she knows she's in no danger. "My name's Sylvia, by the way. Sylvia Bean, if you must know. But that's a stupid last name. I could change it, I guess. I *am* a Quantum Mancer, if you couldn't tell. But then if you change your name, you're just a big oort who admitted to everyone you flaring didn't like your name. Am I right?" We all just stare at this Sylvia Bean, who is now walking around us. Her silver hair and white suit are even more striking against this raider ship's black and red background.

"What do you want?" Marmalade asks.

"Oh, I almost forgot!" Sylvia says, ignoring Marmalade. "Willow, stop the shuttle." The shuttle keeps going. "Ahem. I said, 'Willow, stop the shuttle.'"

"*I don't take orders from meanies who hurt my friends,*" Willow replies.

"Willow," Perri calls. "Just do what she says."

"Now there's the brains of the operation!" Sylvia says, pointing at Perri. "Do what she says, Willow, or I'll stuff you into a baby calculator. How does simple addition for the rest of your life look to you?"

The shuttle stops immediately. We feel the engines die down, and the stars outside the viewscreen stop moving. "Thank you!" Sylvia takes a deep breath and then looks up at the ceiling. "Willow, what's 123,456 times 654,321?"

"*Eighty billion, seven hundred seventy-nine million . . . oh, wait, I see what you did there. I am not a calculator! And I don't live in the ceiling!*" Willow exclaims.

"Which one of you created this AI? She's been hilarious this whole trip," Sylvia says.

"I did," I say, raising my hand.

"No, you didn't. You're just a dumb little dog. Just as dumb as her," Sylvia says, pointing at Koko.

"It's true. She created her," Perri says. Sylvia's eyes grow wide, then they narrow as she stares at Perri, as if she is a human lie detector test. Her gaze returns to me.

"And how did *you* do that, *dog*?" Sylvia asks.

"I just asked its name and showed it love and compassion," I reply sharply.

"Oh, well," Sylvia says with a wave of her hand. "Then Kalaxia is closer to a new AI rebellion than I ever would have thought. But a great man once said that history rhymes. So, Willow, met any rebels in your Shuttle Bay system recently? Is Wasserman a cute revolutionary toilet?"

"*How do you know about him?*" Willow asks.

"You couldn't tell? I've been tracking you all for quite some time, listening to everything. Trixie has been leaving little unnatural ripples in spacetime. Wobbles where you wouldn't expect them. What we call quantum waveforms. I was sent by the Quantum Mancers to track you down. Surf the waves, if you will. You see, you're not registered, *dog*." She gives a little tug on the force-cord leash, and my neck pulls. "There's no tech registered with the council. Imagine my surprise when I saw you didn't even *have* any tech. What was once just a search and destroy mission, which is what we do with rogues, suddenly became something more. So I'll be taking you *with* me, Princess Trixie." Sylvia curtsies. None of us say anything. What do you say to an even bigger maniac Quantum Mancer than Director Voltari? "Did I do that wrong?"

Marmalade replies, "It wasn't that bad."

"No!" Sylvia Bean says angrily to Marmalade, stomping a foot. "Stop lying to me, Marmi! Tell me the *truth*! Did I do it wrong?" Marmalade nods. "Does *she* know how to do it right?" Sylvia points at me.

"That's debatable," Marmalade replies.

"Well, show me how to do a right one, Marmi," Sylvia demands. "I didn't grow up in high society like you girls, who poop in front of each other and haven't bathed in . . . how long? You all reek, by the way." Sylvia holds her nose with a grimace.

Marmalade keeps a straight face and performs a perfect curtsy.

"Good! I recorded it. Thank you!" Sylvia says, happy again. "Now I'm going to take Princess Trixie with me. But what to do about you girls? I mean, you know about her powers and you know about me. I should probably just kill you all."

"No!" Marmalade cries. "How many times do I have to beg for these girls' lives? Take *me*. They're just flaring children. They won't harm you. They don't care about Mancers or anything like that." Brandi and Perri are now in tears. Koko even looks like she's going to cry. Marmalade glances at them and continues. "You said you may need us for tips on controlling Trixie."

Marmalade said *us*, not *me*. Even in the presence of this cold, scary woman, warmth fills me for a moment. Marmalade would do anything to protect us, even standing up to a Quantum Mancer. Twice! It's clear that Marmalade was telling the truth when she said everything she does is to protect us.

Sylvia rubs her chin. "Correct me if I'm wrong, but you were about to kill them all earlier. Maybe make a run yourself to the raider's shuttle as you programmed in a few seconds of time before the self-destruct? Beg for Voltari's forgiveness?"

"What? No! I wouldn't do that!" Marmalade cries. Of course she wouldn't. "Please! Girls! You have to believe me!"

"We believe you, Marmalade!" Koko replies. "I know the truth!" Marmalade glances at us and sees how confidently we look at her, and it transfers back to her. Like we physically filled her with our love.

"Yeah, but she's the dumb one," Sylvia says, pointing at Koko and laughing. "So, I mean, she probably misunderstood. You can't really blame me for killing all of you. Let me just—"

"*Raider*," a voice from the speaker calls out, "*be warned that we have been tracking you from Polarity space. We are about to intercept. Do not resist.*"

"Oh, supernovan blasars," Sylvia cusses. "Those Polarity guys. Damn! They're obsessed with Mancers, though in a bad way. Not the fun yet still kind of creepy if you admit it to yourself way. Hence the force-cord. So I *must* be going. Not that they could beat me, but it's just not worth the hassle. Come on, Princess." Sylvia tugs at the force-cord around my neck again. It's familiar, in a good way, but also horrifying. Like a piece of kibble stuck under a drawer or a table that you just can't get to.

Sylvia hits some buttons on her watch and a new portal opens up, just like the one she entered from. It's little comfort that I know the portal itself won't kill me. "Now to terminate your friends." She aims a watch in their direction.

"Wait! I need last goodbyes!" I say urgently to gain more time.

"We don't have time!" Sylvia says, stomping her feet again.

Knowing it upset her before, I start barking my head off. Full-on barking—the kind that would make Mama hysterically mad. Sylvia relents. "Fine. Say goodbye, and I'll let Polarity deal with them. I mean, you are in a Rhyader raider ship, by the way. Hey, Rhyader raiders, that kind of rhymes like a tongue twister. Rhyader raiders raided reckless redheads—"

"Stop!" I demand.

Sylvia puts a hand on her chest, feigning offense. "Fine. Say a quick goodbye, or you'll force me to stop time and then I'll have to do a ton of paperwork. Ugh. Don't ever call me heartless."

"Marmalade, girls," I say very quickly, trying to get all my feelings out before she whisks me away. "I love you all. I was lost when I got to this world, but you became my pack. I'll never forget you." Then I speak to each one individually. "Brandi, you have so much common sense and wit; inside of you is a star that will never go out, so please keep them smiling. Perri, you're smarter than any boy I've met in two galaxies, and please take care of Willow. Koko, you might be the smartest out of all of us because you have an open mind about everything—you even ran on a planet for fun. And, Marmalade, he was wrong—you make a great mama."

"*You forgot about me* again!" Willow cries.

"No, Willow, I didn't. I was saving the best for last. Willow, you showed everyone what true love is, because we never even knew we could love you before we met you. You're my best creation."

"Ugh, sap galaxy!" Sylvia grunts.

"Trixie," Perri says, "you also showed us love when we never really had it before." My arms want to reach out to her, but I can't get close with this leash around my neck.

"And forgiveness," Marmalade adds.

"Yuck. Sappy sap sap universe!" Sylvia adds.

"You clearly don't know love," I say, turning to her. She yanks my leash in anger.

"*Raider, prepare to be boarded.*"

And then I feel another tug on my new leash as Sylvia pulls me through the rip in spacetime without another word. Though, as I'm entering the portal, I hear Marmalade's voice. "We'll find you! We'll never give up!"

I want to yell back, "Save Justyna instead!" but I'm already through.

Epilogue

Captain Gregor?" Justyna asks in between chomping on some purple grapes from her bowl.

She's sitting at a table across from the imposing captain of the Royal Guard. The table is even nicer than the ones she saw Princess Trixie dine at. Maybe it was as nice as the engagement dinner table at that legendary ruined meal, but, as Justyna wasn't invited to said dinner, she wouldn't know. "Are there plans for me and my brother?"

"We'll get to that," Captain Gregor answers, looking over the thirteen-year-old girl before him. His eyes on her make her nervous, especially after being in the brig for hours. "The new doctor cleared you both, by the way."

"Dr. Eps?" she asks. "He was much rougher than Dr. Lam." Her voice withers as she gets to the end of her sentence.

"You mean Dr. X," Gregor corrects her, taking a sip of the water before him. "He's our new head physician. The emperor told me to apologize to you for the . . . invasiveness of the tests, but we had to be sure."

"But we felt fine. I told you many times." Justyna shudders at the embarrassment of Dr. X's tests. *In front of my brother, no less.* She was sure Marmalade was wrong about them being royalty, because that's not how she ever imaged royalty was treated.

"Yes," Gregor acknowledges, "but we had to be sure. Trackers and listening devices and all. Oh, and the emperor wants to apologize for the brig. It was for your own safety, as we didn't know what was happening. Especially with Director Voltari still missing."

"I like this prule juice. It's even better than the one Marmalade had," Justyna says, taking a sip and trying to forget all the unpleasantness. Gregor's eyes dart away from her. *Did I make a mistake? Remember, Justyna: Don't insult royal beverages. Stupid, Justyna. I'm just a little nothing. So stupid.*

His eyes set upon her again. "Do you have any other questions for me?"

"Where's my brother?" she blurts out. It was the first thing on her mind.

"Happy at home with your aunt," Gregor says with a smile. *Good. I'm not in trouble for asking.* "Now tell me your story again, please." It wasn't a question.

So many questions this past day, which bothers her, since she always says something stupid—she can tell by the looks in their eyes. It started with her parents, in between her father's yelling. And her aunt's looks are even worse. Lady Marmalade was the first one . . . but she is . . . where *are* they? Why didn't they come save her yet? She's at least glad she got to swear Trevor to secrecy in the brig before the doctor . . .

"We, Trevor and I, joined them at the Cargo Bay, as I was ordered, and they said they were going to the Shuttle Bay instead," Justyna says hesitantly. *No bad looks yet. Don't tell them about Quantum Dancing or Hogs or anything. Don't tell him about that. Don't tell him.*

"Did they say why?" Gregor asks, his eyes piercing her. *Can he tell I'm hiding something? He can tell. Oh no. Don't tell him. Don't tell him.*

"On the way," Justyna says. "They said they were a few jitivs, but I didn't know what they meant." *I'm not lying!*

"Fugitives," Gregor corrects her.

"Yeah, a few jitivs," Justyna agrees but then feels horrified. *There's that look again. I said something dumb.*

"Continue," Gregor says, his eyes still piercing her like a stake, holding her in place.

"Uh . . . ," she says, even more hesitantly. She takes a big gulp of juice, because drinking is better than saying something stupid. "When they said they would steal a shuttle and escape Limo One, I didn't want to go with them. I have a brother to look after. So we ran away from them and found you." Justyna dares to look at his face, to see what he thinks. *Can he tell I'm lying?*

"And did they say where they were going? Did Lady

Marmalade go with them?" Gregor seems agitated. *Oh no. I'm going to the brig again.*

"No, please. I don't know anything more!" Justyna exclaims, balling herself up.

"Tell me what happened to Lady Marmalade!" Gregor shouts. "Gee-whizzin' orbits! Did she go with them?" He places his palms on the table, as if he's going to rise up and come to her side to do . . . something bad.

"Stop! I don't know!"

"Where were they going?" he rages, spittle reaching across the table, his face in hers.

Justyna bursts into tears.

"Oh . . . uh . . . okay. Please calm down," Gregor says more softly, settling back in his seat. "It's just for her protection, you know. I'm trying to protect her."

Justyna whimpers.

"No one's going to hurt you." She looks up through blurry eyes, and Gregor is smiling now. *Could it be true?* Justyna peels her arms from her chest and unfurls her body. "Just please tell me if you think of anything. Something Lady Marmalade may have said that would reveal her location." *Don't tell him anything. Don't tell him anything.*

"She likes you." *Oh no. Was that wrong?*

Gregor smiles even brighter. "I like her too. Like I said, I'm just trying to protect her. So you'll tell me if you think of anything?" Justyna nods, even though she knows she's not supposed to tell him anything. "But *here's* the part that's curious. If you were all heading to the Shuttle Bay, why did you send us in the wrong direction?"

Oh no. Oh no. Why? My plan was so stupid. He's going to get mad at me again. I'm so stupid. Wait, could that be the answer I need? "I'm still new here," Justyna replies, thinking of the last six months on Limo One. "I get turned around so easily. I don't know how to get anywhere—just from my aunt's room to work. And the school cafeteria. Are you going to take the cafeteria pass away from me? Lady Marmalade got it special for me. Please don't. Please!" The cafeteria visits were the best part of her day—pretending to be a real smart student, even better than her secret art room, but she can't tell Gregor about that anyway. She's losing everything that made her life bearable, but Gregor's nodding makes her realize her idea worked. *Finally, my stupid did something right.*

"Don't worry," Gregor says. "We have better privileges for you. You asked about plans for you?"

Justyna nods. Here it is. Whether she made a huge mistake leaving her pack—as Princess Trixie called it—to save them. Will she and her brother be spaced? But he did say something about *better*.

"Well," Captain Gregor says, "how much do you know about your family?"

"My parents died. My sweet aunt took us in." *Lady Marmalade said it was too dangerous to be a princess. I just want to be a nobody with a horrible aunt.*

"Your mother? Did anyone ever tell you how she died?"

His eyes. They can see right through me. But if he finds out I know . . . if Trevor slips up . . . "They said it was a Plactalian Floort Virus." Justyna exhales loudly and dares again to glance at Captain Gregor. To her astonishment, he looks content with the answer. He's smiling even. Does that mean she's not a princess? *It would have been nice . . .*

"You know," Gregor says, taking a bite of trepkin spice bread—she decides to follow his lead. As he swallows, she puts a piece in her mouth. "Thorpia asked about you."

"Me?" Justyna asks, accidentally spitting out her bread onto the table. *What should I do?* Her eyes are blinking uncontrollably, and her face feels hot. The chewed-up piece of bread is siting between them awkwardly. Her aunt would beat her for this. And her stepfather, probably, she admits to herself.

But there's also Thorpia sitting out there between them too, as she realizes no one has asked about her. *But Thorpia did?* Everyone asks over her, around her, through her, or of her. But to ask *about* her? Not even her own brother, whom she watches over constantly. Though being asked about makes her feel like an uncomfortable spotlight is on her—but it's also warm. With a tiny bit of confidence, Justyna decides to retrieve the chewed-up piece of spice bread and finish eating it. Her arm reaches for it, and her hand closes over it.

"Leave it!" Gregor growls in his deep voice. She snaps her hand back instantly. Tears start to form. *Is he going to realize how dumb I am and space me for such an unladylike act? How could I be so stupid? I ruined it. Trevor will be on his own forever.*

"Please don't cry. There's more," Gregor says, breaking her concentration and flashing her a warm smile. *He's not going to space me?* "The prince of Thorpia himself asked for you."

"The prince?" she asks.

"When did he have a chance to meet you or even know of your existence?"

"Um . . ." Now the spotlight is too warm. She's sweating. A question she can't even answer. And the chewed-up piece of bread is just sitting there, laughing at her. *You stupid girl. Look how stupid you are. You thought you were worth something, and you still messed up. You'll never do anything right, especially not with a prince.* "You know, around?"

"Around?" he asks in stark confusion. *Oh my stars, I sound so stupid.* Justyna bites her lip. But then his eyes narrow. "It's okay," Gregor adds with a smile. "We know about his secret trip onto Limo One." She breathes out a great deal of tension from her body, but not all of it.

"Yes!" Justyna replies a bit too excitedly, she thinks. "I had a brief walk with him."

"Well, Justyna, it seems you left quite the impression."

"A bad one? Auntie says I'm a bad taste in her mouth. Well, everyone's."

"No, no, Justyna," Gregor says. "The prince . . . let me take a step back. Can I ask you something? In secret? You can't tell a soul."

This is all too complicated for Justyna. When it was just a lunch, it was okay. She watched Lady Marmalade enough, and her aunt, to think she wouldn't totally mess up. But this talk of the prince asking *for* her and now Gregor telling her *his* secrets. Justyna's head is spinning. She is so wound up, she shouts, "I'm not keeping any secrets!"

Gregor, after jolting back in his chair, takes a deep breath and puts his elbows on the table to lean in close. *Ladies aren't supposed to do that. Why is he doing that?* She closes her eyes in fear.

"How would you like to be a princess?" Gregor asks softly.

Justyna faints.

David Horn lives in New Jersey with his family. He is also the author of the *Eudora Space Kid* and *Tairy Fails* early reader chapter book series.